WHITE MAGIC

By

Peggy Wragg

Jeff, Kim and Echo for their continued support and encouragement.

NEIL	ELLIE	ALEX	MUM	JEAN
Wellies	Jumper	Book	Coat	~~Socks~~
Shoes	Chocolate	Noodle	Shoe's	~~Bag~~
Jumper	Smellt	Biscuit's	Sweet	Biscuits
Gloves	~~Tea~~ ~~lights~~	~~Xplender~~	Cushions	~~Keyrip~~
Whiskey	~~Glass~~	Tea	~~Biscuits~~	Calender
DVD	~~Accessory~~	~~Chocolate~~	~~Biscuits~~	
Biofresse	Biscuits	~~Biscuits~~	Jumper	
Sweaty		~~unglue~~		
Accoutrer		Tea		
Socks				
Top				
Seeds				
Book				
CD				
Socks				
Pane				

Alan
Beer
Chocolate
Dog

Susan
Jumper

Ainsley
Smelly
Money
Dog

Thomas
Smelly
Chocolate
Money
Dog

Kerri
Crumble
+
Biscuits

Melanie
+ family
Choc + Toffees
Han - Smelly Melanie
Smelly Chocolate
Banfax

AIG

CONTENTS

CHAPTER 1

Friday, 3.45 pm. The Arrival.

A summons from Satan's earthly prince of darkness had spooked and given him a hard-on, but during the uneventful flight back from Tangiers Brett Watson considered those eventful past few days.

The offer Mohamid Van Jonger had tried to force him into accepting was dangerous and he'd declined the venture. At the age of thirty-four Brett was a cautious negotiator and shrewd entrepreneur having cultivated his company into a secure position from the dying embers of the retired directors and had started to enjoy life with growing enthusiasm.

Brett Watson knew his discussion with Mohamid was going to be a non-starter but nevertheless felt a muted urge to listen to his putrid blueprint.

His company had expanded to such a size he'd been forced to increase his own staff and appoint a co-director so enabling him to develop the international side of the business, leaving his new right-hand man Aston Appleton to run the more mundane elements of company procedure. In so doing Brett had made a major circumspect error and he began to see the company traversing down roads he wouldn't have considered viable himself. However, the profits were at their highest level and he remained cautiously pleased.

Brett couldn't quite adjust to the methods Aston Appleton used, feeling he was manipulating some of their clients, and the mental warning bells had rung during the Tangiers trip. Somehow Brett knew Aston was involved yet couldn't be sure how.

The seat belt warning light flickered on as Brett shook himself back to the remaining day ahead. A stewardess reached down and removed his empty glass but the look of surprise on his face must have startled the young woman as she immediately offered an explanation, reminding him of their imminent arrival at Heathrow. Her perfumed aroma filled his head; she was stunning yet Brett had been oblivious of her until that moment and smiling, watched as she headed back towards the galley.

Her fragrant body set his mind wandering; he really wanted to be with his wife at that moment in time. Brett and Rebecca Watson had been married for just two years and although very much in love never felt they saw enough of each other. Christ, he'd missed her this trip and yearned to be back within her warm embrace.

He noticed how clammy the palms of his hands had become and was acutely aware of yet another stirring sensation developing deep within his groin. Attempting to avert this subconscious train of thought, Brett again considered the trip to Tangiers and remaining few minutes of his flight, but it was without effect.

His tightening trousers strained around him as the erection became evident and grew into painful proportion. Brett smiled in shy acknowledgement to himself as he considered his present predicament sat on board the Boeing 727 landing at Heathrow. He was a successful business executive sporting an enormous growth which made him feel like an excited teenager who'd never made love and knew he was about to gain his manhood.

The aircraft jolted as it touched down, making him wince since his penis was now so large it felt explosive. How he wanted to be with Rebecca. If she'd been there and seen his current state Brett knew she would have laughed and that made matters worse. Arriving at the ramp people started to move about the aircraft and in no time at all its cabin was almost empty.

For some reason Brett always needed to be away from an arriving plane as fast as possible and usually the unloading of passengers seemed a slow process yet today, when he could have used more time, the procedure had been swift.

With his erection now in decline he started towards the cabin door, his black leather briefcase being carried in front to hide any remaining evidence of his sexual desire. The stewardess who had spoken to him not fifteen minutes earlier smiled as if she knew about his growth and its current rapid decline. Brett passed her by whispering, "Bitch," under his breath.

The effort of passing passport control, baggage reclaim and customs uninspired most travellers and he was no exception. After the routine questions having been answered to some pompous young customs officer trying to be a hero, Brett made his way to the terminal exit.

En route a line of bell boys waited waving placards with passenger names scrawled on them. He was surprised to see his own name on display and made his way over to the young lad who declared the message. A feeling of apprehension welled within him as the boy passed a sealed white envelope to Brett who then thanked him before continuing on his way towards the terminal doors.

Outside the air was cold but fresh and was a welcome relief from the humid airport building. Brett Watson was not in the habit of reading messages in front of others and elected to open the envelope once seated in his car.

It seemed to take an age before he reached the car park but the cold September air cleared his mind. Watson fumbled in his pocket for the key and locating it, opened the door, throwing his briefcase and small suitcase on to the back seat. He climbed in and sat admiring the polished walnut banks of dials and smelling the aroma of leather, all of which were a part of his new Aston Martin. He drooled over this car, considering it to be the finest ever made. It was his own £120,000 emblem of success.

Brett tore open the white envelope the bell boy had given him as his eyes scanned the message and horror filled his body. He read it again to make sure he'd understood.

BRETT WATSON RETURN TO YOUR HOME BY 6.00 PM TODAY. YOUR WIFE IS OUR HOSTAGE. WE KNOW WHO

YOU ARE AND WHAT YOU ARE. SHOULD YOU CHOOSE TO BE LATE, REBECCA WATSON WILL CEASE TO LIVE. YOUR CAR IS OF COURSE BUGGED FOR OUR BENEFIT ONLY.

He threw down the typed message, started the Aston's big engine and made for the motorway.

The time was 5.01pm.

CHAPTER 2

Friday, 3.00pm. Central London.

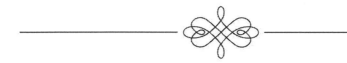

Rebecca Watson glanced down at her watch so relieved to see how quickly time had passed since her real interest was to be home by 4.30pm and prepare her body for Brett's return home. She hated his foreign trips but didn't complain, knowing he was always under pressure especially since having expanded the company.

Rebecca looked around her small shop; she glowed with enthusiasm and felt proud to think it was her own. The small perfumery had done well in its first year with Brett encouraging and helping her to overcome many of the pitfalls which could have ruined that small empire.

Usually by this time in September the major perfume houses had sent their Christmas stock and although Rochas was still to come, the shop bulged with small sealed boxes in brightly embossed colours.

Rebecca had a final look around at the cut glass light fittings, mahogany cupboards packed to overflowing and engraved glass display units before padding over the thick carpet to speak with her relief. Mrs McDonnald was a quiet elderly lady of some standing and particularly good at running the shop for Rebecca when she felt the need for a holiday. Rebecca approached Mrs McDonnald, saying, "Alice, I'm off now, will you lock up tonight as I want to be home when Brett gets back from Tangiers. He hates that place."

Alice McDonnald smiled at Rebecca knowing how much she loved Brett and acknowledged her concern.

"That's alright, my love." Alice McDonnald sighed. "Don't worry about coming in tomorrow. I am sure a day off would do you good."

Rebecca turned, waved to the other two assistants knowing Alice would maintain control and headed out into the mid-afternoon air. The sweet aroma of the shop left her instantly as the London traffic roared past. She turned and walked down Oxford Street to the underground car park which Brett had insisted she use, much to her disgust as it was incredibly expensive and considerably overrated. During her short walk she didn't notice any of the fancy shops but wondered about Brett and just thinking of him made her crave for his body. He was six feet tall, dark, hairy and knew how to make love with awe-inspiring passion. Rebecca realised she was wet for him and quickened her pace towards the car park. Behind her followed a small puny-looking little man of indistinguishable features who Rebecca wouldn't have given a second glance. She didn't notice him but he watched her with growing interest. He had been watching her every movement for the past few months.

She reached her car, a second hand XR3 which Brett didn't like but it suited her needs. He'd wanted her to have a brand-new car but she insisted for driving around London this was more than adequate. Rebecca drove out into the mainstream London traffic passing the puny little man who concealed himself from her view near to the payphone. He turned, picked up the phone and dialled. The ringing seemed to be endless before it was answered. He began to shake but although not enjoying this job so far, found the money was good and up to press easily acquired.

"'Control', she left at 3.25pm. Usual car."

There was no reply from the other end, just a click as the receiver was replaced. Christian Beck swayed but gathered his balance and headed home to his one-room pit. He'd done as the instructions demanded and felt relieved the task was completed. Little did he know it was only just the start of things to come.

Rebecca gathered together her thoughts and steering the car through London onto the M25 motorway, loathed this section of the journey but knew the prize was well worth the effort. The miles passed by with endless streams of high-speed traffic chasing the afternoon sunlight.

Leaving the motorway her mind relaxed, allowing the day's turmoils to be wiped away. The journey from London to their smart suburbia home usually took just over an hour yet perhaps it was the thought of Brett making love to her that evening which made the arduous trip so brief.

She turned down the leafy glade of Lenton Parva, its trees turning to shades of bright orange, red and brown. Rebecca loved the autumn yet always resented the passing of each summer with those long, warm days. She turned the car into the drive, stepped out and walked briskly over the gravel surface to the front door. As the huge front door eased open she slipped her sensual body into the cavernous hallway and closed the door firmly behind her. Everything was still, quiet and peaceful.

Rebecca called the maid but to no avail. She'd asked Martha to come in especially as Brett was coming home but it was not uncommon for her to be out shopping at this time during the afternoon. The morning mail lay stacked on the antique sideboard but Rebecca decided to take a shower before attempting anything else. She climbed the huge spiral staircase and entered their bedroom. Her skirt fell to the floor with uncontrollable ease, the silk blouse shed from her well-developed bosom and the fine lace underwear slid away revealing a succulent, tender body. She glided over the shag pile carpet towards the en-suite bathroom with every intention to pamper her slender, suntanned body. The shower water was hot and she was excited as allowing her own hands to massage the firm, large breasts Rebecca became totally transformed.

Hans Zenna slipped out from the large double wardrobe in the Watsons' bedroom and tiptoed towards the bathroom. He didn't want to harm Rebecca, especially having watched her undress with such ease.

Hans had admired her female form the like he'd never witnessed before. He slid back the shower door and placed his thumb on the pressure points of her neck just as his martial arts training had taught him. Rebecca Watson, stunned by this intrusion had no time to struggle before collapsing into his strong arms.

Hans Zenna carried Rebecca towards the four-poster bed, laid her gently down and surveyed the room for a bath robe. He couldn't help admiring her body; she was stunning but he knew the current task was all important to his future survival. Hans wrapped her in a bath robe he found and gently tied her hands behind her back. His powerful arms slid underneath her glorious form and picking Rebecca up Hans headed towards the lounge downstairs, being careful not to damage his most precious cargo.

The lounge was lit by the late afternoon sunlight as Hans entered the room and laid Rebecca's stirring body on the sofa. He stood back, admired her yet again and wondered how many men could have carried out this operation without having explored her wonderful body. Hans Zenna was different and determined but "Control" had located his weakness, he was gay. Hans knew if he didn't follow "Control's" instructions his career within the Civil Service would be shredded.

The door chime echoed within the hallway and Hans sprung back to attention as he knew this was one of "Control's" people. Easing open the large front door, Alexis Matos stormed past him with a sense of impending urgency. Zenna was aware of a powerful woman in their presence and after securing the door followed her into the lounge.

Alexis Matos stood with her black-leather-clad legs slightly apart, her hands fixed firmly to her side and long black hair brushed back past her brown face. She viewed the room, then Zenna and lastly Rebecca Watson who had started to waken. Matos grinned while her body trembled before she uttered in forceful yet clear Arabic tainted English.

"Well then Zenna, did you feel the bitch or are you still a gay, crooked bastard?"

Zenna felt rage but contained his impulsive desire to kill Matos and turned away. An hour and twenty minutes had passed since Rebecca entered the bedroom yet he considered that to be the longest and most tedious period in his life. Hans Zenna felt angry, exposed and most of all destroyable.

CHAPTER 3

Friday, 5.50pm. Lenton Parva.

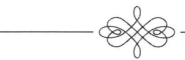

Brett Watson made good time. The journey from Heathrow to their home in Lenton Parva normally took just over an hour but today he made the Aston Martin work overtime and turned into their drive with ten minutes to spare.

Brett felt the car slide to a halt on the gravel drive but was more intent on finding Rebecca and lifting his large frame out of the car noticed his once clean tailored suit looked generally worse for wear.

During the drive home after reading the message the airport bell boy had given him, he attempted to consider every possibility. Twice Brett almost rang the police but refrained from that line of action as the undertones of the message pointed to him dealing with dangerous criminals. He considered who to Christ would have a motive for holding his beloved Rebecca as a hostage. The only answer which came to the front of his mind reflected in his trip to Tangiers and even more alarmingly, Aston Appleton.

Brett almost ran to the large front door, noticing someone moving inside the house, and opening the door headed straight into the lounge. Alexis Matos heard the big Aston Martin enter the drive and motioned Hans Zenna to take his pre-arranged position behind the door. Alexis let the safety catch off the .38 revolver and stood in readiness as before when Zenna had entered the room with her black-leather-clad legs slightly apart. It was almost a trademark.

Brett Watson burst into the room and was faced with the revolver pointing straight at him and froze.

"One wrong move and she will die," Matos hissed in her Arabic-splattered English as Brett's eyes shot over to the sofa and his heart raced as he saw his sexy wife lay there with her hands tied. He started to move towards her.

"Stay exactly where you are," Matos snapped. "If you do as you are told then you will both live, if not you'll share a coffin."

Brett froze again; he couldn't bear the thought of these bastards hurting his wife and it tore him apart to see what they'd done so far. Anger started to grow inside him. Brett felt sure he could overpower this bastard bitch who continually pointed the gun at him. He could do it, he felt it, but at the same time he felt a large hand on his left shoulder which shook him back to reality. Hans Zenna remained out of sight but felt the vibration of Brett's thoughts. He would have helped Brett, dearly loving to destroy Alexis Matos, but knew it was "Control" he must destroy.

Brett was forced into an easy chair as Zenna moved round the room and stood in front of him, taking the Matos woman's gun. He pointed it in Brett's face, saying, "Relax and we'll get out of this in one piece."

Brett looked up at Zenna while his muscular body towered over him. He noted the clean edge the man had, his fair hair, smart casual appearance and easy manner which the woman clearly used. Alexis Matos he regarded with intensifying hate; her skin-tight leather clothes, long black hair and coloured skin made her more evil to look at as the seconds passed. She strutted up and down the carpet as if waiting for him to make a move so she'd tell Zenna to kill Rebecca.

Brett's eyes flashed towards his wife. She lay still but Brett could see tears running down her perfect face. He wanted to go to her but Zenna made sure any possible escape route was blocked.

The mellow ticking of the grandfather clock was broken by its chimes announcing it was 6 o'clock as Brett wondered how long Rebecca had been at their mercy. The last hour had been bad enough for him yet Alexis Matos looked relieved to hear the clock chime. She darted to the phone, punched in a long number and waited. It seemed an age to Brett before the coloured woman's call was answered.

"Control, both your birds are in the nest as planned. I'm going to open the next stage of your schedule."

Brett sat horrified. He suddenly realised this was not a game but something fucking dangerous and he was the key. His mind demanded to know who was attempting to operate this devilish plan. Who the hell was "Control" and what were these two bastards going to do next? He was sweating.

CHAPTER 4

Friday, 6.00pm. London Office.

The suite of offices occupied by Rosco International were quiet with the hustle and bustle of the day having passed. Stood at the window overlooking the Thames, Aston Appleton watched the traffic pass over London Bridge. His mind was never idle but at that moment he was considering his next move in the cat and mouse game he was playing with Brett Watson's life.

The phone ringing took him by surprise and lifting the receiver noted the time as being 6 o'clock. Alexis Matos' check-in time, he considered, and his heart jumped as she relayed her message. Aston replaced the receiver to his private phone, sat down in his leather office arm chair, poured himself a large double brandy and lit yet another of his favourite deadly heroin smokes. This game he was going to win; he'd all the odds in his favour, it was well planned and he'd picked the players himself.

Aston's crooked grin cracked his weather-beaten face as he considered the pain Brett Watson was suffering, the money he personally was going to make and finally the thought of taking full control of the company really made him feel happy. His crooked grin turned to a full smile and then he laughed quietly to himself at first but later his laughter filled the entire room. He was evil and he knew it, everybody knew it except Brett but far more important he, Aston Appleton, was "Control".

Historical

Aston Appleton and Brett Watson were both thirty-four years old. They first met whilst still at Oxford University and during their final year shared the same living quarters. It was fate which at that time they both considered had brought them together and they appeared to do everything in unison, enjoying each other's company. Brett had considered Aston a firm ally but even from their early months together Aston always disliked playing second fiddle to his companion. Brett Watson was an ace student. His midterm grades were always better, his sporting ability received more acclaim and he was very popular with the women. He always purveyed himself as a smooth, well-dressed, intelligent Romeo while Aston was constantly in his shadow, never quite breaking through Brett's impermeable barrier of success.

As their finals approached Aston had to study with increasing concentration to even have a chance of obtaining a degree. Brett on the other hand was a natural, he did little work towards his finals and sailed through with Honours.

Their final year in close contact started in good humour but as it drew to a close Aston's hatred for Brett was well developed, even though they were both subconsciously oblivious to these thoughts.

On leaving Oxford Brett moved into a well-paid position with Rosco while Aston had struggled to obtain a meagre position with Choans. Both companies dealt entirely with locating positions for very highly qualified engineering personnel, advertising the positions, obtaining suitable candidates and then passing them over to their prospective employers. Both Rosco and Choans charged a large fee for their services but Aston considered Choans to be the more viable company as it dealt internationally, unlike Rosco's. Both men kept in constant touch to begin with even though Aston's hatred for Brett was only apparent to himself. Aston Appleton realised the potential at Choans and like Rosco's it was run by elderly directors who in his opinion were only fit for the graveyard. Aston's mistake was to let this thought be known and as a result the directors made damn sure Aston Appleton worked harder for less remuneration.

Brett's rise to fame was very different. He came to terms with Rosco's ability and as time drifted by worked his way from negotiator to associate director. Brett Watson began to filter his ideas into the company including diversifying to the lucrative property deals around London's Dock Lands.

This proved highly profitable for Rosco's, ensuring their long-term financial stability while the City became acutely aware of the company and especially Brett Watson's ability. Everything he handled turned into profit. Although still a dedicated bachelor at the time, he was continuing his panache for success developed less than five years before at Oxford with a true spirit.

Aston Appleton reviewed Brett's career with horror. Every time he learnt more of Rosco's recent developments he winced, knowing the old buffoon-like directors were not responsible for this success. He knew just who to blame and that made him all the more angry since he could do bugger all to match it.

Historical

It had been seven years since the two men had left Oxford.

Choans' share of the market had over the last two years declined beyond belief. Aston Appleton felt cramped and cheated as his twisted mind couldn't even consider how to approach beating Brett Watson. Rosco's on the other hand had grown from strength to strength. They had excelled in the original mode of the company as a skilled personnel recruitment house and had made glowing profits with land development. It came as no surprise to the City when Rosco's two elderly directors retired and appointed Brett Watson to run the whole company in its entirety. Naturally Brett was delighted and found no difficulty in raising the capital to finance his taking over the company. He felt as if the world was his playmate; he'd aimed for the top of the tree and arrived but knew this was only the start. Brett had already planned his approach for the company's development, the planned first stage, however, was now complete.

Within two months of him being the sole director of Rosco's he made a successful bid for Choans. Their directors had been only too pleased to sell their ever declining concern and did so for a meagre five million pounds.

Brett Watson closed Choans down overnight, stripping all its assets and transferring them to his own original company. Choans' old offices were sold and Rosco's became Rosco International.

Brett had wanted Choans for their international contacts which he knew to be secure and these he proposed to develop in harmony with his ever increasing salient foreign land deals. Brett had observed Choans personnel and was only prepared to offer one position, that being his associate director. He lifted the phone's receiver, punched in a local London number and the call was almost immediately answered. Brett recognised Aston's voice and told him outright of his offer.

Aston Appleton winced but accepted as his brain ticked in accelerating palpitations. Replacing the phone, Aston couldn't believe his good fortune, that bastard had made him an offer and he swore to Christ this was going to be the start of Brett Watson's decline.

Within the hour Aston Appleton's arrival was announced by Brett's sumptuous secretary and as Brett watched his office door swing open, allowed his eyes to follow Aston's entry.

Initially Brett was stunned to note how Aston had aged. His auburn hair was now mainly grey and looked to have retrogressed dramatically. The charcoal grey suit hung on his drawn, stooping body and his once full face was thin, heavily lined and tired looking.

Brett's expression must have portrayed to Aston the shock of his appearance as the last time they'd seen each other Aston looked twice the man standing before him on this occasion.

"Aston, thanks for coming over so promptly," Brett said and standing up, moved around his exquisite leather-topped desk to shake Aston's warm, sweltering hand.

"I was surprised to hear from you," Aston acknowledged.

"Well," Brett said, seating his sturdy frame back in a large, soft leather easy chair and motioning to Aston to do likewise, "I know we have had our basic differences over the years in a professional capacity but I wanted someone from Choans to continue with the foreign contacts. Naturally I've checked out all the options and since I am aware of your ability I considered you to be the most suitable candidate for the position of associate director. You must understand, however, I will still maintain control of the company but feel sure our future relationship could secure Rosco International's increasing growth and profit trends within the international scene."

Aston Appleton regarded Brett throughout his speech and couldn't understand how he'd maintained his youthfulness. His large frame was as sturdy as ever, and there were no signs of any grey hair, it still being well groomed and full bodied. Aston could feel the heckles of hatred growing but quickly brought them back under control.

"I'm grateful you have considered me for the position, Brett, and will endeavour to not only work with you and for you but to develop the company's influence," Aston had answered in his usual curt manner. Both men smiled, discussed terms of employment and parted with a cool limp handshake. Aston Appleton went back to his car planning Brett Watson's downfall with a satirical chuckle of untold glee.

CHAPTER 5

Friday, 6.00pm. Lenton Parva.

Alexis Matos slammed down the phone after speaking to "Control". Her face beamed with sinister delight whilst making for a black holdall in the far corner of the room deposited by Hans Zenna. She withdrew a roll of wide surgical tape, cut off a short length, made her way to Rebecca and placed the tape over her mouth. Up to this point in time Rebecca had been still and quiet, partly through fright but mainly through her inability to move. As Alexis put the tape over Rebecca's mouth her fear rose and she started to shout for Brett, shaking her face from side to side, but all her movement and whimpering yells were in vain. Brett made a concerted effort to go to his wife again but Hans Zenna kept him down; he was still holding the .38 revolver.

"Now listen very carefully," Matos yelled.

The aggressiveness of her tone instantly stopped Rebecca's sobbing and made Brett freeze.

"The plan is as follows. Hans, you are to stay here and look after the Watson woman. If she gives you any trouble break something and when every bone is broken, kill her. 'Control' says any resistance must be met with agonising pain. We," she motioned to Brett and herself, "will return as soon as possible, probably in a couple of days if everything goes to the plan as arranged by 'Control'."

Rebecca's eyes filled with tears and grew in sheer horror of being left gagged and bound for so long. It was not the home coming she'd planned for Brett and the only thing running through her mind now was him being taken away from her for so long. Her body quivered with uncontrollable fear.

Alexis Matos strode over to Hans Zenna and stood directly in front of Brett. She was obviously enjoying her moment of power.

"You and I are going to take a short trip," she announced in her Arabic-tainted English which seemed more pronounced than ever. For the first time Brett saw the glimmers of a smile flash across her face. Hans dragged Brett to his feet; his legs felt useless with fear while Alexis stood back allowing Zenna to remove Brett's jacket before later passing to her for searching. Hans frisked Brett for any other objects which may have been of interest to them but Alexis noticed how slowly Hans was doing the job and turned away as she realised Zenna was enjoying himself.

Alexis again went to her black holdall and withdrew two pairs of white overalls, the type Brett had seen mechanics wear. She passed Brett one pair and told him to get in them. He hesitated but the sight of the revolver and Rebecca tied up eased the pain of receiving such curt instructions. The overalls were a perfect fit and Alexis Matos motioned him towards a pair of white training shoes with red markings along the sides. Brett Watson went towards them with his every move being monitored by Hans Zenna and as he bent down horror filled his inner stomach. The distorted bloody body of their maid Martha lay behind the easy chair in which he'd been sitting. Her face was bruised and her flaxen hair smeared with bodily waste. Brett took another look but didn't feel Hans Zenna pull him like a limp dog back into the centre of the room.

Martha had been with them since their marriage two years ago. They'd grown to love her little ways and she had treated both Brett and Rebecca like her own children. Brett had always felt sorry for Martha, she had no family and they had accepted her motherly ways into their household with open arms.

Alexis Matos felt her own contentment as she watched Brett discover the maid's body. She now knew they had touched yet another tender spot in the Watsons' life. Martha's murder was not planned but Hans had discovered the maid when breaking into the Watsons' house almost four hours before. She had made frightening gestures towards him with a large meat knife; he'd retaliated, grabbing the knife from her and without thinking had plunged it deep into her heart. The elderly lady sunk on to the lounge carpet behind the easy chair and Hans went to the Watsons' bedroom to hide in readiness for Rebecca and calm his shaking blond body. Martha's remains were surrounded by a large pool of blood steadily soaking into the carpet.

When Alexis Matos arrived and saw Hans had not only carried out his instructions as issued by "Control" relative to Rebecca but disposed of the maid as well she thought better of him. She would rather have not been involved in this whole affair but "Control" had made sure there was no escape for any of them.

The maid had been known to Appleton but normally didn't work at the Watsons' home between Thursday night and Tuesday morning. Today was Friday and Martha's dedication to the Watsons had been her downfall. She shouldn't have been there, if anyone asked questions, Matos decided, and put the event out of her mind with some difficulty.

Alexis Matos recovered Brett's passport and credit cards from his jacket, pushing them into her black holdall as she nodded to Hans who knew she was almost ready to leave. Zenna pushed Brett towards the lounge door and looking towards his wife, he felt utterly distraught. He couldn't believe this was happening to them. Alexis took her revolver back from Hans and looked at him with the knowledge that if she didn't succeed, both their lives would be destroyed.

Outside the house she came back to her senses and although feeling saddened by her actions on the Watsons, ushered Brett past his gleaming Aston Martin and out onto the road knowing she still had to conform to "Control's" demands despite loathing every second of it. Lenton Parva seemed serene and untroubled; the night was almost upon them with stars dimly beginning to showing themselves. Brett checked his watch, it was a little after 7.00pm when they walked towards a white Ford Transit van with the bold red letters of R.A.M. Royal Air Maroc painted on the side. These were exactly the same initials which adorned his white overalls. Matos forced Brett into the driver's seat, threatening him again with

Rebecca's security, and told him to head for the staff service entry gate at Heathrow's terminal two. If only she'd told Brett of her plight.

Brett drove with greater care than ever before, it had been a long time since he'd driven a Transit. He recalled the time as he and Rebecca had moved into the house on Lenton Parva just before they married and felt tears running down his face but knew they were tears of anger, not joy this time. Alexis witnessed this display of emotion and she felt for him.

Brett didn't speak throughout their journey, he still thought it was all some kind of bad nightmare. It seemed to take an age before the service entry gate was reached but just before they arrived, Alexis Matos attached an airport security pass to his left lapel. The guards at the gate only took a brief glimpse at them as they appeared bored with the number of airline staff passing through and after all, what were another two? Brett considered making himself known to them by yelling for the police but the vision of Rebecca being hurt and Martha's distorted body made him reconsider his actions.

Alexis guided him to the ramp where the Royal Air Maroc jet stood waiting with airport lights shimmering all around it. Her knowledge of the airport was impressive and Brett was convinced beyond all doubt this was no five-minute operation. She demanded he park the van close to the aircraft steps before they climbed out and armed with her revolver, she told him to board the plane with her following him.

The glare of warm, comforting cabin lights hit Brett. He knew whoever "Control" was had gone to immense planning tactics to achieve a result he as yet knew nothing about. Brett noticed the airplane was already loaded as he was forced to take a window seat right at the front of the cabin with the Matos woman beside him and as he did so felt the plane being pushed away from the ramp.

As they boarded the cabin staff had acknowledged them as airline employees with their bright, crisp new overalls, hence no alarm radiated from the crew at all. Brett was alone, frightened and accompanied by an eccentric woman who still carried a revolver which pointed in his general direction.

Lenton Parva was dark and quiet yet there was a dim light shining from within the Watson household. Rebecca had managed to gain control of herself again despite Brett and the Matos woman having been gone just over an hour even though it seemed like a lifetime. The regular movement of the grandfather clock had managed to secure a degree of calm and Rebecca was starting to wonder for the first time since her ordeal had started that maybe, just maybe the whole affair would pass without further incident if she did as her guard told her. Although still bound and gagged she knew danger was all around. Her mind wandered but was quickly awakened by Hans Zenna moving Martha's body out of the room. Alexis Matos had told him to dispose of the maid's body but the method and means Hans couldn't determine, so for the time being he considered the garage as being the best place. He couldn't bear to think of his past actions relative to the maid yet alone spend any further time with the body in the same room. Rebecca had seen Brett's facial expression when he discovered Martha's body and she had worked out for herself what he'd found. It certainly coincided with Martha not being around when she came home since she'd definitely asked Martha to come in that day. Rebecca felt remorseful and guilty over Martha's murder, she was already blaming herself but the sight of Hans Zenna removing her body made her weep and turn cold.

Martha had been a great friend to the Watsons.

Hans Zenna returned to the lounge and drawing an armchair close to Rebecca, he noticed the fear in her eyes but sat back, allowing time to meander past. Hans drifted to sleep recalling how he'd become involved in this dirty affair.

Hans Zenna was German by birth but had come to England whilst still only a boy. At ten years old he recalled the move. His father was Jewish and although the war years were long past, the Zennas considered their fortunes would be better laid down elsewhere in the world. His father had a great respect for the English and loved England yet the move had been difficult, but after many years proved fruitful. His father's bakery was a success and Hans had claimed British citizenship. He'd done well at school and studied law at London University, graduating with a degree. He was no fool and his parents were proud of him especially since he was their only child. After graduation Hans applied to join the Civil Service and although he'd experienced difficulties in convincing the authorities of his determination he was accepted. Good fortune shone on him and his promotions came quickly. He worked hard and eventually gained the position of permanent secretary to a junior minister of government.

At the age of thirty-two he was well admired but Hans kept his private life away from his working environment, much to the disgust of the women he worked with, who would have loved to share his bed.

Hans looked after his body, frequently visiting a martial arts club with gym and went jogging most mornings covering nothing less than five or six miles. His six-foot frame was broad and well put together. His blond hair always well cut complimented his suntanned skin. Hans Zenna knew he looked good and for most of the time felt good.

During his years at university he'd discovered something about himself which frightened yet excited him. He had been approached by another student and together they had formed a homosexual partnership. Hans couldn't explain why or how but during the last years of the university term, he had lived with this man and enjoyed the exciting lovemaking they created.

After leaving, Hans had tried to straighten out his sexual drive and attempted to make love to some women but could never manage a solid, hard erection. He never passed sperm into any woman.

Three months prior to him abducting Rebecca Watson and just after receiving his promotion to permanent secretary, he went into a bar in London's West End for a quiet drink before heading home. He hated the rush hour and usually carried through this ritual to avoid the worst of the crush. As he sat at the bar a small, puny little man entered and came to sit beside him. At first Hans didn't notice but became aware of someone watching him and turning he saw his old homosexual partner. Hans didn't know whether to be horrified or pleased but they sat, talked and drank into the small hours of the morning before going back to the man's apartment and they made love as he had not done since his days at university.

Hans had been shocked to see how his old lover had withered and to hear of his failed business. He'd not known the whole of their homosexual act had been photographed and his lover was receiving money for the film.

To say he had been shocked when the pictures came through the post coupled with the telephone calls from someone calling himself "Control" was very much an understatement. Hans was threatened, he knew if he didn't follow the instructions he was repeatedly given "Control" would send the photographs to his superiors which would ensure him losing his job and disgracing his elderly parents. Hans was given no alternative.

He woke up with a sudden start as the grandfather clock chimed and Hans realised he'd been asleep for nearly two hours. He instantly thought of Matos and Brett Watson, her threats, "Control" and his own future. Hans knew very little about "Control's" plan, only his own duties which were sufficient to redeem the negatives concerning his wild night of homosexual passion.

Rebecca had also drifted to sleep but awakened when she heard the curtains being drawn. Hans walked over to her and carefully removed the surgical tape from her mouth. He sat her up, smiled and started to remove the ties from her hands. Looking at him and managing a small, meagre smile, Rebecca believed an ally to be in sight. It was 10.02pm.

CHAPTER 6

Friday, 5.15pm.

The Royal Air Maroc Boeing 727 would soon be approaching the runway, Brett considered, as the taxi time had seemed longer than usual and he wondered if this was the same plane which had flown him into Heathrow a little over four and a half hours before. Alexis Matos wriggled a little in her seat but Brett was still covered by the revolver hidden discreetly under her loose-fitting overalls.

Brett felt the large airliner turn, noticed the uniform lines of runway lights and within seconds the surge of power from the three rear-mounted Pratt and Whitney engines. The aircraft built up speed, quickly lifted away from Mother Earth and forced its way into the dark night.

As the seat belt sign was turned off Brett still didn't know of his destination for sure, although he assumed it was to be Morocco since this was their national airline. He turned to look at Alexis, moved a little towards her and in a voice he couldn't perceive as being his own whispered, "Since you've frightened the living shit out of me, used my wife as your hostage and are still pointing that ruddy gun toward my stomach, would you care to enlighten me as to which part of Morocco I, correction, we are heading for, or is it a part of the master plan I'm not supposed to know?"

Alexis Matos turned towards him and relaxing her hold on the gun looked at Brett as if he was not there. She turned her dusky coloured face towards the front of the aircraft and flicked back the long black hair with her free hand. Brett considered he'd just been put in his place but in a few short seconds she turned again obviously having considered her reply.

"Mr Brett Watson, you are the subject of a very evil man's desire to see you suffer, possibly die, just to satisfy his own egotistical and financial gain. Regrettably many more of us are having to suffer so I suggest you sit back and enjoy the rest of the flight. It could be our last."

Somehow Brett depicted a note of sincerity in her voice as the harsh Arabic-tainted English had mellowed a little. Throughout the remaining hours of the two-and-a-half-hour flight no further communication was made and neither of them slept or ate. Brett was deep in thought worrying over Rebecca whilst Alexis considered her future in the light of the past twenty-four hours. Her hand never left the revolver and he considered she was a hard woman carrying out a mission which was not entirely pleasurable for her as he wondered if the real truth would ever be known. Brett only glanced towards her once or twice during the flight after their initial confrontation but on both occasions could have sworn he saw tears oozing from her wild, mysterious eyes.

Feeling the whine of the engines change Brett guessed their descent was well underway. The cabin staff had been busy throughout the journey and he had allowed his mind to wonder as to who Alexis Matos had in mind as being "a very evil man". Who the shitting hell could want to do this to him? But all reason eluded Brett. Sure, he had rivals within his working environment, yet he was having difficulty tracing anybody who would go to such extremes.

The aircraft touched down and Alexis felt the undercarriage come into contact with Mother Earth. The plane rolled to a halt by the terminal building as she demanded Brett get out of his seat and make for the doorway yet any trace of the mellow undertones he'd detected during the flight had vanished. The cabin staff acknowledged them with a shy smile, their white airline overalls giving them a pass to disembark from the plane before normal fare-paying passengers.

As Brett made his exit the hot night air struck him. It was like walking into an open oven. The lights of the terminal were dazzling but he could make out the name of the airport above the concrete roof. "Tangiers," he whispered to himself, feeling fear and anxiety inflate his tired body. To the left of the aircraft steps a dark Rolls-Royce was parked. As they descended from the aircraft and walked towards the Rolls, Brett recognised it as the same car which picked him up only days before on his own scheduled visit to this stinking city. He looked around with total disbelief. How the hell could Mohamid Van Jonger have done this to him? He'd been his friend for so many years but it looked to Brett as if Mohamid was "Control". *The stinking two-faced bastard*, he thought. "I knew I shouldn't have got involved with these fucking dirty Arabs," he muttered under his flaming breath.

Brett's temper craved to get the better of him yet Matos sensed his feelings and pushed him into the car but his patience snapped as his arms lashed out at her. Alexis had already backed away from him so as to avoid his anger. The revolver appeared once more and Brett's outrage instantly became inert. He sluggishly scrambled onto the car's back seat with Alexis close behind him.

The Rolls-Royce slipped away from the aircraft's side whilst Brett's mind churned alternative methods of attracting the customs staff attention as they passed through the exit. The whole exercise was futile as waving them through the airport gates the Rolls headed for the ancient walled city.

None of the other passengers had witnessed any of this episode, except one. A small, puny little man seated in row 10F watched the whole incident and made his report to "Control" once he arrived at the hotel.

Brett couldn't understand Mohamid's reasoning for acting in such a barbarous manner as was now apparent. He didn't consider their conversation of earlier that day, in which Mohamid had hinted at a drugs trade triangle to be a suitable reason for this current harassment. Then again he considered the vast sums of money which could be made in that business but Brett had rejected the idea outright wanting Rosco International to remain free of such dirt money. It seemed that conversation couldn't have taken place only the same morning since so much had happened since.

The Rolls sped towards the old walled city of Tangiers which always made Brett feel apprehensive at the best of times. Tonight was no exception but with an added ingredient, he was petrified.

Drawing to a steady halt outside the Rembrant Hotel the car door was opened by a large Arab dressed in his national caftan, displaying an Arabic sabre strapped to his side. Brett was hurried into the hotel's entrance with Alexis Matos following close behind as the liveried doorman took a firm hold of Brett's arm; his grip was painful.

Watson could smell the Arab's pungent aroma, it not being unlike the silty stagnant drains from within the Kasba and he winced at the thought of being in close contact with this heathen. Although having left this same hotel earlier that day Brett noticed no familiar faces during his swift propelled transit across the marble floor. Nobody looked and nobody cared. He felt degraded, an unimportant lump of inconsequential meat.

They reached the office door at the far end of the hotels reception lobby. The stinking Arab opened it, almost throwing Brett into the room's centre whilst Alexis glided in behind him. In the midriff part of the room Mohamid stood clad in a black pin stripe suit; his outwardly sharp features which normally displayed no emotion looked utterly distraught to Brett. Alexis made straight for Mohamid, threw her arms around him and hugged him with tears flowing freely down both their faces.

Brett straightened himself and stood upright, rubbing his arm the big Arab had gripped so vigorously. He coughed as both Alexis and Mohamid looked towards him. Their sorrowful eyes told him a story containing an evil venom but he needed to know more, a whole fucking lot more. It was 11.15pm.

CHAPTER 7

Historical

Mohamid Van Jonger was a self-made millionaire and had grown up in the Kasba under the stigma of being mixed race. His mother was a Moroccan and his father Dutch. They'd met before the Second World War made their home in Tangiers and struggled for the remaining years of their lives. Mohamid recalled how his parents had loved each other despite their squalid lifestyle. They'd always provided sufficient for him yet Mohamid couldn't remember wearing shoes until his early teens.

As his seventeenth birthday approached his parents both contracted T.B. and died. Being alone and a cross breed in a city wrought with crime was not a good start for any young man. The Second World War gave Mohamid a chance to build up a small mobile shop based inside the dirty caftan he continuously wore. It was a source of lasting entertainment to the passing military how he managed to carry such an array of cigarettes, dirty books, watches, rings, silk, stockings and drugs hidden within the garment.

Throughout those endless war years Mohamid learned to trade and make money, very often having to make a hasty retreat from unsatisfied customers.

During all his early years of development Mohamid retained his faith in Allah, prayed like a good Muslim yet was always on the lookout for a fast fortune and eventually the opportunity arose. One sweltering evening in the then very seedy Rembrant Hotel, Mohamid played poker with the elderly owner and six less savoury characters. The stakes were high but Mohamid maintained a cool level head as each of the players dropped out of the tournament and the betting became more intense. The amount of money on the table grew and eventually the hotel's owner had nothing left but his building. Mohamid bet his entire night's winnings against the hotel yet being a greedy Arab the owner, who loved a true bet, couldn't resist trying for Mohamid's money. They were the only players left around the table, the die was cast. He recalled how silent the smoke-filled room became as the cards were dealt. Each of the two players attempted to outstare the other but in a fit of impetuosity the hotel's owner displayed his hand and laughed with excitement whilst moving the money towards his greedy slobbering body. Outraged by this action, Mohamid demanded his own cards be permitted to show his loss or gain. The older man sat transfixed as Mohamid opened up the winning hand. Each of the men in the room let out a river of local dialogue followed by a series of fist-shaking actions. The new owner of the Rembrant was only twenty-nine, had no experience of running a hotel but was so determined for this to be a success the whole incident made him ache. Mohamid never played poker again.

As time rolled past he learnt how the hotel worked, how to deal with people, their painful requirements and turned the Rembrant into the best hotel in North Africa. It provided him with an excellent standard of living and pampered to his every need.

*

Many wealthy Arabs and Europeans frequented this hotel including a Moroccan shipping tycoon bringing his young daughter with him as his personal assistant. She was in her late twenties and Mohamid now in his early thirties was smitten with her at first glance. He made advances towards her and she capitulated to his passionate overtures, becoming pregnant within a very short space of time. By this period in his life Mohamid was no longer a back-street scruff looking to shake off his low-level tags but a respected wealthy man in the ever growing city of Tangiers. He could now afford the best of everything and frequently put this into practice.

Before meeting this young woman Mohamid had taken himself a true wife who was the daughter of a prominent lawyer within the city and had assisted him in the hotel's development. His wife of only a few months was a true Moroccan, shy, traditional and didn't object to anything her husband said or did. This was the known and accepted Moroccan custom.

The making pregnant of an unmarried Muslim woman was one of the worst offences Allah's creed depicted. The situation was made worse by the woman's family being so influential within the shipping fraternity but once her parents knew of the pregnancy and she had named the father. Mohamid was summoned to their grand villa on the Atlantic coast of Tangiers City.

The meeting was serious and subdued; both the girl's father and Mohamid knew the act he'd committed was punishable by death according to Muslim law. They struck a bargain while the girl sat sobbing against the open window, allowing the sweet smell of jasmine to waft around them.

Once the baby was born it was to be sent away from Tangiers and brought up by Mohamid's mother's tribe high up in the mountains. He was to pay for all the child's upbringing, education and future life. In addition he was to pay the girl's parents a substantial sum of money once a year for the next ten years yet wincing at the thought, Mohamid knew he had no alternative if he wished to remain in Tangiers. The remaining part of the deal was for no other person except her father and Mohamid to know of this understanding, at least this would protect the unborn child and her mother's family from the stigma of having betrayed her culture. Mohamid knew it meant her life would be spared.

Once the baby was born, her mother never saw the child again and her family didn't make contact even though Mohamid maintained his regular payments as they'd agreed. He was a man of his word.

As time ticked past Mohamid made more frequent visits to see his illegitimate daughter, she grew up quickly and he made more of her on each visit. His only true wife was unable to bear children and Mohamid had considered that to be Allah's curse for his wrongdoings in earlier years but he still loved and cared for her.

Van Jonger knew he couldn't bring his daughter into Tangiers until she was at least twenty-one; that, he considered would be soon enough but he wanted to give her the very best yet for the present, he could do no more.

*

The age difference between Mohamid Van Jonger and his illegitimate daughter was thirty-two years. She had developed into a full-grown sensual woman who took care of her bodily appearance. When she reached twenty-one Mohamid summoned her to Tangiers but by this time he was fifty-three. They had spent many hot, sultry evenings talking of the past. The young woman always listened intensely and never pressed Mohamid, she was just glad of his company and loved him.

It came as a great shock when he told her in future, she'd be introduced as his "second wife". At first the young woman couldn't come to terms with Mohamid's reasoning. She could never be a true Moroccan woman, unlike his only wife who just accepted the young woman as a free spirit in her own right. Mohamid wanted everything for her but was unable to give her the greatest gift in life, sexual love. This was a deep regret to him and it hurt as she had grown into a ravishing, smooth-skinned goddess.

As the years passed by his true wife began to acknowledge the young woman's role in Mohamid's life and although they shared the same living quarters, little was ever spoken about her past. Mohamid's hotel became more successful and he decided to move his own living quarters away from central Tangiers so providing his two ladies with more freedom. He purchased a large villa well clear of any populated area facing the eastern Mediterranean Sea. The building was perched high on a cliff top and he filled it with the best of everything. The large windows were draped with heavy velvet curtains, marble floors were dotted with skin rugs and large pieces of antique furniture added a cool air of ambience to the airy building. The grounds were lush with lemon, orange, banana and olive trees with extensive lawns, patios and fountains. It was the most perfect retreat.

Whilst taking breakfast at the mansion one morning the first and worst shockwave struck Mohamid. It had been some time ago since he'd felt such pain and his eyes wandered towards his "second wife".

Mohamid Van Jonger's Villa. Friday, 7.30am.

The message which had made Mohamid shiver lay in front of him resting on a large silver tray brought in by the house boy.

Mohamid Van Jonger, you've never been punished for the rape of a young girl you didn't marry some twenty-eight years ago. We know all about you and how you've avoided your countries laws. If you don't want to die. have your illegitimate daughter go to London's Heathrow terminal two on the 9.00am flight today from your fair city. Enclosed is a security locker key. In the locker further instructions are awaiting for her. when she reads the instructions she will carry them out as detailed. If not, she will die, you will die and your family will be chastised forever. Further instructions will follow for you later.

The key slid onto the tray as Mohamid picked up the letter, it was typewritten and naturally unsigned. His cool nature prevailed but on leaving the table he beckoned the young woman to follow. Dutifully she pattered along the marble floor behind him and as they entered Mohamid's study, closed the door behind them.

He was not a big man and at the age of sixty he'd held his youth well. The grey-black hair was always well cut and his beard followed suit yet when dealing with Moroccans he preferred to wear his white robes, but today his black pin-stripe suit was looking equally good. Mohamid crossed the room and stood by the window, he turned to the young woman and showed her the typed letter he'd received. She coldly folded the sheet of paper, looked at her father, turned and left the room. Alexis knew her own history and more of her father's than was perhaps good for anyone to know. She went to her rooms, dressed herself in black leather trousers with shirt, collected a black leather holdall and made progressive moves towards the car. Alexis felt hate for whoever was doing this to her beloved father but he'd done so much for her, it was now time to repay at least part of the debt.

Driving to the airport she considered the letter her father had received and while the security box key lay on the seat beside Alexis she considered her mother, how she must have been and if the love for her father had been anything other than a small light flickering for just the briefest of glimpses. Alexis felt distraught and lonely.

The young woman arrived at the airport and boarded the flight to London feeling apprehensive of the near future. Mohamid Van Jonger had watched his daughter leaving and he'd wondered how anybody could have discovered their secret. His mind was in turmoil as the phone rang.

"Mohamid Van Jonger, you've received and acted on my instructions I trust?"

Mohamid was about to launch into a heated reply but thought of his daughter.

"Yes," he replied. "My daughter is aboard the flight to London. May I ask to whom I'm speaking?"

"You may ask, Mr Van Jonger. Shall we say you can call me 'Control'."

Mohamid considered his reply and carefully asked, "What is it you expect from me and how did you come by this information?"

The voice at the other end of the phone did not waiver. Mohamid knew it to be an English male but couldn't detect any sign of weakness.

"How the information was obtained, Mr Van Jonger, is only for me to know. Today you are being visited by Mr Brett Watson and the purpose of your meeting is to discuss the possibility of Mr Watson purchasing land on your behalf, shall we say in foreign countries not friendly to yours. I wish you to suggest another type of venture. One which if it succeeds will save your daughter, yourself and many others including Mr Watson from sure death. On the back seat of your Rolls-Royce you will find two suitcases. Each case is packed with cigarette lighters. You will notice the lighters are made in your fair country but have engraved upon them a map of Cyprus. The reason for this, Mr Van Jonger, it is necessary for these rather special lighters to be delivered to a colleague of mine based on that island. You will also notice them to be larger than one would expect. For your information, to secure the safety of your daughter's life, I will tell you not to tamper with any of them. They are very expensive to make and contain pure heroin. You will no doubt try to light one of them. Each lighter contains sufficient fuel for a sixty-second burn. Your job, Mr

Van Jonger, is to persuade Mr Watson to deliver these lighters to Cyprus. I don't expect him to accept your offer during the scheduled meeting you have arranged but your daughter will, however, bring Mr Watson back to the Rembrant tonight. I trust you will not allow him to leave without my prior instruction."

The phone went dead as "Control" concluded his speech. Mohamid replaced the receiver and sat down on the nearby sofa, stunned.

*

Mohamid sat for nearly an hour as the contents of the conversation with the English man calling himself "Control", ran through his troubled mind. He made his way through the palatial mansion and headed for the Rolls-Royce, opening a rear door only to see two tan suitcases facing him. Carefully he removed one and under the shade of a nearby olive tree opened the case to find it was filled with the garish coloured lighters the man had mentioned. "Tourist junk," he mumbled. Mohamid inspected one of the lighters closely and indeed they were bigger as the English man had said. Whoever had produced them knew the stakes were high, they were expensive and well made despite their colours. He played haphazardly with one lighter, attempting to value the drugs this innocent item contained, but replacing the article closed the suitcase lid and put it back into his car. Mohamid decided to take the cases to his hotel office and leave them to fester.

Driving from the mansion towards Tangiers the chauffeur cautiously steered the Rolls through unusually heavy and noisy traffic as Mohamid sat slumped next to his two suitcases on the rear seat. Being distinctly marked, these cases constantly caught his eye but he was still stunned at the thought of someone actually having the nerve to come so close to his mansion without being seen.

Pulling up outside the Rembrant, Mohamid eased himself and the cases from the luxury of the Rolls' sumptuous upholstery and entered his hotel a little more harassed than normal. Once in the sanctuary of his private office Mohamid allowed his body to relax and take stock of the situation. For the first time in many years Mohamid knew he was being used in a most sinister manner to better another man's financial resources.

Friday, 11.00am. Rembrant Hotel.

Mohamid Van Jonger and Brett Watson had enjoyed a successful business relationship for only a few tender years but the trust and satisfaction of their rapport had developed into a true friendship.

As Brett entered Mohamid's office for his scheduled meeting, Mohamid had decided to mention the venture concerning drugs only briefly. He knew Brett would be back again that day accompanied by his "second wife" and he couldn't risk agreeing anything that may hinder her safe return.

The meeting between these two men had been convivial, paving the way for a large land purchase by Mohamid and they'd both agreed it would be better if the Moroccan government were not informed. As their conversation broadened Mohamid became increasingly aware of discussing a trade in drugs but Brett had been shocked by his doggedness and declined any possible involvement.

Mohamid considered the Englishman calling himself "Control", knew Brett Watson well. He'd responded exactly as the man had suggested.

Friday, 11.15pm. Rembrant Hotel.

The tense atmosphere in Mohamid's office dissipated as he walked towards Brett and embracing him, felt relief with Alexis back in his company. Slowly Brett responded but with considerable caution while Alexis moved to the open window still clad in the white airline overalls. She leant slightly towards the opening and drank in the warm, fragrant night air.

Brett felt Mohamid and Alexis had a common bond but it was not until he introduced her in his formal manner that Brett knew Alexis to be his "second wife". He had met Mohamid's true wife many times and always admired her but assumed she was the only one.

Alexis crossed the large, well-furnished office and took hold of Brett's hand. Feeling an instant charge of current release into his inner body he felt total exoneration for her recent actions. Rebecca seemed miles away and Brett was smitten as Alexis spoke.

"I am so sorry for having done this to you and your wife, please, how can I ask for forgiveness even in time? But Mohamid is threatened."

Tears began to flow down her smooth skin whole she spoke in tones of such tender passion but Brett didn't hear a single word. Alexis fumbled a little, handed Brett the .38 revolver she'd been waving at him for so long and made her exit, saying a shower would make her feel a whole lot better.

Mohamid and Brett sat talking till the sun rose next morning. They both related their knowledge of the events experienced so far and between them tried to isolate the man calling himself "Control".

Brett realised he'd been hasty in assuming Mohamid to be "Control" as they discussed many things but although telling of much, Mohamid didn't expand the truth concerning Alexis. Brett still didn't know of Mohamid's shameful pride.

CHAPTER 8

Friday, 11.15pm. Rosco International Offices, London.

Aston Appleton drew heavily on his heroin cigarette and the brandy sild down his throat like pure silk, warming his arduous body. He checked the time, withdrew his master plan from the private safe located within his large desk and delighted himself by following the coloured lines plotting his evil scheme. It gave him an orgasm, the first in many years.

Aston didn't hear his private phone ringing at first but then lunged towards it. He'd been waiting to hear from his puny little man in Tangiers.

"Van Jonger, the Matos woman and Watson are all at the Hotel Rembrant as required."

The little man's voice seemed distant to Aston who boomed down the phone in return, "Well carry on to the next part of your schedule, keep me informed at the allotted times and don't forget how much I'm bloody well paying you."

Christian Beck heard Aston replace his phone and feeling inside the pocket of his cotton jacket withdrew a clean white sealed envelope with "Mohamid Van Jonger" typed in bold letters across the centre. He drifted towards the reception leaving the envelope on the counter to be found by one of the clerks and bending a little, he daintily pushed a small plastic carrier bag to one side of the counter just out of sight from passing clients. Christian moved towards the hotel's entrance and making his exit, climbed into a nearby taxi heading for the airport.

Historical

Aston Appleton wanted money and power yet this he had decided could be obtained at the same time as destroying Brett Watson. Since Brett had taken him onboard at Rosco International, Aston had weaved and dodged his way around their clients trying all the time to find a loophole from which he could manoeuvre. He was intent on using Rosco money to finance the growth of his own fortune and arranged for some of Rosco's capital to be transferred into a Moroccan bank. He told Brett the interest reaped from this investment would be of benefit while the goodwill created may ease the passage of any future business with Mohamid Van Jonger. Aston knew of Brett and Mohamid's latest venture and this he considered to be his loophole to secure more confidence with Brett hence eventually opening the door of fortune for himself. Although at the time Brett had seemed to reserve his opinion concerning the ethics of Aston's proposed investment he cleared the plan and the money was moved to Tangiers, all three million pounds worth.

Brett Watson became suspicious when the company money started moving from one bank to another and not gaining any interest.

This was in fact being paid by the banks but directly into Aston's own account and he was then using the money to purchase heroin. Aston knew if Brett discovered company money was being syphoned his plan would fail. He had to move quickly and cover his tracks since Brett was already asking questions and demanding to view bank statements.

*

Aston Appleton knew all the financial crooks within London's square mile. He'd used and broken people in the past but his withered, stooping frame was well known to many for his direct hit tactics, lacking only in compassion. He'd first met Christian Beck at London's Savoy Hotel and sensed he was a man of good education but with no true morals. Aston checked out Christian's background and was not surprised at the summarised conclusion. Beck's small private investigation concern had failed mainly due to him not attempting to conceal his homosexual disposition. He was broke and in appearance almost reflected the image of Aston himself.

For the first time in his life Aston Appleton took pity on another human being, inviting Christian to his fashionable penthouse in the Dock Lands. The two men discussed may aspects of life yet the meeting was concluded with Aston offering him a job. Christian was to work directly for him with strict instructions not to discuss their plans with anybody. Aston told him of his requirements but not the reasoning; he didn't wish for Christian to know any more than was necessary.

When Beck left Appleton's penthouse he had immediate duties to perform which he intended to conclude as quickly and efficiently as possible. Christian walked back to his seedy one-room flat clutching the money Aston had given him as a retainer. His mind considered who he could approach to secure the type of information Appleton wanted yet Beck knew he was becoming involved in some type of blackmail but wasn't aware of many details. He recalled the instructions he'd been given and just for a brief moment wondered about the ethics involved, however, feeling the wad of notes in his pocket put any doubts out of his mind.

The next day Christian Beck commenced his tactful observations of Rebecca Watson and on inspecting his past diary of affairs decided to relocate Hans Zenna. The media had given some coverage to Zenna's recent promotion and Beck knew he could cash in on his good fortune. It didn't take any effort to locate Zenna on Christian's part and approaching him in the West End bar he frequented, found his own body yearning for the man he'd once enjoyed such explosive shared passion with.

Beck had to report to Appleton each day and provide an update of his findings. He'd told Aston of Rebecca's daily routine, the people she met and the places she visited all with accurate gusto. Beck had not enjoyed Appleton instructing him to sleep with Hans Zenna again yet alone to photograph the whole affair since he'd already decided to entice Zenna to his flat, but photographing themselves together whilst performing such lovemaking as they'd done years before, didn't turn him on. Christian had thought Appleton would have been satisfied to know of a permanent secretary who was gay but gaining this type of proof was something else.

The arrival of the special camera with more money convinced Beck he had no alternative and removing some of the slats from the louvered wardrobe door, Beck fixed the camera in place. Hans was a big man and if he knew he was being photographed, Christian felt sure it would mean certain death for him.

Beck carried out his paid duties with reservation even though he'd enjoyed himself with ecstatic pleasure. The film and camera were duly returned to Appleton yet Christian never saw the developed printed photographs.

A few weeks elapsed after his affair with Zenna and although he'd maintained his observations on Rebecca, reporting them to Appleton with monotonous frequency, no new instructions arrived. He was bored by Rebecca's regular routine while Aston prepared the final touches to his blueprint.

The morning post landed heavily on Beck's faded carpet. He sauntered across the floor wiping sleep away from his eyes and observed the large brown envelope. Swaying slightly, he lifted the package, ripped it open and emptied the contents onto his unmade bed. Christian read the neatly typed instructions, looked closely at the four airline tickets and counted the wad of new fifty-pound notes which tumbled with the tickets. His heart was thumping.

*

Aston had developed Christian Beck's film himself as he wanted to be sure of the operation's privacy and in so doing decided Beck must die at the appropriate moment in time. His face again supporting a crooked evil grin. Scrutinising the photographs Aston considered Beck had done an excellent job despite some of the frames being a little dark; they left no stone unturned. Every position, posture and part of their lovemaking had been recorded. Packing one set of the photographs into an envelope for Hans Zenna's consumption, Appleton viewed Zenna's body feeling the pangs of jealousy at his well-endowed features. He was sure the shots would empower him to control Zenna, manipulate him and then finally destroy him.

Zenna's first encounter with Aston Appleton's tactics shook him. The photographs represented a part of his life he was unable to overcome and he'd looked at them for hours feeling bitter, unable to believe his old partner would stoop so low. During the course of the next twenty-four hours, Hans found it increasingly difficult to concentrate as his mind continuously wandered back and forth to the photographs.

As he sat one evening in his rented accommodation allowing the street below to offer the only illumination, he was startled by the phone ringing. He reached over, picked up the receiver and didn't have time to utter a single word before his inner body was dominated by a sinister voice booming at him.

"Hans Zenna, you will have by now received a series of photographs taken by my associate. If you agree to follow my instructions, then once the operation is complete the evidence held in my safe will be destroyed. Do you understand?"

Hans Zenna answered in a husky voice, "I understand."

The voice at the other end instantly reacted without altering pitch.

"Good. I want all the information on a man named Mohamid Van Jonger. I know you have a file on him due to his relationship with British business men and I require it by tomorrow night."

Hans attempted to say it was going to be difficult and if caught he'd lose his job but that would happen anyway if he didn't agree to the man's demands. He continued after a short lapse as if allowing Hans to absorb his instructions so far.

"The removal of such a file I know to be difficult, hence the reason why you will only take a copy. This you will leave in a plain brown unmarked envelope in locker number 106 at King's Cross station. I already have a skeleton key to open this locker. In a further twenty-four hours after six thirty tomorrow evening, you are to return to that same locker and using your own key open the door to receive your final set of instructions. If you fail at any point the photographs will become public knowledge."

Hans didn't have time to think of any alternatives, he'd listened to the instructions intensely, knowing blackmail for the very first time.

*

Throughout the course of the next day Hans photocopied the thick file on the man Van Jonger and was surprised how easy the task had been. The file was drawn from central records without question and Hans had replaced it some seven hours later, chatting to the elderly clerk as he passed the documents back to her. By five o'clock that afternoon he'd pushed the thick pile of paper into the specified brown envelope, sealed it and was on his way out of the building.

Whitehall was busy at that time of day and Hans hated all the traffic, people, pushing, shoving, it always choked him. He would have dearly preferred to have gone towards his West End pub but since his meeting with Christian Beck, he'd not ventured in that direction.

Hans heaved his strong body through the crowd and onto the underground. The journey to King's Cross although short was tedious and as the train stopped Hans almost fell out onto the platform. He ran up the escalators, stopping only for the ticket barrier, firmly gripping the brown envelope and searching for locker number 106 in the main hall, Hans felt sweat trickling down his damp back. He inserted the coins into the locker, opened the door, threw in the envelope, snapped the door shut and withdrew the key. He noticed the time, it was only five forty-five.

Hans tried to collect his mind and body together, walking briskly towards the station's taxi rank. He was unaware of pushing a small elderly lady to the ground as he clambered into the first available car and shouted his home address at the driver. A crowd gathered around the old dear but the taxi driver could see she was unharmed although clearly shaken and he started lecturing Hans about manners but he didn't hear a single word. The hot, scalding urine running down his trousers went unnoticed by both of them.

*

Aston Appleton arrived at King's Cross station a little after seven that evening and the station was still a hive of activity. He walked over to locker number 106. His key he knew was a perfect fit and the locker door swung open. Aston removed the envelope, slinging it under his arm whilst placing Hans Zenna's next set of instructions into the tin locker. He closed the door and headed back to his office.

CHAPTER 9

Historical

The richness of Appleton's office engulfed him as he strode towards the leather arm chair ripping open the envelope. The volume of paper it contained surprised him and he read well into the night enjoying all his sinister private thoughts.

Aston Appleton contemplated his strategy but his hatred grew and he reverted to his favourite target. He loathed Brett Watson but cherished everything he symbolised. Aston had never beaten Brett at anything but this time he intended to change that dramatically and make Watson suffer right up to the dying moments of his life. He wanted Watson to feel remorse for always putting him into second place, being better than he was at everything they'd attempted and for the job he'd given Aston. Nothing was going to stop him getting what he wanted and that meant everything Watson owned, controlled and loved.

Aston recalled how he'd first met Brett's wife Rebecca and how he had been beaten on that occasion. At the time they were all still single looking to satisfy the needs of life none of which were truly evident to them.

He had been walking along the South Bank whistling yet enjoying the spring air after having concluded a most satisfying deal for

Choans and securing an ally in the Middle East when he'd walked into this dazzling young woman. Aston knocked her off balance and he'd re-approached her to apologise for his mistake, a gesture not normally offered by him but he instantly thought he loved this woman at first glance. They had talked for a short time whilst he helped her recover and she seemed interested in him but Aston noticed her wedding ring finger was bare. He shone with delight and fell to his knees pretending to be looking for something as Rebecca watched and laughed at him before asking in her smooth feminine voice what he'd lost. Aston recalled his reply about looking for her ring and Rebecca, informing him of her unmarried status gave him fresh hope which allowed the showman in him to flicker for a rare moment. The whole incident only lasted a few brief seconds, it was the only time Aston had a real affair of love.

Within the batting of her eyelids Aston thought he could see his future. The taking of a really beautiful wife who was clearly from wealthy stock would enhance his position at Choans and may be even possibly encourage the two old directors to give him some leeway. He desperately wanted to be recognised and considered this chance meeting with such a sexy woman to be his ticket to success. He asked her to dinner that evening and to his utter surprise she accepted. They walked a little further, made arrangements for the evening and went their separate ways until later. Aston watched her walk away from him, unaware of her body moving like silk blowing in a gently scented breeze. He was considering other possibilities.

*

Aston Appleton drove into Grovener Mews being careful not to attract any attention to his ageing Rover car. It was not something that had ever worried him up until that moment when he thought he was destined for better things. He calmly presented himself at the front door and was surprised when Rebecca opened it, stepped daintily over the threshold and walked briskly past him towards his car. He ran after her and opening the door enquired of her well-being. She acknowledged Aston but he felt this was not the same woman he'd asked out to dinner earlier that same afternoon.

Little was said for the first few moments and Aston felt particularly uncomfortable. He wanted this woman as she was going to be the creator of his new success. He wanted to show the world, he wanted to be seen with this woman but most of all Aston demanded to be noticed. It was for these latter reasons he elected to take Rebecca to the Café de Paris which he knew to be the playground of many aristocratic and influential people, with which he would dearly have liked to be acquainted. Rebecca was delighted with Aston's choice of restaurant but failed to understand her own reasoning for accepting a dinner date with a man she'd never met before until that day. She'd decided it was not love but a need for some light entertainment.

The Café de Paris was radiating its usual warm elegance as they entered. Rebecca dressed in a white flowing gown stood some three inches taller than Aston who although attired in his dinner jacket was still unable to offer the image of a dashing knight. They were escorted to their table where the champagne dressed in a white drape was dutifully opened and poured. The heavy atmosphere of their surroundings was beginning to relax Aston.

A fine meal of pictorial elegance was served, consumed and discussed. The sweet-scented aroma of Rebecca's perfume lingered and Aston was totally off his guard as Brett Watson approached their table. Aston Appleton knew he'd lost again to Brett as he slapped him across the back, making him choke a little, and asked how he'd been during the past few weeks. Aston couldn't retrieve his breath fast enough before Brett demanded a formal introduction to his beautiful female companion. He knew he'd lost her as soon as Brett had made a gentle bow, apologised for intruding, kissed her on the hand and asked Rebecca to dance with him.

They danced all evening and through most of the night as Aston sat watching every move, drinking heavily until he fell off his chair onto the floor dragging several empty champagne bottles with him.

Brett and Rebecca never saw Aston again that evening after leaving his table. They only had eyes for each other it was definitely love at first sight.

Brett had driven Rebecca back to her Mews house, escorted her to the door and went inside. They both knew they desired each other and skipped the usual hideous charade of coffee or unwanted drinks. The bedroom was dimly lit, radiating cool tones of pink and white.

Fragrant aromas of exotic perfumes filtered from the bathroom as

Brett watched this goddess clad in a silk negligée drift towards him and he could see with sensual delight her breasts gently moving. Her erect nipples were clinging to the silk with pending excitement but Brett's eyes couldn't penetrate the garment any further. He went towards her, placing his lips firmly over hers, and explored the deepest parts of her warm, soft mouth with his excited tongue. The room was warm, her perfume aroused him beyond any feeling he'd ever known and he could feel his brow becoming moist but more obviously his erection was growing at an alarming rate. Brett knew if he didn't control himself, the first time she touched his penis Rebecca would be showered in sperm.

Brett slipped the negligée away from her perfect shoulders and allowed it to fall to the thick pile carpet. His hands enwrapped her large breasts and stroked them with gentle, excited ease. Rebecca tore Brett's shirt away from him, longing to see his naked body. Her fingers ran down through the hair on his chest until they met his trouser catch. She knelt before him, his fingers running through her ash brown hair as she undid his buckle and peeled the trousers and underwear away from his excited body. She fondled his colossal cock and stroking his balls with increasing deliberation placed her mouth over him, allowing her tongue to encircle his swelling organ.

Brett drifted with excruciating pleasure, it being almost intolerable. He wanted to come out of her mouth but the more he tried, the more Rebecca forced him to remain. Brett shouted to her he was losing control but still she wouldn't release him and Rebecca took him to the brink. She felt him stiffen so as the skin would break and moved her face away, pushing Brett onto the bed. They rolled over each other with Brett's fingers caressing, exploring and exciting her. She was wet and wanted to feel that enormous cock slide inside her. Brett made her climax many times as she had almost made him before allowing his explosive erection to penetrate deep inside her. At first he moved gently, allowing them both to feel the beauty of their bodies. He could feel his balls touching her smooth inner thigh as her fingers ran down his damp back, scouring painful marks with her nails but Brett didn't notice, he was too intent on trying to make the moment last. He slid smoothly in and out of her until they couldn't stand the untouched pleasure any longer. Brett didn't need to quicken his pace, his penis was so erect and Rebecca was so ready, the time was perfect. He felt sperm leave his body with jet-like speed and feeling the searing hot liquid penetrate deep into her body, Rebecca moaned with satisfaction. This was the fountain of life.

They slept soundly that night wrapped in each other's arms. The next morning broke with rain pelting against the window but Brett and Rebecca didn't care, they made love again with utter and absolute devoted tenderness.

Two months later they married and moved to Lenton Parva, Brett gained control of Rosco's and Rebecca started planning her own business.

*

Aston Appleton woke amidst dustbins in a small alleyway near the Café de Paris. He was sporting a mammoth headache and was wet through. The early morning rain continued as Aston became acutely aware of his current plight. He recalled drinking heavily, hating Brett Watson who'd stolen his companion, being very vocal to a waiter and being thrown into the alley. He stood up, gained his balance and gingerly took a few steps. Realising his arms and legs were still a part of him, Aston made his way towards the noisy London traffic which was deafening. He loathed himself and the world but he passionately despised Brett Watson. Aston made his way home on foot, reasoning the damp air would sober his scruples and ease his thumping head.

He decided during the trek back to his trendy apartment Brett should be put in his place, after all he'd stolen another woman from him just like at Oxford all those years before.

Aston embarked on formulating a strategy to annihilate Brett Watson, regain his ghoulish hold on Rebecca and totally embezzle Choans company funds to his own betterment. Brett, however, had yet another bombshell waiting for Aston in the wings.

CHAPTER 10

Friday Evening, 10.00pm. Lenton Parva.

As Hans Zenna untied Rebecca's petite hands he noticed she was still trembling and conspicuous of her fear for him, wanted desperately to tell his story. Hans felt they both needed to bring out the ally within themselves even though he knew deep down he'd no right to this respect. They had a common denominator in as much as they were both threatened but Hans didn't know it was "Control's" hatred for Rebecca's husband which had secured his present predicament.

Hans sat back in his arm chair close to Rebecca and admired her sensual body. She sat almost petrified to make any movement; her eyes were sore with having cried the tear ducts bone dry but he wanted to tell her, yet couldn't speak as his mind became totally cluttered. Hans was ashamed about his involvement, his sexual problem which he badly wanted to overcome, but most of all having so patently hurt such a gentle woman. He found the whole affair obscene and couldn't determine how it would end despite "Control's" promises. He was churning so much through his mind Rebecca's first words went unnoticed. As she leant towards him, touching his knee as if to wake him, Hans instantly froze, took stock of his plight and relaxed. *Maybe she understands*, he thought, knowing that not to be true but still living in hope.

Rebecca again shook his knee as Hans came back to the real world.

"Can you tell me when my husband will come back?"

She muttered these few words in a quiet, shy voice yet Hans must have looked startled by this intrusion into his private world since at first he couldn't offer an answer but then later started to form his reply.

"I'm only a small cog in a particularly dangerous time bomb," he whimpered. "I can't tell you when your husband will come back. I think it will be within the next few days, certainly before the end of Monday if my instructions are correct."

Rebecca was clearly not satisfied with his answer and although still scared, she tried to control her emotions, forcing herself to continue in an uncertain, uphill, questioning manner.

"I don't understand why you are doing this to us. Why did you kill Martha? What have we done to deserve this treatment?"

Rebecca's eyes filled with fresh tears again and they began to trickle down her cheeks. She tried hard to fight the impending flow but although her body felt tired, drained and exhausted she sobbed with uncontrollable passion.

Hans couldn't bear to watch her and turned his head away but Rebecca's sobbing echoed through his tormented mind like a villainous mimicking angel of the occult.

He moved over to the sofa and sat gingerly beside her, taking her hand into his grasp. Rebecca's crying eased and her head turned towards him as she became aware of a terror-stricken individual whose warm, soft hand transmitted shockwaves of tenderness, anger and need. Rebecca, although unsure of Hans knew at last she had an ally.

Gradually as the late evening turned into night they spoke more of the events which had forced them together, causing such distress. Rebecca listened to Hans with uncomfortable ease; the last few weeks of his life must have been unbearable, she'd considered and the thought of this man murdering Martha faded from her mind even though the bloodstained carpet was now clearly visible. She knew after her brief discussion with Hans he wouldn't have entertained these macabre acts unless he'd been forced under considerable pressure and after many hours of listening to his narrative, Rebecca knew the driving force of this nightmare to be blackmail. She tried to console him many times as his voice crumbled into sobbing undertones of melancholy remorse.

Rebecca, although understanding Hans joined him and they cried in unison, Hans for his actions and the grief he caused, Rebecca for herself, Martha and most of all for Brett.

The night matured into early morning and they still talked of each other's plight with Rebecca learning how little Hans really knew of any master plan. She listened to him intently and in so doing allowed her placid nature to be replaced with true anger. Hans told her he couldn't let her out of his sight and although understanding, she had no intention of ignoring their current plight.

By dawn on Saturday morning they'd decided on a consolidated approach to locate the man called "Control". Rebecca had told Hans of Brett's company and his co-director Aston Appleton so at 7.30am on that drab, dark September morning, Rebecca rang Aston's apartment. She was jubilant when he picked up the phone even though she knew Brett wouldn't have approved of this action. Aston Appleton heard Rebecca's voice and instantly started to dehydrate as he listened to Rebecca's feverish but brief summary of events and tried to collect his own shaking torso back into some degree of normality.

Aston replaced the receiver, looked at himself in the huge hall mirror, winced and ambled uncertain of his feelings into the immense living room. He sat on the edge of his favourite easy chair with a sense of failure welling up inside his lower abdomen.

"How the fucking hell have those two managed to combine forces? That gay bastard was meant to keep Rebecca trussed up like a Sunday chicken until he was told otherwise. At least they don't suspect who I am… yet."

Aston mumbled on, not making any sense to himself. He couldn't let this happen; if he failed this time it would be the end for him.

Taking the photographs of Hans and Christian from his bureau safe, Aston allowed his eyes to wander haphazardly over them while his brain was now in overdrive considering all the options. Aston knew if Rebecca found him out then he'd lose again to a Watson. He slipped the photographs back in the safe, thankful only Christian Beck knew of his identity, dressed and leaving his apartment for the Watson household recognised he still had the advantage, just.

CHAPTER 11

Early Saturday Morning. Tangiers. Rembrant Hotel.

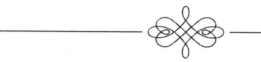

Brett Watson and Mohamid Van Jonger stood by the window which was still open from the previous evening. Together they watched the huge glowing red globe of the new sun rise over old Tangiers. Mohamid regarded the city as his own, it was special to him and he enjoyed acquainting his personal guests with its rich and sordid past, yet under normal circumstances would have been delirious with pleasure at again witnessing the new dawn. In the distance both men could hear morning prayer being babbled from exotic mosques yet neither of them spoke since they were both in penetrating meditation considering the previous day's events. Their nocturnal discussions created a scheme to outwit and find the identity of "Control". Both of them knew "Control" to be a determined Englishman who they decided had created an ominous plot to achieve a goal which at present remained unknown to them.

Alexis quietly entered Mohamid's office and she was not astonished to see neither of them had slept. They didn't notice her as she padded barefoot over the polished floor and was about to surprise them both as was her foxy decorous nature, when the hotel's early morning house boy entered the room, presenting Mohamid with a single white envelope. He scrutinised the clean, expensive-looking document with his name typed clearly across the centre. Mohamid's face drained of colour and dismissing the house boy he averted his deep set, penetrative eyes towards Brett.

Both men were aware of "Control's" presence forcing them apart like magnets of the same pole. Alexis stood quietly, acknowledged the men's irritation and turned to make her exit when Mohamid called to her.

"I think you had better stay, my dear, this is yet another instructive epistle from our sick friend and I've the gravest feeling it will involve all of us."

Alexis went back to Mohamid, gently kissing him on the cheek. This was the first time she had done such a thing in the presence of another man since becoming a woman and Mohamid felt a warm tingling sensation run through him as Alexis's freshly perfumed body touched him. Brett noticed the satisfaction this meagre action caused Mohamid and wished Rebecca could have been there with him. He'd spoke to Mohamid during the night, telling him how they'd been forced apart and Mohamid expressed his sorrow yet still told of the instructions Alexis had received on her arrival at Heathrow only yesterday. Brett, horrified by the accumulating dark deeds had only been pacified by Mohamid's cultured manner promising revenge.

Mohamid took a large flat knife from the drawer of his nearby desk, slit open the envelope and removed the folded sheet of paper from within. With a positive act of defiance he unfolded the document, allowing two drab-coloured airline tickets to float towards the floor. Brett knelt down to pick them up, as did Alexis; their eyes met and for the second time since their union his body was aware of a sensationally beautiful woman. He quickly recalled his purpose, and standing back and moving closer to Mohamid guessed the next act of this macabre tragedy had been disclosed.

Mohamid motioned the others to sit down while he called the house boy back to the office but questioning the frail boy proved fruitless. He was dismissed after having been given instructions to obtain fresh clothes for Brett and make a European breakfast for all present. It became clear this interlude of firing questions at the boy had given Mohamid a few seconds to collect his composure.

"I am heartily sick of this rather immature faceless wonder. If he were a true man of upstanding principles, whether they be right or wrong, a degree of respect could be possible. But this..."

Mohamid's voice was running a tone above its normal pitch and Brett had never heard him talk like this but he witnessed the slight shaking of Alexis's head which told him not to interrupt as he was clearly considering all the alternatives in the light of the latest communication.

"Brett Watson is to accompany your beloved Alexis to the lush island of Cyprus, taking the lighters with them. On their arrival at Larnaca Airport they will be met by my... representative, shall we say. Do as you are told and no harm will befall your two families. 'Control.'"

Mohamid completed reading the letter as his true wife entered the room bringing breakfast. She acknowledged each of them in order of importance and departed from their company after informing Brett his change of clothing was now available.

Brett never understood the Muslim way but since it had been established longer than his own life on this earth he'd accepted the differences. Each airline ticket was clearly written. Their next destination was Cyprus's Larnaca Airport and the take-off time was 9.30 that morning, but that concluded the flow of information. They each sat around the breakfast table, spoke very little, ate very little and allowed time to meander past in private thought before reality was abruptly forced upon them by a large explosion. With the building quivering and crashing glass being clearly heard from the reception area, Mohamid darted towards the door, flung it open and saw the devastation in the Rembrant's foyer. Brett and Alexis looked over Mohamid's shoulder in startled amazement as the telephone in the office rang. At first it was not heard but its persistence attracted Alexis who stumbled over to answer the call.

"This is 'Control'. I hope my small show of strength has not damaged the hotel but just shaken the dust a little. Make sure you follow my instructions and nobody will be hurt."

Alexis was about to replace the receiver after not having said a single phrase when the message was repeated word for word again. She called Brett over to listen. He was stunned and dismayed. That night he and Mohamid had thought of ways to escape the bonds

"Control" seemed to administer over them and their families but this incident confirmed to Brett, "Control" always seemed to be just ahead of them in thought and deed. He turned to call Mohamid while Alexis lay the receiver on the desk but she reached out to hold Brett's arm. They both watched Mohamid move towards a pile of debris in the foyer's centre and kneel down, staring totally transfixed for many moments.

Alexis and Brett went to Mohamid, offering their support as he had done for them so many times in the past. Their chosen words failed to meet the dusty, stagnant air as they saw Mohamid's first and only wife skewered to the floor by a once large, elaborate glass chandelier. Her blood oozed over the once proud floor and tears of despair filled Mohamid's eyes. "Control" had claimed a second victim. The time was 7.45am.

CHAPTER 12

Saturday Morning, 8.00am. Tangiers.

Brett and Alexis forced themselves away from Mohamid, leaving the Rembrant's foyer in a state of repulsive outrage and knowing they had to keep "Control's" schedule, did nothing less than entangle their own formidable hatred of this man for the deaths he'd caused.

They started across Tangiers in Mohamid's Rolls-Royce towards the airport with Brett clutching the two tickets they'd discovered only a short while before. He glanced towards Alexis who was engrossed in deep thought but didn't have the nerve to destroy her concentration. The city rapidly passed by, its personal noisy yet malodorous aroma going unnoticed. They didn't speak on this short journey although Brett wanted to console Alexis on the loss of Mohamid's wife. He wondered if Alexis felt any remorse, after all he'd seen two sides of this remarkable woman within the last twenty-four hours but felt considerably more at ease with her now than on their trip from his home in Lenton Parva to Heathrow.

The Rolls smoothly pulled up at the stairway leading into a huge Cyprus Airways A300 Airbus. Brett had lost sight quite heedlessly of Mohamid's influence, expecting the usual customs routine which he hated so much. Alexis grabbed the two suitcases containing the lighters, opened the car door and ascended into the aircraft with Brett chasing after her, mounting the steps two at a time. He witnessed Alexis thrusting the cases at a pretty stewardess, shrieking instructions for their safe passage. Brett put his hand on her shoulder; he felt she was tense and rigid. Guiding her to their seat in the aircraft's rear, row 39 seemed along way back as they pushed and stumbled past other passengers intent on playing the role of important travellers.

They sat and prepared themselves for yet another arduous journey as the big jet started to taxi with both its 51,000lb thrust engines screaming. Brett always considered taking off and landing to be the most enjoyable part of any flight, although on reflection he preferred to choose his own destination. As the Airbus reached V2 and lifted from the runway he watched with awesome glee the whole cabin elevate to an angle of steep climb. The sheer power used to enable these huge aircraft to fly was fascinating and he wondered how the plane's acceleration would compare against his Aston Martin, but the thought of his car channelled his mind to consider Rebecca. Saturday morning she normally goes into town until lunch time, then onto their favourite restaurant to meet him and allow the hours to slip past while they enjoy each other's sensual company. Today was different. To the best of his knowledge Rebecca was still at the mercy of Hans Zenna, while he was winging his way towards the eastern Mediterranean carrying drugs with a woman he couldn't be sure to trust, despite Mohamid's craving words.

Brett turned towards Alexis; her tense appearance had been replaced with the loving warmth she'd shown at the Rembrant. Tactfully Alexis took Brett's hand and placing it on the inside of her thigh, held it tight starting a conversation that continued throughout the five hour flight.

They discussed many subjects, spending considerable time evaluating the true meaning of love. Brett told of his adorable Rebecca and Alexis spoke of her respect for Mohamid. They discussed the past, the present, the future and their current demise of Lady Luck. For the first time in less than twenty-four hours they were at ease with each other. Neither of them felt the aircraft touch down at Larnaca Airport as Brett's hand still fondled the inside of her smooth, silky thigh even though Alexis governed his movements. They looked into each other's eyes and saw passionate fires burning as the aircraft doors were opened, allowing the sweltering midday air to enter the cool cabin. The startling change in temperature and sound of people shouting outside the plane brought them both back to actuality. Brett's image of Rebecca faded with embarrassment as he realised his feelings for this woman beside him, but he was content to be satisfied with her company. Alexis on the other hand had different ideas. She wanted much more from him and was determined to have him. Their sweaty hands parted as men entered the cabin. The time was only 2.30pm.

Hotel Rembrant. Tangiers. Saturday Morning.

Mohamid was only partially aware of Brett and Alexis as they'd left for the airport. The revolting scene which lay before him disgusted his proud ethics and saddened his tired heart. His wife had been the perfect model of Muslim tradition and this was no way for her to die. The noise inside the Rembrant's foyer intensified while people gathered to view this repugnant sight as Mohamid rose to his full height and at the top of his voice wailed to Allah in earthy Arabic an overture of revenge. The entire place fell silent as fingers of the sun's rays shone down from the lofty windows, picking out dust disturbed by the explosion. The sight of a once elaborate reception was now nothing more than a pile of splintered timber. Mohamid saw none of the reception area and ignoring the milling people jostling to help the hotel's staff made his way back towards the tranquillity of the cool office. Closing the heavy door he felt a whimpering deep within his inner soul. He walked over to the desk and picked up the receiver Alexis had left at the side of the phone. Placing it to his ear Mohamid heard the full recorded message repeated just as Alexis and Brett heard. Slamming the phone down onto its cradle he knew he must follow the plan he and Brett had hatched the previous night but felt tense and bitter, yet most of all revengeful. Glancing down at his hand still holding the phone he watched a small trickle of blood run from beneath the plastic appliance. Instantly pulling his hand away, the telephone fell into two parts. Mohamid clearly didn't know his own strength.

Historical

The conspiracy they'd hatched the previous night was a long shot and that being truly recognised by both of them made the task to locate "Control" no easier. Brett related his findings or lack of them pertinent to Aston Appleton's financial involvement with the Moroccan banks. He told Mohamid how the money was being continuously moved around without apparently gaining interest despite Aston's guarantee of obtaining the best investment rates. It was at this point Mohamid added a most sinister comment which confirmed Brett's mistrust of Aston's conduct. All banks in Morocco offer the same return on invested capital. Mohamid was told the sum Brett's company had invested and without the aid of a calculator he confirmed the return which should have been paid. Brett was dumbstruck. In discussing the various possibilities as to who "Control" was, Brett had been exposed as having been used. It was to what use the embezzled money had been manipulated which concerned them both rather than Brett's loss of integrity and they'd opened each suitcase looking for pointers but neither revealed their pestiferous owner.

Brett felt totally besmalled yet was convinced "Control" operated from within Rosco International's office in London and Mohamid couldn't disagree it was a possibility Aston Appleton may be their man. He'd only met Aston a couple of times and didn't care for his harsh manner and lack of respect for others, but both men concluded as dawn broke this was a line of inquiry which should be checked. Brett knew he couldn't return to London until "Control's" plan had been carried through, fearing for Rebecca. Mohamid agreed and armed with information data to gain access to the company's computer files was to go to London the next day. Mohamid stressed to Brett this was only a theory they were working on which at present looked as if it may develop into fact.

Saturday Morning, Tangiers. 8.00 to 11.00am.

Mohamid took stock of himself, called his chauffeur and went back to his palatial home. He had no intention of remaining there for any lengthy duration but desperately needed to be away from the Rembrant for the first time since that fatal card game had given him ownership. The Rolls swung through the narrow streets and headed towards the villa. Mohamid's day had not been memorable but one thing which had flashed through his mind earlier, suddenly caught up with him again. He removed the letter which had been delivered to him earlier that morning by the house boy from his inside pocket. Reading the solemn message again didn't strike any warning tones over those he'd already felt but as the car passed through a cutting in the road, the sun glimmered through the car window at such an angle as to illuminate the paper making, it transparent. Mohamid's face turned full colour and his body trembled with excitement as he saw the faint letters "R.I." embossed within the paper like a watermark.

He found it difficult to believe that after his stupidity Brett was right with his judgement of Appleton's character. Mohamid kissed the paper, folded it and placing back into his pocket allowed his sun-blessed face to crack with a growing smile of satisfaction. He was pleased Brett was with Alexis, knowing full well she would look after him, but he was now looking forward to his trip to London. Aston Appleton hadn't banked on Brett Watson's support from Islam and Mohamid was going to make sure Aston never forgot the lesson he was going to be taught.

Van Jonger only stayed at the villa long enough to shower and pack a few clothes along with his Smith and Wesson revolver before being whisked off to the airport. As usual no customs formalities were observed as the Rolls pulled up at the airliner's steps. Mohamid clad in a light grey suit with silk shirt and tie looked a formidable figure as he entered the aircraft's first-class cabin. He'd enjoyed London every time he travelled to the city but this time was special, it was electrifying and he couldn't wait. The sweet taste of revenge was going to be good but the finale would be spectacular.

CHAPTER 13

Friday. Midnight At Tangiers Airport.

Christian Beck stood in the departure hall at Tangiers Airport and took a good long look at his seedy profile while his sweaty hands clutched the remains of his current air ticket. Spluttering into life, the public announcement system hailed the pending departure of Royal Air Maroc's flight to Larnaca but Christian felt uncomfortable and his cotton jacket was beginning to look decidedly shabby. His pockets bulged with paper wrappers, an envelope containing money from Aston Appleton and two remaining unused airline tickets. He was hot, tired and wished he was back in his one-room flat in St Pancras. When Aston Appleton secured his services as a private sleuth, Christian hadn't expected the work to entail planting bombs but only following people, watching and reporting.

The flight announcement was heard again and Christian made his way through rows of arranged orange-coloured plastic chairs to the departure gate as he noticed the pathetic duty free shop, the lack of people around him and absorbed that pungent aroma which announced Morocco. There were few people booked on that flight and Christian was able to walk straight over to the Boeing 727, boarding it via its rear stair entry. He stopped halfway up the stairway and cautiously regarded the jet engines mounted each side of the aircraft a little way above his head. Turning, Christian looked back at the shimmering lights of the low-level terminal building with its name standing out well against gently swaying palm trees.

He wondered if he would ever return to this place and absorb its true character, after all the only part he'd seen other than the road to and from the airport was Mohamid's Hotel Rembrant. Planting the bomb had unbalanced his mind; he'd not wanted to destroy any part of someone else's life and truly hoped nobody was hurt but he couldn't understand his attraction to Tangiers. The city seemed to be drawing him and if he'd stood there a second longer knew he wouldn't have taken this, his allocated flight.

Christian walked up the cabin of an almost empty aircraft, noticing the number of Arabs on board certainly outweighed the Europeans. He began to feel uncomfortable again as he took a window seat just past an emergency exit and buckling himself in felt the plane jolt as it began to move. Christian didn't take any notice of the cabin crew's pre-flight instructions as he watched the airport buildings disappear. His cotton jacket was wet with his own perspiration and carried ground-in marks of accumulated dirt.

Accelerating down the runway and soaring into a dark night sky with cabin lights dimmed, a silence settled over the passengers broken only by rushing wind and engine noise. A sole stewardess walked past and seemed concerned for his health yet Christian denied any fear, putting his sweating down to the heat of the night in Tangiers, but he couldn't fool himself. Actually he was really terrified, his hands shook, his body and clothing were wet through as he tried to control his emotions. Christian stood up and noticing none of the nearby seats were occupied removed his wet jacket, emptied all his pockets and sorted the contents into scruffy piles.

He opened his wallet and as usual there was no money contained by the dividing sections so slowly, as if it was his last earthly duty, he sorted through all the piles of paper and wrappings. Christian had not banked the money Aston Appleton had sent him along with the four airline tickets; he'd had no time since their arrival a few days before. Fumbling through the remaining fifty-pound notes and counting nine hundred pounds in all, Christian sat in astonishment but still couldn't determine why he'd been chosen for these tasks. After all, nobody else wanted to employ his services. As he sat gawping at the now crumpled notes he noticed the top two shared the same numbers. Panic struck home again as he fingered the remaining money, checking all the letters and numerical codes. His heart was pounding, his hands sweaty again as he realised all the notes contained identical letter and numerical combinations. The money he'd considered to be his own was in fact nothing more than a pile of waste paper.

Christian sat and allowed his dwindling enthusiasm to utterly drain. He thought he was rich but this was not to be the case and rummaging through the remaining piles of paper he found the typed instructions sent to him by Aston Appleton. Beck viewed the remaining two tickets with some degree of caution. It crossed his mind with staggering ease these may also be fakes like the wad of money Aston had sent but he stuffed the notes into his wallet, not knowing why, but their presence seemed better than nothing. Folding his remaining tickets Christian placed them in his trouser pocket knowing if they were lost he would be well and truly in the mire, yet if they were fakes he could maybe, just manage to work his way back to London.

Christian gathered the remaining piles of paper and stuffed them into a sick bag for disposal. He rang the stewardess call button and waited but as the young, dusky woman approached him, he ordered a strong black coffee with whisky chaser. Regarding the man with a little uncertainty she confirmed his request and thinking it may ease his apprehension disappeared into the galley. Christian sat back with an evil grin on his face as he intended to pay for the drinks with one of Aston's crooked notes and swaying a little, the stewardess brought him both beverages but as he offered her the note she announced all drinks were free. Flabbergasted by this development, Beck had again been cheated but by someone being generous! He drank the coffee, sipped his whisky and considered what should be done next.

Christian Beck was not generally a dreamer but he'd had many a knock during his life right from being a boy. He was brought up in the rural county of Staffordshire and being an only child had been really spoiled. His parents had provided well for him, concluding his education at London University, but during that time the majority of derogatory comments fired at him related to his size and unfortunate shape. Other students ribbed his stooping form, his ginger hair, being a country boy and especially for not mixing with girls.

Christian was bright in the classroom and in examinations but couldn't handle the real world. He knew he was different at a very early age yet couldn't determine by what degree and it was only after finding a pornographic magazine at the age of fourteen which offered confirmation of his own suspecting aspirations. Christian recalled sneaking the glossy pages into his bedroom and pondering over the size of other male organs but even now as he considered the various possibilities he could feel movement within his groin. No practical act of defiance against the betterment of society or his parents took place until he'd met Hans Zenna; the temptation had overwhelmed him. His parents learnt directly from him about his sexual inclination and they asked Christian to leave the family home, considering it was they who'd failed him.

After that point in time Christian never considered his morality as being open for debate until now. Suddenly he felt lonely, cheated and isolated from the world as he opened his wallet yet again and checked the notes; they were still fakes but the photographs of his parents were very real even if a little tatty. He looked at the airline tickets withdrawn from his pocket still not knowing if they were genuine and lastly he looked at himself feeling disgust as he reached for a sick bag from an adjacent seat, allowing the contents of his stomach to flow freely into the bag.

The stewardess who'd attended Christian an hour or so before rushed to his assistance. She fussed around him like a broody hen, forcing him to turn tail towards the airliner's rear lavatory and small although the compartment was, it felt blissful despite the increased engine noise. Christian looked down at his trousers; they'd once matched his jacket but were now a intermixture of putrid colours. He tried to sponge the stained material but with little effect. The mirror reflected a bedraggled individual who for all intent and reason had not washed for many months. Christian's sense of smell confirmed his visual assessment. He reeked of everything which smelt putrescent.

After the best part of half an hour he emerged from his sanctuary only to be pounced upon again by the same stewardess. She fluttered around him, commenting on his bettered appearance before spraying him with an air freshener and then guided him back to a different set of unoccupied seats.

Christian watched her go before attempting to retrieve his possessions yet the smell of stale sick filled his nostrils, but he retreated before the effect caused him any further discomfort. As he seated himself, turning on the overhead light he began to relax. His jacket pocket contained a leather-clad note book, it was the only quality possession he'd left in this world and he fingered it with a degree of passion. Ripping out the first few pages he started to write down his recent life story with an old ballpoint pen.

Christian continued reasoning with himself as to why he found his predicament really frightening and in so doing the bombing of Van Jonger's hotel came into clear perspective. He'd never understood other human beings, only ever having cared for and loved himself, yet perhaps it was because of this he found himself in a position with no money, two dubious tickets, no friends and somewhere over the Mediterranean Sea. In fact, all he knew from his instructions was that he'd be met at Larnaca Airport.

Prolonged writing gave him a little cramp in his left hand but he wrote down everything which had occurred since meeting Aston Appleton including all the sordid instructions, the places he'd been and the people he'd hurt. Raising the stewardess yet again brought a flood of interest from her as Christian tried to ignore her comments and concentrate on the matter in hand. He'd called her as he wanted an envelope at least the size of the note book and was surprised when she returned so promptly waving a brown packet. After considerable deliberation she liberated her interest in Christian and attended to one of his fellow passengers as he slipped the note book, Aston's last typed set of instructions and four of the fake fifty-pound notes into the envelope. Sealing the package, he wrote in capital letters across the frontage and then called back the stewardess.

She trotted playfully towards him, delighted to be of service again despite the ungodly time of the day and he asked her to sit down beside him for a few brief moments. Shamelessly looking around, she slipped into the seat next to Christian's and in a quiet tone of voice he asked if she would ensure the bulging brown package be put aboard a London-bound flight as soon as possible after their arrival at Larnaca. The stewardess looked blankly at him as he brandished one of the fake notes under her nose. Smiling a distant grin she regarded the package and was deeply shocked to see who the recipient was to be as her facial expression changed, forming serious stress lines over her delicate forehead. The young woman acknowledged Christian's request, took the package from him and disappeared leaving him holding the fake note. *Can't give the damn stuff away*, he considered as the aircraft made a bumpy landing at Larnaca.

Christian left the aircraft as quickly as possible, walking towards yet another terminal building armed only with his passport, watching his attentive stewardess hand the package over to a British Airways cabin attendant. That, he considered was his insurance policy to get even with that rattlesnake Aston Appleton, but knew he would never see London again.

*

It was a little after 5.30 on Saturday morning as Beck made his exit from the airport buildings. Dawn had settled down into a fine, hot morning and Christian became conscious of this being perhaps the last daybreak he would witness. He felt slightly drunk with his own success in securing the insurance policy's passage aboard a London-bound flight yet he instantly sobered up as two well-dressed gentlemen of Middle-Eastern extraction approached. They confirmed his identity and parcelled him into the back of their white Mercedes car. Christian Beck identified a flourishing sense of impending doom as they sped away.

CHAPTER 14

Lenton Parva. Saturday Morning, 7.30am.

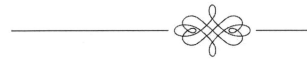

Rebecca replaced the receiver after speaking to Aston Appleton and looked over towards Hans Zenna. The lounge looked dull and large yet Rebecca, although not having slept, radiated a glowing warmth as Hans approached her slowly, very slowly pulled Rebecca towards him with the gentleness of a tender loving father. Averting her eyes away from his, she permitted herself to be held close as he gently caressed her subtle lavish frame. They stood for many moments allowing their bodily vibrations to intercommunicate before Rebecca eased herself away from his clutches, moved a pace or two from Hans and turned towards the lounge door. She noted he looked like an innocent school boy wrongly accused of smoking behind the cycle shed as making her exit, Hans followed. asking in a crisp, bright tone, "Where are you going now?"

She started to climb the huge spiral staircase but without turning or faltering replied, "I'm going to take a shower, change out of this bathrobe and dress in something more fitting the occasion. You can make some breakfast if you like. The kitchen is…"

She stopped herself realising Hans knew his way around their house and not wanting to aggravate this preposterous situation any further continued, "Well, you know where it is. Help yourself to whatever you want. I'll have toast and coffee with a glass of orange juice." She continued up the stairs, entered their bedroom, kicked off her slippers and sat on the four-poster bed but the shag pile carpet felt soft to her feet as she pondered over her current predicament.

"What would Brett do if he were here?" she mumbled to herself.

The feeling of loneliness had expired as she'd learnt of Hans Zenna's past and how he'd become involved. Although Rebecca couldn't forgive him she knew he was only trying to protect himself yet was unclear in her own mind as to the events of the past twenty-four hours. Something was very wrong but despite his admissions she now felt safe with Hans. Brett would come back, she considered, but still felt it necessary to determine who was behind all this revolting wistful strategy. Her heart was pounding with a desire to know but most of all she wanted their life to return to normal. It had taken many hours during the night to persuade Hans that Aston Appleton may be able to help them, but she managed and he'd conceded. Rebecca knew Brett wouldn't be keen on involving Aston but it was the only line of action she considered which may bear fruit.

Slipping out of the bathrobe, Rebecca went to the en-suite bathroom and entered the shower where it had all begun for her the previous afternoon. She washed her slender, suntanned body thinking only of Brett as the soap streaked over her perfect bosom and steam from this scalding hot water enveloped the whole cubicle, forming a roasting sauna. Hans said he couldn't leave her and she knew he'd not let her out of the house but Aston's pending arrival made her feel as if communication with the outside world was still possible, yet there was a nagging pain in her mind which overshadowed the perfect picture of Brett's return. She wondered where he was, what he was doing and if he was safe.

Turning the water off, Rebecca opened the shower door, grabbed a towel and dried herself. She went back into the bedroom, stood in front of her delicate dressing table, picked up Brett's photograph, raised it to her lips and kissed it, muttering, "Forgive me for what I am going to do but I know you will understand, you always do. I love you."

Replacing the photograph and dressing in a pale cream silk blouse with a deep golden pleated skirt, she slipped four sleeping pills into her pocket and started towards the door as Hans called from the stairway that breakfast was ready.

Gracefully descending the stairs, Rebecca's ash brown hair was still wet but her own plan was now securely memorised. She needed to be with Brett, didn't totally trust Hans and was sceptical of Aston Appleton. After all, she'd been the one who'd dumped him for Brett just over two years before. Now Rebecca regretted having rung Aston as she thought he may try to use this occasion to get even with her.

Entering the well fitted kitchen, a glimmer of sunlight splashed through the curtained window. The breakfast bar was set for a feast and Hans stood displaying a shy smile of amusement while his strong blond features towered above her as he moved a chair and gestured for them to sit down. They sat, ate, drank and talked for some considerable time. Rebecca had ample opportunity to slip the sleeping pills into his drink but couldn't bring herself to carry out the act as Hans seemed so much at ease with her and she realised trusting him beyond all doubt was a necessary evil to secure survival.

*

Aston Appleton had calmed himself considerably since Rebecca's phone call and driving the difficult distance from his Dock Lands apartment to Lenton Parva considered he was still in control of the whole situation. He'd estimated the bomb at the Rembrant Hotel would have by now exploded and the recorded message become known to his pawns. Aston had regarded his plot as being a classic jewel; everything was in accordance with his designs except Hans and Rebecca but they were only of minor concern to him.

Aston's old Rover had seen better days but he wasn't bothered. It was dirty, tired and certainly didn't function very well. The cloth seats were stained, torn and like the carpet reflected his own tatty appearance. Turning into Lenton Parva the small electronic device he'd used to follow Brett's new Aston Martin beeped with continuous alarm. He'd fixed the corresponding part of the device to Brett's car, enabling him to follow from Heathrow at a safe distance without being observed since Aston wanted to ensure Brett had taken the bell boy's message seriously. As it transpired he couldn't have kept up with Brett since the Rover was outstripped on all counts. Aston Appleton turned off the device and parked on the road outside the Watsons' house. He slithered out of the driving seat, slammed the door closed and walked over the gravel driveway towards the front door. As he passed Brett's gleaming silver blue car he allowed his own car key to run along its entire length leaving a deep gouge with that chilling sound of metal scraping against metal.

Pressing his stubby, sticky finger on the door bell, Aston could hear the chimes echo inside and stood in readiness for Rebecca's greeting. Hans and Rebecca were about to drink their coffee while discussing the possibilities for the day as the door chimes rang and Hans sprang up, headed out of the kitchen, knowing only of how Rebecca had insisted this man be contacted. Now he was very much against the idea but at four o'clock in the morning it seemed a feasible solution. With Hans out of the room Rebecca's impulsive reactions took over. She ground the pills into powder and mixed it into Hans's coffee, stirred the dark liquid and prayed the particles would dissolve quickly. Her all-encircling strategy was for Aston Appleton to tell them what course of action should be taken, for Hans to fall into a deep sleep and hence allow her to gain Brett's freedom unhindered.

As Aston entered the kitchen he helped himself to the available coffee while Rebecca viewed him with a want for knowledge. He looked around and enjoyed the sweet dark liquid which was destined for Hans Zenna as Rebecca sat in total astonishment watching her frail plan evaporate into thin air.

Aston stayed at the Watsons' home for only half an hour and during that short space of time felt he'd convinced them both to act in accordance with Hans Zenna's orders. He told Rebecca with impartial glee it appeared to be the only safe way to ensure Brett's return home, since neither of them knew who was "Control". Aston had watched Zenna throughout and although conveying the appearance of a helpful family friend, couldn't help but recall the photographs of his well-developed body. Aston felt his eyes wanting to close as the drug took effect; he wanted to sleep and although trying to fight this sudden desire knew he was failing. Like a flashing thunderbolt he realised he'd been drugged and possibly blown his own cover so quickly making his exit suggested he'd urgent office business despite Rebecca's plea for him to remain. Aston made his way towards the front door totally unaware of Hans Zenna thanking him for his advice and almost falling over, staggered towards the car. Reaching the Rover Aston fought to keep his eyes open, unlocked the back door, clambered in, locked the door behind him and lay grotesquely across the back seat falling into a deep sleep harbouring thoughts of having been exposed.

The time was 10.00am.

CHAPTER 15

Lenton Parva. Saturday, 10.00am.

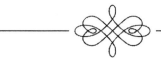

Hans had watched Aston Appleton stumble, stagger and sway as he'd disappeared out of view from the house and closing the door felt uneasy. Zenna was not the most observant of people but he'd detected a note of discord in this man. His whole brief scenario seemed a little too well prepared as he didn't flinch or appear to be concerned by the kidnapping of his own company director and throughout his half-hour stay always seemed to be watching him with a knowing smirk.

Wandering back towards the kitchen he knew something to be wrong but wasn't sure of himself and rejoining Rebecca at the breakfast bar Hans noticed her desperate appearance. He couldn't help but detect the colour fading from her face and large pools of tears accumulating within her once sparkling green eyes. He knelt down in front of her, gently taking a hold of her petite hands and attempted to comfort her sobbing body. Tenderly Hans led her away from the kitchen into the lounge, poured them both a large whisky and they sat as Rebecca told him of her failed plan.

After many moments of deliberation Hans knew it was still necessary to convince Rebecca of his true form even though he thought he'd achieved a satisfactory truce between them and a degree of forgiveness after their all-night vigil. Hans felt tired but was aware that without her support he wouldn't stand a chance of morally surviving the remaining weekend.

Hans moved his muscular body and sat beside her. He'd already told Rebecca of his homosexual inclinations and his regret of being different. She'd seemed to accept all his actions and gave credibility to his being but now he must elaborate on some of the finer points to convince her beyond all doubt, he was trustworthy. Hans recalled for her his return to King's Cross station as instructed by "Control" to collect further instructions from locker 106.

Historical

It was 7.00pm as Hans had entered the station's main concourse but was conspicuous of people watching him even though they were all perfect strangers and only carrying on with their own business. He was afraid someone would recognise him from the previous evening as the man who'd knocked down an elderly lady. He'd stayed well clear of the taxi rank in case the driver noticed him and started lecturing him again or wanted some recompense for cleaning up his urine. The evening air was cool as he made his way through the milling crowd but each of the florescent lights seemed to be pointing at him like a criminal returning to the scene of the crime. He was sweating again, felt uncomfortable and was conscious as his hand floundered around the deep trouser pocket for locker key 106. It seemed to take an age before again standing in front of the tin locker, Hans realised he was shaking uncontrollably. Cautiously he removed the key, inserted it into the keyhole and the door sprang open, declaring its sinister contents. Hans stood looking in awe at the envelope unable to bring himself to touch it but felt as if a single pair of eyes were penetrating his body, forcing him to take the locker's contents. Merely thinking of the photographs back in his flat subdued his shaking hand as he picked out the envelope, slamming closed the locker door. Slowly as if not to attract any attention he walked out of the station and into the busy street.

Electing to walk back to the flat his hatred of crowds became frighteningly evident. People appeared to be directing themselves at him from all angles, his head was spinning, his shirt damp with sweat and his knuckles white with fear.

Hans couldn't recall walking home or even how long it had taken, he was just so relieved to open the flat door, slump inside and shut out the world behind him. He turned on a small table lamp in the tastefully furnished lounge, ripped open the envelope and removed the typed message. He gingerly unfolded the sheet of white paper and read.

Well done, Mr Zenna. I will be in touch with you when your next set of instructions are available... "Control".

Hans couldn't believe it, that bastard was playing games with him and he vowed revenge. In a fit of sheer determination he ripped off his clothes, went to the bathroom and took a long hot shower.

Historical

Almost a month drifted past before Hans had any further communication from "Control". His life had started to gain a degree of normality despite the photographs which were a constant reminder of a looming problem. Once or twice he'd visited the West End bar in which Beck had approached him but he never stayed long. Hans called on his now elderly parents and generally paved his way for society to expel him as he was convinced "Control" would never free his spirit.

He arrived home one evening late to find a pile of mail waiting for him scattered over the hall floor. There was the usual volume of junk mail, bills and letters but a single expensive-looking white envelope caught his undivided attention. Collecting the remaining assortment of mail he sat in the lounge and opened the white envelope. It was typed and matched the previous communications from "Control".

Even having prepared himself throughout the month as he'd

waited for "Control's" next brief to arrive, it was still a shock when it came. As time had progressed onwards he'd come to expect this may occur at any time but he sat fingering the quality envelope before carefully breaking the seal and removing its contents. The thick paper folded into three segments was unsigned and its typed contents met Hans with sedated pain.

You are to go to Lenton Parva and ensure entry into the Watson household. You will be there by 3.25pm tomorrow, Friday. Once you have gained entry you will conceal yourself as necessary until the arrival of Mrs Rebecca Watson. At an appropriate time within an hour of her entry she must be abducted and sedated by a method of your own choice. It is stressed no harm must befall this woman on any account. You will take Rebecca Watson into the lounge suitably incapacitated and wait for my envoy to arrive. You will follow all instructions as issued by this person to the letter… if you don't wish the photographs of yourself and Mr Beck to become public knowledge.

Hans twisted and shuffled around in his seat as he'd related these events to Rebecca. She gazed woefully towards him as he removed the typed message from his pocket and handed it over for her inspection. She read it twice before folding the document and handing it back to Hans, cried with flooding tears forming rivers running down her delicate clear face. He moved closer to her and allowing Rebecca to rest her head on his shoulder, assured her he had no intention of ever inflicting pain. They became involved in deep conversation, Hans attempting to avert Rebecca's mind away from current events while she wanted to tell Hans of her own history. She knew more about Hans and his life than any other person in the world with the chilling exception of "Control". He could only put down the opening up of his personal chronicles to her as being a mark of his increasing respect. In fact, Hans knew it was more than that, much more, yet despite his reservations of the female sex he was aware of a growing electric current passing between their two souls. The acute ringing of door chimes deflected any further intercourse between these two enchanted mortals.

Rebecca, composing her elegant form stood up, straightened her skirt and made a graceful move towards the front door. Hans, hearing the door open and Rebecca's excited squeal, rushed out into the hallway but his hasty manoeuvre was halted as he came nose to nose with the cold steel barrel of a Smith and Wesson revolver.

The time was 3.15pm.

CHAPTER 16

Heathrow Airport. 1.30, Saturday Afternoon.

Mohamid Van Jonger enjoyed his flight to London, having sufficient time to consider the demise of his wife and continue to plot Aston Appleton's destruction. He considered many possibilities but his main priorities were to secure the successful return of Brett to Rebecca and he to Alexis. Aston's degeneration was just a matter of formality relative to time since he'd formulated his approach, the first port of call being the Watsons' household as Mohamid had faithfully promised Brett he'd ensure Rebecca was safe.

His passage through Heathrow Airport involved a series of rigorous questions by the customs service but Mohamid wasn't used to this treatment as in Morocco his face was the best passport any mortal could desire. He conformed to the requirements demanded of him and in so doing ensured his free transition through all the airport's austere regulations. The mid-afternoon air hit Mohamid with breath-taking effect. It was cold and damp yet although the sun glinted occasionally through breaks in the cloud, the atmosphere felt oppressive. His last trip to London had been during the height of a summer when despite being rain soaked, the atmosphere felt more conducive to his Moroccan upbringing.

Mohamid Van Jonger made his exit from the conglomeration of

airport buildings forty-five minutes after he left the Royal Air Maroc jet. He'd often wondered how the western world would exist if the frontiers of bureaucracy were removed and the ethics of his own country instilled into the populace. His black taxi was a definite downward move from the luxurious transport he'd learnt to expect but in this instance a low-key profile was essential to secure a successful conclusion.

The taxi dodged and weaved its way through the heavy Saturday afternoon traffic as it transported him towards Lenton Parva. He'd demanded the most direct route but knew full well the journey would still take a good hour. Mohamid sat admiring his contrived strategy whilst stroking his beard and re-arranging the smart light grey suit. His cool level-headed nature secured his lean figure into a fighting force of immense power and despite his sixty years Mohamid was filled with valorous energy. The small but expensive overnight bag perched on the seat beside him contained only a few overnight garments, a lavish white caftan and his Smith and Wesson revolver.

As the taxi nosed its way into Lenton Parva Mohamid prepared himself for the first duty in resolving this distasteful state of affairs. Disabling Hans Zenna may prove difficult according to Brett so as the car drew up outside the house, Mohamid had his faithful revolver at the ready and gracefully alighting from the aged vehicle asked the driver to wait for him while he made his way towards the large front door. He didn't notice Aston Appleton's old Rover parked a little further down the avenue but admired Brett's gleaming Aston Martin despite the nasty scratch along its side.

Mohamid made his presence known to those inside and holding his Smith and Wesson revolver, prepared himself for a face-to-face conflict with one of "Control's" partisans. He was shocked to see Rebecca answer his call but delighted no harm had befallen her magnificent body. Her utter surprise at seeing him was established by a jubilant excited shriek yet as Hans Zenna moved quickly into the dimly lit hallway Mohamid pushed his way past Rebecca, raising his revolver just in time for it to halt Hans moving any closer. The two men stared at each other. Hans was obviously taken by surprise whilst Mohamid clearly wasn't sure of his next move but Rebecca intervened and placing her petite hand on Mohamid's arm forced him to lower the revolver. She turned, closed the front door and suggested they all went in the lounge.

Mohamid's instincts told him these two had already resolved their initial conflict and as they each sat down with Hans remaining close to Rebecca she launched into a difficult dialogue.

"Mohamid, it's good to see you again and so much has happened, I don't know where to start."

Tears were beginning to form in her eyes but she gradually unfurled all the events as they'd occurred. Mohamid sat and listened to every word she said complimented by an occasional comment from Hans. Rebecca told of how Hans had become involved, their initial conflict, Martha's death and Brett's abduction by a woman called Alexis. Hans was about to embark into a lengthy discourse as to the credibility of Alexis but fortunately Mohamid cut him short.

"I feel it is necessary for you both to know a series of facts not yet at your command. I and my family are also involved in this conspiracy much to my personal distaste."

For a brief moment the room fell silent as they each became acutely aware of "Control's" sinister presence.

"I've listened to you both and your story is not dissimilar to my own. If you will both permit me to continue."

Mohamid's voice was quiet yet positive; he stood up and strode around the lounge, stopping to look with admiration at the grandfather clock. The mellow ticking created an air of sophistication while the bloodstained carpet caused him grief. He turned to face Rebecca and Hans who'd remained perfectly hushed as if knowing this was painful for Mohamid and began to reveal the events which had them entrapped. He didn't quite tell of all the underlying reasons for his involvement, principally his relationship with Alexis, but their faces clearly drained as he announced Alexis was his "second wife". Mohamid turned away, looked out of the leaded window towards a picturesque garden and continued.

"The message received at the villa was clear and very much to the point. Alexis was to come to London, pick up further instructions at Heathrow and return to Tangiers with Brett. She knew nothing more and was acting purely to protect myself. It is perhaps for the best she didn't know any of you prior to this unsavoury affair."

Mohamid described the bomb blast, the death of wife number one, how the hotel he'd built up seemed to have turned against him and his sorrow for causing so much pain. They all started to talk at the same time attempting to comfort each other but Mohamid's superior manner prevailed as he regained his confidence which was only briefly destroyed. He continued.

"Alexis is not as she may have seemed to you both, actually she's a caring, loyal woman with much to give the world society. I know she regrets having offended you both, as do I, but as you will see no choice was given. Rebecca my dear, Brett is safe and well. We spoke last night of the veiled character calling himself 'Control' and formulated a scheme which may expose him, hence my rather hasty journey to London. Initially Brett wants me to convey his wishes and inform you he and Alexis are now following 'Control's' plan. Cyprus is their next destination."

Again the room fell silent as Rebecca felt tears trickling down her cheeks but the warmth of Hans Zenna's hand holding hers secured a degree of well-being. Mohamid took a seat opposite them and continued.

"It's possible we may know 'Control's' identity and it's my part of the deal to consolidate with irreputable proof our worst suspicions. In the meantime Brett and Alexis are going to follow the instructions as given with rebellious integrity."

Rebecca and Hans both sat with eager impatience waiting for Mohamid to enlighten them as to who the finger of suspicion was about to descend upon. However, as if anticipating their question Mohamid considered it a cautious and prudent gesture to say no more until proof was obtained.

"I want to know who is behind all this," Rebecca demanded. "But most of all I would like to join you in the quest for proof."

"That, my dear, is most noble of you, but I must insist you remain here with Mr Zenna. You will be safe, secure and away from any impending danger. Two people have already died through related circumstances and I don't wish for any further sacrifice to be made." Mohamid concluded his lecture by offering a sincere smile of encouragement to them both but Rebecca knew Mohamid meant business and he'd already taken more risks than could have been reasonably expected.

She was about to inform Mohamid of Aston Appleton's recent visit but he cut down her words by preparing to depart and asking them if they'd any of "Control's" messages available for his inspection. Hans felt in his trouser pocket and handed over a crumpled white sheet of paper relating to "Control's" instruction on the abduction of Rebecca. Removing his own communication from this sordid individual Mohamid briefly observed the paper's quality and the form of the varied instructions ensured he knew them to be from the same person. Before he made his final parting gesture to Rebecca he asked Hans if he'd any idea how "Control" would end this nightmare but the negative answer only coincided with his own assessment.

Escorting Mohamid to the front door, he told Hans to be especially cautious and guard Rebecca with unsurrendering dedication. He announced his intention to return, delicately kissed Rebecca's hand and was gone. They stood facing each other as the front door swung closed and their bodies' advanced sexual communication system took up a firm hold. His six-foot-tall, strong blond body dwarfed her succulent, slender form as he purposefully lowered his lips onto hers.

For the first time in his life Hans Zenna wanted to make love with a woman, not just any woman but Rebecca Watson and her beating heart pounding with excitement could be felt in the surrounding atmosphere. They gingerly made their way upstairs knowing full well what had to be done. For the first time since they'd encountered each other they were totally relaxed, interlocked and lustful.

The time was 5.00pm.

CHAPTER 17

Larnaca, Cyprus. Saturday, 5.45am.

The white Mercedes quickly settled down to a steady speed of 50 miles per hour as they left the airport terminal and Christian Beck feared for his life as the temperature outside the car began to climb. Summer in Cyprus had been particularly sweltering and although it was now September the heat didn't appear to have diminished. He'd already decided in his own mind Aston Appleton wasn't going to allow him to enjoy his old age or even possibly the next day, he knew too much, didn't care enough and was expendable. Christian's clothes were again damp with his own perspiration as the car made its way past a salt lake bordering the airport. He'd not taken much notice of any surrounding countryside for a great many years but the sight of accumulating pink flamingos padding around the salt flats averted his mind from any impending reduction in life span to admiration of a dazzling natural spectacle. The sheer beauty of pink and white against an arid green-brown backdrop brought him to realise life was unequivocally precious, especially his own. This pageant jolted his mind into action, he wanted to live, he wanted to enjoy living and what was more he'd decided to take the world by the scruff of its collar and extract all possible goodness if not for himself for his parents. Damn Aston Appleton and damn these two beings sat in front of the car as Christian smiled to himself. It had taken nothing more than a flock of delicate wild pink flamingos to ensure his own true understanding of life.

The car moved sedately past this tranquil setting and on towards the town of Larnaca. Gradually the buildings grew larger in size as they approached the towns limits yet the two smartly clad gentlemen in the front seats had hardly spoken a single word since they'd confirmed his identity at the airport. Their entry into the town itself was heralded by the two men commencing a conversation in their own native tongue. Christian didn't understand a word of their discussion but knew the language to be Arabic, yet their exchange appeared to be frank, to the point with a degree of attached maliciousness. The car slowed to a more sedate pace as traffic increased. Christian Beck considered making a clean getaway from the car as they stood at traffic lights in the town itself but put the idea out of his mind knowing Appleton and his sinister web of evil wouldn't let him live in peace. Apart from this he'd started formulating his own scheme to better himself and knew this could only be complimented by the package he'd ensured was by now well on its way to London.

The car moved forward and made its way along the wide palm tree lined boulevard towards a well populated yet sophisticated marina. The big Mercedes was steered positively through crowds of people walking aimlessly and enviously looking at the expensive collection of glamorous yachts. As the car drew to a gentle halt Christian regarded this luxury cruiser moored at the side of their car with considerable envy. It was enormous and radiated expensive taste yet he sat transfixed, knowing he was about to enter a world he'd only ever read about. The two gentlemen who'd escorted him from the airport were now on the quayside and opening the door nearest to him suggested in a most forceful manner he was expected aboard.

Christian slid out of the lavish car and shaking himself, looked at the huge seagoing vessel. He noticed the Cypriot flag hanging from the mast, the Greek flag limply dangling at the stern and an array of expensive fittings adorning the entire ship. Standing aside of him, the two men manoeuvred Christian in a most positive manner towards the ships gangway. Unable to help himself Christian regarded the sheer magnificence of this gleaming white emblem of grandeur with inspired contempt. His glazed, absorbing attitude focused on the proud bow displaying in black letters with gold shadowing the vessel's registered name, *Brave Goose* was clearly owned by people of influence who knew their fortune and he wondered how on earth Aston Appleton had become involved with such people or at worst he may even own this fantastic-looking vessel. The thought of Appleton made him shiver but his dreaming was rudely interrupted by his two escorts forcing him up the gangway. Although raised at a steep angle Christian staggered up as quickly as he could, being pleased to reach its climax and stepping on to the level teak deck was met by a member of *Brave Goose's* crew. His original escort went back to the quayside and standing guard over their white Mercedes watched him with an evil eye. Leading Christian towards the ship's stern his new host passed neat wooden doors, large oval curtained windows and well stowed nautical equipment. His eyes couldn't absorb the imposing splendour of the current environment yet looking skywards the upper deck seemed equally well furnished and surrounding a curvaceous white and gold funnel, the expensive sun loungers were laid out to a vacant informal pattern.

As they reached the ship's stern the aft deck opened up in front of them. Christian's host clearly wasn't impressed by his wandering eyes and disgusting appearance. He was still wearing the same clothes he'd left London in on Friday evening so coupled with his own sweat and putrid activities on the flight to Cyprus, Christian knew he didn't cut a particularly dashing figure. By contrast his host crew member was attired in freshly pressed white slacks, white rubber-soled shoes and white short-sleeved shirt with the ship's name embossed across the chest. Christian hadn't taken much notice of him as they'd walked down the deck until turning onto the aft part of the ship; he was dark in appearance, taller than himself and was clearly a European, possibly Greek. The man never spoke as he turned on Christian and spinning him around, pushed him onto the steel cabin wall. His hands started working their way up his body feeling for any weapon or concealed instrument of death. The search was most effective and meticulously executed down to the point of checking the heels of his shoes. Christian watched the sailor through the corner of his eye as his hands wandered all over his puny frame. Although the situation was totally alien to him, Christian found the whole affair to be so exciting he felt his body becoming sexually aroused by the man's presence. This series of thoughts didn't remain embedded in his mind for long as the big sailor almost picked him up, spun him round and telling him to wait where he was, disappeared through the large, heavily tinted glass patio doors. As the door slid closed Christian now on his own again attempted to dampen his excited body yet couldn't see beyond the glass doors and hence had no idea who was behind the austere black glass but felt as if he was being watched.

Christian wandered around the aft deck; the two men who'd brought him from the airport still stood guard by the white car but despite feeling apprehensive he was aware of his own self-assumed importance. The teak deck was warm underfoot yet the awning covering this part of *Brave Goose* was still and prevented the sun's intense rays from burning his exposed thinly covered scalp. He made his way ambling past a suite of wicker furniture to the sternmost part of his current environment and looking down into a clear green sea Christian hadn't realised how far out of the water this lavish symbol of eminence sat. For just a few brief moments he was spellbound but the moving sun traversed a sufficient part of its daily journey around the heavens for its powerful rays to not be averted by the canvas awning and penetrate his vulnerable human membrane. Moving out of the sun's directness Christian heard the patio doors slide open he turned and was faced by two members of the crew, each one being dressed identically. Speaking in English with a most prominent Greek-based accent his original onboard host told him to step into the ship's main saloon. Christian Beck had no alternative, he attempted to straighten his stooping form and clearing his throat marched past the two sailors towards an uncertain future. Aston Appleton had informed Beck he'd be met at Larnaca Airport but other than his remaining two airline tickets with stated destinations he'd no other source of knowledge.

Passing from brilliant daylight into the secluded dark saloon, Christian was unable to identify any of the cabin features yet alone who was present. As he became accustomed to the reduced lighting concentration levels he gradually began to make out the features of his surroundings and with whom he was clearly having an audience. The cabin was cool, furnished like a luxury hotel with exquisite taste and diffused an air of utter tranquillity. At the far end of the saloon facing the patio doors Christian had made his entry by, there was an enormous highly polished table totally devoid of any personal features.

To the left of the table stood a man clad in brilliant white robes with a colourful headband, he was clean shaven, looked to be in his late twenties and was obviously a wheeler of great power. Beside him sat a much older man and Christian estimated his age to be perhaps late eighties or possibly early nineties. His attire was not dissimilar to the younger man's but his withered body couldn't transmit the same element of power. Moving a little farther into the saloon Christian was aware of the older man being in a wheelchair and as the patio doors were closed the two sailors stood like sentries each side of the black tinted glass.

The cabin was silent as all eyes were on Christian; he didn't know what to do with himself but was alarmingly aware beads of perspiration were running down his back with sheer undiluted fear. He stood and froze to the deep pile carpet totally unaware of the thoughts running through the mind of the younger Arabic-looking gentleman standing by the perfunctory table. The atmosphere grew unbearably heavy as the younger man and Christian stared at each other with intimidating suspicion.

At last, just before Beck was about to embarrass himself, the old man spoke out, diffusing that intense moment. His husky voice was not comprehensible to Christian but the younger man moved and started to manoeuvre the wheelchair away from the table towards where he stood. As they approached with slow determination Christian began to wonder of his fate and if his worries concerning living were about to be obliterated or confirmed. He still didn't have any idea as to who these people were, if this was their ship or what was expected of him to any great degree.

The two men halted in front of him and Christian noticed the old man's eyes. They stared into space with a glazed awkwardness not known to him before. It must have been obvious to the young man as Christian gawped but perhaps becoming more obvious was the old man's total lack of movement. The only part of him which had flexed during this audience so far had been his mouth and lips, everything else appeared to be frozen. Silence reigned no longer as the young man spoke in perfect Queen's English.

"Please be seated, Mr Christian Beck. We are pleased to have you aboard our meagre floating home. You will forgive us for not having met you at the airport but my father found the early hour offensive.

Permit me to introduce ourselves, my name is Winston Al-Hassan and this is my father formally the Berber of Marrakesh. You must excuse our most unforgivable behaviour but we understood from Mr Appleton his onward emissary to be of more respectable appearance."

There was a deadly pregnant pause after he'd finished his opening dialogue yet Christian Beck was surprised and full of bewilderment as to why such obviously wealthy people were tied to Aston Appleton. Looking directly at Winston Al-Hassan, Christian spoke as positively as his nervous disposition would allow.

"It's been some considerable time since I've been permitted to spend any period on my personal hygiene. Also I had a most uncomfortable flight from Tangiers to Larnaca, suffering a bout of air sickness due mainly to a lack of sleep, change in diet and the almost intolerable temperatures experienced in both countries."

Christian was intending to continue but Winston cut in with electrifying speed.

"Well Mr Beck, you now have some time to catch up with yourself. Your flight out of Larnaca is not until much later today so we would like you to rest and treat our ship as if it were your own. Yiannis here will take you to your cabin and ensure a fresh change of clothes is made available for your onward journey."

Winston Al-Hassan clicked his fingers and the sailor who'd escorted him around *Brave Goose* instantly sprang into action. Christian's audience with the Al-Hassans was clearly over as Yiannis the sailor ushered him past the two Arab-looking gents and out of the saloon.

Closing the door behind them, Yiannis led the way down a narrow but carpeted passage as they heard the Al-Hassans erupt into a highly vocal argument. Their voices were still audible as they started to descend a small spiral stairway leading to a lower deck but Christian couldn't help himself any further, he asked Yiannis if he was Greek, who were the Al-Hassan's and if they owned *Brave Goose*.

The hunky sailor merely answered he was a Greek and they did own the ship as he stopped outside a cabin door. Again he asked who were the Al-Hassans and defiantly demanded to know what were they arguing about but Yiannis didn't even look at Christian as he unlocked the cabin door. It swung open, he stood back, gestured

Christian inward and in so doing said they were arguing about him. Beck didn't expect Yiannis to follow him into the cabin but surprise appeared to be the order of the day. Closing the cabin door, Yiannis demanded Christian should remove all his clothing so he could check the sizes prior to obtaining a new set. He pointed out the small en-suite bathroom, silk bathrobe, clean towels and service call button.

The cabin itself was only small, housing a three-quarter bed, wardrobe and chair. A small, circular, curtained porthole was only just above the waterline but the dark quayside excluded a great deal of natural light from entering. It was warm in the cabin and the air smelt fragrant as Christian started to remove his clothing. He emptied his pockets making sure the tickets and fake money were still intact as he stood in only shoes, socks and underwear. Yiannis made it clear these were also to be removed and in doing so exposed his entire body to the Greek. He watched the sailor push his clothes long past their best into a black plastic bag yet as Yiannis concluded his work, turning to leave the cabin saw Christian's male organ begin to rise with suggestive jerking movements. The sailor dropped his plastic bag, watching Beck climb onto the bed and moving over towards him sat beside his horizontal body. Christian Beck's stiff penis seemingly interested Yiannis as he firmly placed his large pawlike hand around the erect flesh and started to move the whole skin up and down. Quickening his pace, Yiannis made him reach the point of no return and Christian expelled his sperm, splattering it over his hairless chest. The large stocky sailor stood up and far from being excited himself, unzipped his trousers, pointed his limp cock over Beck and urinated, laughing uncontrollably.

He couldn't believe this had happened to him as Yiannis zipped up his trousers, picked the plastic bag from the floor and leaving the cabin, grinned at him showing two rows of perfect white teeth. Closing the door Christian heard the lock turn and jumping off the wet bedding tried to open the door but sure enough he was locked in, naked, stripped of his remaining morality and very much a prisoner. He leant against the cabin bulkhead knowing full well he'd been raped. What else was left for him?

The time was 7.10am.

CHAPTER 18

The Berber Of Marrakesh. Historical.

During the third and fourth centuries before Christ was born, small Berber kingdoms were being established in many parts of Morocco. Their origins were particularly hazy and nobody truly knows from whence they came but theories link them to the Celts, Basques and even Canaanites. Over a thousand years after these powerful kingdoms flourished the Berbers spread their wings and constructed mighty empires ruling North Africa and parts of Spain.

Since these early years Morocco had been governed by outsiders so reducing the influence of its own Berber regime, yet traditional customs and languages remained. In time the National Revival under the Alaouites had been replaced by the effects of various world wars and most Berber kingdomships had almost been obliterated. In 1956 Morocco was again united under the independent rule of an Alaouite but too late for the Berbers to reinstate their past glory.

Berber Al-Hassan's family had like many of his counterparts from Fez, Meknes and Rabat graduated from being kingdom rulers to very powerful tycoons of varying degrees. Shortly after the century's turn the Al-Hassans found themselves being deposed from their native Marrakesh through forces beyond their extensive control. The whole family inclusive of devotees moved to the European equivalent of Sin

City, Tangiers. It was here they made their new home, purposely building a grand villa on the secluded Atlantic coast. Berber Al-Hassan, as he was still known, diverted the family's enormous wealth to form a shipping company of unprecedented magnitude which as time slid past grew beyond his most excitable dreams. The name Al-Hassan became so well-known and internationally acceptable the family had immense difficulty in maintaining their personal yet individual control. Despite a large number of direct and indirect relatives working within this sizable organisation, Berber Al-Hassan's wife maintained a low yet positive profile. She followed the true Moroccan principles as laid down centuries before relating to feminine roles in Berber life. Her main function in their society was to care, pamper and produce a steady blood line of male children as this was essential to guarantee continued growth of the company, preserve the Al-Hassans' name into future eras and secure a guardian benefactor during their dwindling twilight years.

The birth of a daughter formed an unwieldy rift between senior members of the Al-Hassans' family as for years they knew how important a male child would be and its designated fundamental role couldn't in their eyes be effectively performed by a woman. As Berber Al-Hassan came to terms with his daughter's presence on earth he began to take an increasing interest in her well-being and she developed into a bright, intelligent child which continued throughout her ripening years. His accumulating interest in her began to force traditional elements of the family's culture into change. Such developments were becoming a ready source of heated exchange within the company elders and many times Berber Al-Hassan had to calm the frustrated ingredients of his forward planning. He personally wanted to see the company grow but was aware new trade with Western society was not successfully cultivated by Arabic or Moroccan methods. These high flyers from countries like America and Great Britain preferred to trade with people they genuinely understood and since his wife was unable to bear him a male child, he elected to teach his daughter the company business with aspirations of her being able to develop such lucrative markets.

Al-Hassan knew he'd have an uphill fight to convince the family elders this would be an effective trade development. During his announcement at their regular weekly meeting the Berber spoke with apprehension as he laid out before his family members a trade development scheme to secure a profitable future. He'd watched their faces as the plan had been disclosed and detected no true resentment until his daughter was mentioned. Carefully the Berber had attempted to play down her involvement but the family was wise to his move since they knew he wanted to manipulate them into accepting her. Al-Hassan's gamble didn't pay off, the room erupted with ferocious fist-shaking jargon at noise levels he'd only ever heard during the Mellah uprisings many years before.

The battle raged for days; his daughter was confined to the female quarters of their large villa while he attempted to calm each family member and time progressed with an endless river of growing concern but proved to be a tepid healer. Berber Al-Hassan although not having the full backing of each family elder commenced his strategy of future development, initially by employing his daughter as his personal assistant. They followed each other around like shy lap dogs uncertain of breeding while the business world of Tangiers watched from a most vigilant distance.

*

Berber Al-Hassan and his daughter were beginning to create a formidable team as their general approach coupled with charm and intelligence began to outstrip the ageing family members' comprehension. Time had definitely proved to be a respectable healer as the Berber had given little by little more responsibility to his only daughter and although still calling her his personal assistant she began to handle far more of his routine business concerns, accompanying him on all but the most delicate of meetings.

It was during one such outing to an important meeting held in Tangiers their lives changed, not instantly but within only a few unbearable grief-stricken and calamitous months. The Berber's meeting was to be with Middle-Eastern Arabs which unfortunately precluded her from actually being involved. They would only deal with the Berber but he insisted she came as one day they may weaken and agree to discuss business with her present. He knew this to be a most unlikely event but he considered it to be as good an excuse to be seen out and about with his daughter as any. She was beautiful, intelligent, socially aware and he was proud of her.

The rendezvous took place in Tangiers gleaming showpiece Rembrant Hotel but as they entered the foyer Al-Hassan was swiftly whisked into the conference room, leaving his glamorous twenty-eight-year-old daughter open to Mohamid Van Jonger's passionate advances. Mohamid was young, ambitious, virile and hungry. The sight of this single woman so captivated his body he knew despite being married, he had to make love to her. At first her alluring body rejected him but as time passed and their visits to Mohamid's hotel increased so his advances became more and more consolidated. Finally she submitted to Van Jonger's sexual provocation with cyclonic hunger; he was her first man.

The act of passion took place in a suite of rooms not occupied that day and as they enjoyed each other. Mohamid felt he'd only really taken delight in eating forbidden fruit with a piggish willingness. He'd watched her dress after they'd finished while laid naked on their love nest. She never spoke to him again after he'd penetrated her cherubic body but her eyes and stone glazed look told Mohamid she already regretted having laid eyes on him. The young woman left him on the bed as she made her way out of the room and down to her beloved father. Mohamid on the other hand wasn't satisfied. His body still rigid with excitement wanted more and reaching over spoke to his wife on the telephone demanding she should come to him straight away. Naturally being a Moroccan woman her primary duty was to please her husband but even she was surprised to see him laid naked and erect on the large double bed demanding her body.

*

Each time Berber Al-Hassan came to the Rembrant, Mohamid watched for his daughter but she never appeared again. Some four months after their few moments of sexual passion Mohamid had almost forgotten her vowing he'd never touch another woman again other than his wife. The call from Al-Hassan's villa came very much of a shock to him especially when he'd been told of the reason for him being summoned but Mohamid dutifully attended the Berber's villa with a degree of regret. The meeting was serious and subdued with almost intolerable undertones. His daughter was no longer the radiant beauty he'd lured into his bed but a rather large, tatty young woman who appeared not to look after her appearance. Al-Hassan himself seemed to have aged a great deal since the last time he'd been seen at the Rembrant. His face was drawn, covered with lines of worry and his once sparkling eyes which used to beam seemed grey and withdrawn. Mohamid's gaze drifted back to the woman sobbing by the open window; her face was heavily bruised obviously a mark of her father's disgust. Berber Al-Hassan told Mohamid in no uncertain manner as to what he'd destroyed by asserting such animal passions on his daughter. Her life, he stated, was destroyed, disgraced and possibly to be removed from the earth's face unless they could now come to some agreement. Mohamid knew if he didn't agree to the Berber's terms he would be hounded out of Tangiers and this young woman stoned to death.

*

The announcement of Al-Hassan's daughter disgracing the family name wasn't met with predictable results from the family's senior members. They listened to the arrangements the Berber had forced Mohamid Van Jonger into agreeing with contempt, before adding their own terms. Al-Hassan concluded his speech knowing full well they'd all told him not to involve his daughter in the company business and he'd failed them. More hurtful to the family was the disgrace being imposed upon one of Morocco's most noble, old and highly respected families by one of their own kind. The room fell silent as a spokesman for those present rose to his feet and without casting a glance at Berber Al-Hassan informed him of their terms. He would be permitted to remain in Tangiers as their own Berber in name only until the child was born. Once the event had taken place they were happy for the child to be brought up by Van Jonger, using any surname but their own. However, since this would always be a constant threat to their security they'd decided the Berber Al-Hassan, his wife and child-bearing daughter would be deposed from their remaining family, Tangiers and Morocco. Moreover, should any of them feel the need to return they would face death without question but since his bloodline had been the ruling family for many centuries they felt it necessary to furnish him with a sum of money for his continued existence elsewhere. This money was to be a single lump sum payment not tied or repayable but as a mark of their respect for his forefathers. Again the room was silent as the man stood down from making the family's announcement. Yet despite being devastated, Berber Al-Hassan was not surprised. At least they wouldn't kill his own family as had been done in the past for such disgraceful acts. His head was implanted in his hands as he tried to accept their terms but by the time he was ready to speak the room had emptied. The Berber looked around; his wife and daughter were the only ones left and standing up he knew this to be their destiny. His fingers twitched with unease and felt as if the sands of time had trickled away between them without him knowing.

*

Each day of his daughter's remaining pregnancy passed with snail-like speed as he considered what should be done but was unable to form a conclusion. The family, however, carefully avoided his own cell of intimacy as they grew further away from their outcasts.

When Al-Hassan's daughter went into labour she was attended by second-rate medical staff, a continued sign of the family's lack of interest. She pushed and heaved for many hours, the pain almost crippling her small frame. Her mother and father stood close by despite her unsavoury actions as she was still their only child. The young woman's body was saturated with perspiration as she gave her final moments of life to create a new human being.

The small baby girl came into the world as a new dawn broke heralded by her grandmother sobbing for joy at the birth and for sorrow at her daughter's death. Al-Hassan approached his dead flesh and blood, wiping the girl's brow gently, reciting a prayer of divine forgiveness. Their tiny baby granddaughter seemed so much at peace with the world, they both hoped she wouldn't ever grow up to hate it. An attending nurse loomed over them and whilst wrapping the tiny baby in a soft, warm shawl explained the baby's mother, their daughter, had suffered massive internal bleeding during the birth. The nurse turned, picked up the tiny human bundle and left the room as both Berber Al-Hassan and his wife looked towards each other. He put out his hand, she took it and they drew each other together, knowing for the first time in many years how much they loved one another. They spoke of the lifestyle they'd lost, the daughter they'd lost and the granddaughter they'd never see again as the family chauffeur appeared. It was the end of an era but they both had a will to live and create a new life together.

CHAPTER 19

The Berber Of Marrakesh. Historical, Part Two.

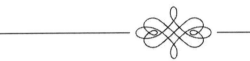

Since being forced out of Tangiers the Al-Hassans had woefully moved to and settled in the state of Lebanon, making a comfortable low-key living. The Berber's business tended to deal with small, high-cost, low-risk goods being imported or exported around the world. He only employed one or two people and the company's turnover was kept to a nominal sum. There was no real ambition, he didn't have to struggle to stay alive any more, in fact the small business had only been set up to keep the Berber's mind occupied. Most of their income was secured from the returns made against financial investments guaranteed by money they'd been expelled with from their traditional home.

During the seaward journey from Morocco to Lebanon the Berber and his wife had many days to consider the fortunes which lay ahead. They had passed through difficult patches during their life but always with the family in support. Now it was just themselves in a great big hostile world. Taking a passage by steamer from Tangiers to Beirut gave them both time they'd needed to create an attitude of adaptation, to consider and reshape an uncertain outlook. It was then the Berber knew if their money was correctly invested a particularly comfortable lifestyle could be attained without ever having to work again. Between the two worlds of known and unknown it was decided a life of luxury was of no consequence until they had a family again to share in its possible rewards. Neither of these two eloquent beings were spring chickens but with such an adventure ahead the romantic effect of seaborne travel coupled with their total commitment to each other resulted in a major decision. Once settled in a new developing country they would again try to produce their own loyal family cell.

Time passed by with frightening rapidity as the Al-Hassans settled to their new environment. The young city shrouded by ancient history offered a sense of intrigue which gave Berber Al-Hassan a complete new lease of life. His wife encouraged him to develop their small business concern and for the first time during their marriage felt as if he really needed her loving support. Between them their life took on a totally new, exciting outlook and all this was peaked by his wife becoming pregnant during the most beautiful time of the year. The lush orange and lemon trees were in full blossom issuing a fragrant aroma of perfect harmony.

*

It was early winter as their second child was born, a boy they named Winston. Berber Al-Hassan and his wife were without doubt the happiest two people on earth. Since the death of their daughter and the loss of their granddaughter they'd longed for this sensational moment. Both mother and father decided the child's upbringing should be considerably more Westernised than their previous life had permitted. This was considered the most suitable education format which in time would stand the future Al-Hassan bloodline in an excellent position to display worldwide a cultivated balance of East and Western culture; it would be nothing short of unequalled excellence.

After the birth of Winston life settled down to a more sedate pace. The young Al-Hassan quickly became aware of his parents' importance in years past but was never tempted to question beyond his limited understanding. His mother was nothing more than perfect, she gave all which was possible plus very much more while his father, now with a real added cause to be successful began to expand the previously meagre business concern in readiness for his son and heir.

As his father's business gained considerable momentum, Winston's father grew away again from his mother and began to treat her as he'd done years before in their Moroccan environment. Winston's mother could see the Berber slide back into his old ways with frightening consequences and they began to argue over the smallest of petty details. He started to spend less time with his son who he'd idolised with painful force from his conception and their house became a place of evil sanctuary for him as he elected to remain for longer periods of time at his ever expanding powerhouse of an office. Berber Al-Hassan was committed to provide for his son as he'd never provided for any human being. The financial investments grew, the business became profitable and Al-Hassan tended to forget who really cared for him.

Some Years Later

As far as Winston's father was aware the whole world was again at his mercy and when a representative of Choans appeared on the scene bearing golden promises the temptation proved excessive. A young, mean-looking man at that time, Aston Appleton had a nose for money. Choans' mainstream business wasn't pulling any startling strings for him so he'd decided to branch out and although financing his deals with Choans' money, intended these arrangements to expand his own personal wealth. In short Appleton was moonlighting using company money, lining his own pocket and being a true trickster.

The now ageing Berber had become greedy for power and success and money. Aston Appleton although only a young man had identical objectives and as these two human hurricanes met, a dark satanic thunder cloud loomed over a nearing horizon. From the start of their relationship it was clear only one of them would be a winner. Berber Al-Hassan was old, crafty and worldly wise while Appleton although having youth on his side was a disaster waiting to happen. Their meeting was brought about by a third party from London's exclusive stock exchange society and in oblivious innocence a chance comment by one of the society's jobbers had paved the way for Al-Hassan and Appleton to meet. The Berber wanted to invest more money through the London financial markets and naturally Aston was only too pleased to assist, at a price to be paid direct into his own bank account.

Aston Appleton had taken advice from one of his less than reliable sources in the City as to which company would provide the best return on a large investment and the inside information which filtered back favoured an airline. United European Express was brand new, had a dynamic board of directors, a completely new approach to air travel, new aircraft and heavy debts. Its floatation on the stock market was as usual, designed to raise working capital and Appleton bought some thirty percent of the available shares on behalf of Berber Al-Hassan. The airline felt it had a secure future, secure investor and a fresh member to its board of directors who it was hoped would influence the licence of their routes into Beirut.

For a short while all associated parties were content. Al-Hassan and Appleton didn't meet again and the airline developed into a profit-making concern with a glittering future until one of their aircraft crashed on take-off, slamming into a taxiing Boeing 747 with a full payload of passengers. The value of United European Express shares dropped overnight by almost eighty percent as the Civil Aviation Authority isolated the cause as mechanical failure through bad maintenance. Berber Al-Hassan was forced to resign from the company and sell his shareholding at an unprecedented loss. The shock of this whole affair, especially the loss of almost his entire fortune, caused him to suffer a stroke which left him totally paralysed and entrust him to a wheelchair for the rest of his life.

Aston Appleton watched as United European Express stock dropped in value. The developments of this unfortunate affair inspired him into collecting as much capital as he could obtain in readiness to purchase the stock himself once he was convinced it had reached its lowest monetary worth. He knew the airline wouldn't go out of business since the financial commitment of the bank ensured the company had weathered the worst of this dreadful accident. At precisely the correct moment Aston purchased a significant proportion of the airline's stock. He knew of Al-Hassan's departure from the company and the fortune he'd lost but he didn't damn well care a cent. Now it was a challenge for Aston Appleton to make money prove his worth to the world, secure a seat on the board and finally leave Choans far behind.

During this period Aston began to feel Choans were cheating him out of a more senior position in the company and he started to voice his opinion concerning the directors' wisdom, methods, anything he could criticise he did in style. It was his own stupidity which secured his meagre position at the declining company and so as a major shareholder of the airline, he felt at least as if there was something positive to be achieved. However, in his usual cocky manner he'd launched himself into a project without concluding the background research. Aston didn't take the trouble to isolate the airline's other major investors but if he'd done just a minor study he'd have found Choans' prominent position as a shareholder in United European. His captious comments on Choans' performance were filtered by design of the directors to the airline's board and at that moment in time Aston Appleton's investment strategy became null and void. The unease which both companies attempted to assert over Appleton would have broken any normal mortal but he kept on fighting, considering he was superhuman and eventually with clouded bitterness a confrontation took place at United European's headquarters. Aston demanded a seat on the board of directors in accordance with the company regulation ruling on share value but his application was denied with venom. In a fit of unsecured anger Appleton relieved himself of the pressures and United European's stock, making a handsome profit. His shares were naturally bought up by Choans who for a short while reaped a profitable reward. The fuel crisis, however, brought the value of their investment to straining point and when Rosco made a successful bid for Choans, the airline stock was evaluated, condemned and disposed of with frightening rapidity.

*

The news of Aston Appleton buying up United European's stock after such immoral failings and at rock bottom prices certainly didn't improve Al-Hassan's health. Since having been confined to his wheelchair most of his business had declined to a minor trickle of unprofitable failures. Confined to their indistinctive residence in Beirut, Al-Hassan watched the world go by through drawn curtains; his brain was all that functioned since his stroke. He had no time or patience for his wife and her untimely death of old age, exhaustion and hatred didn't worry him at all. Thoughts of passing glory ran around his mind but since leaving Marrakesh all those years ago when he was a younger man, nothing had ever been either stable or everlasting except his Winston.

Berber Al-Hassan and his son had not been close since Winston was a young boy, yet despite all his failings, he had tried to secure his son with a rich, profitable and respected company to take over when he knew the time to be right. Failing hurt his stubborn pride with excruciating pain. It had been their joint decision to send Winston to England for the best education money could obtain and Eton had been happy to accept the opportunity of proving the Al-Hassans correct.

Winston's education was a glorious success and the college was quite rightly proud of their latest sensation. The world and Winston were destined for great things but his father's stroke and mother's death precluded him from joining the band of fortunate young noble millionaires. He returned under duress but with the intention of remaining in his home town of Beirut for as short a time as was possible. Winston wanted just like his father to conquer the world and he felt London would offer him a better chance than Beirut, but the sight of his once able father brought him down to reality with a lesson of cold intent. Being in a wheelchair had made the Berber very bitter and he knew with his wife dead Winston was his only hope of a comfortable, secure survival.

*

As Winston Al-Hassan came to terms with his enforced lifestyle he put the prospect of joining London's elite out of his mind at least for the foreseeable future. He and his father spoke of the past, the family's high points and failures including their expulsion from Morocco which was deemed to be the reason for their current demure standing in life. Berber Al-Hassan knew they should be living in a far more exotic environment to at least maintain a degree of status for their aristocratic name. The old man now in his eighties eventually told Winston all about their past with one exception. The sister Winston had never known produced a baby girl but both mother and child had died during birth. Berber Al-Hassan lied but he couldn't risk Winston going to Morocco to find his niece with a death threat issued so many years ago still playing on his mind. He prayed Allah would forgive him but he needed Winston's affection so very, very much.

Their hours of discussion, argument and frank exchange of views led to a bond between them becoming so exceptionally strong the old man felt quite secure. The events which had taken place and been recited by his father had as he'd wished, ensnared Winston into taking over what remained of the family estate with one sole objective. Aston Appleton, Winston declared was responsible for his father's state of mind and loss of fortune which should have been his. The books of credit he vowed must be balanced.

Their strategic approach to displace Appleton was the mastermind of Winston Al-Hassan, the twenty-six-year-old Arab, who Beirut knew to be an up and coming force. Since taking over from his father all family fortunes, decisions and business events were in his control. Winston steadily sold their interests in the city of Beirut and surrounding areas. He invested in safe concerns knowing any further losses would kill his ageing father and coupled with their income from the Moroccan expulsion money Winston finally secured the family name on to a steady, secure and profit-making route. His final move in regulating his father's affairs was to sell their home complete with surrounding land. For too long the Al-Hassans had lived out of the limelight but with the income from the house sale Winston purchased the luxury seagoing vessel *Brave Goose*. At first the Berber didn't approve of the idea and right up to his dying day always said such a base for their operation would leave them vulnerable, but Winston didn't agree.

Larnaca Marina. Saturday Morning.

The grandeur of *Brave Goose* still filled Winston with superior motivation but as he stood by his wheelchair-based father, the vision of Aston Appleton's envoy made him realise his current purpose. Their exchange of words had been limited before Winston, instructing Yiannis to take Mr Beck to his cabin below, turned on his elderly father. Their voices were raised and Winston became more and more aggravated.

"How dare that evil bastard Appleton send a tramp like that to do business with me?"

He stared at his father who attempted to defend his own position but Winston cut him off, bellowing at him in no uncertain manner for having even entertained dealing with such a man in the past. This exchange of views and defence of each other's position continued for some time before Yiannis re-entered the saloon carrying a black plastic bag. He stood upright, brushed down his hair with the free hand and said to Winston, "I've collected Mr Beck's clothing as you instructed, sir. They're in this bag."

He was going to continue but with a heated tone, Winston replied, "Throw them overboard into the sea and keep that little worm locked in his cabin until I am ready for him. You'd better obtain a new set of clothes for him as I promised but nothing expensive."

Yiannis took the black bag, dropped it over the ship's side between the quayside and the ship where Christian Beck's cabin porthole was situated before getting on with his other duties totally without regard for what he'd done. Winston knelt to the floor in front of his old father, kissed his hand and softly said, "Our revenge will be your lasting life. May Allah bless us and bring our enemies to the table of their slaughter."

CHAPTER 20

Larnaca Airport. Saturday, 2.30pm.

Brett Watson and Alexis Matos barely noticed the duration of their flight from Tangiers to Larnaca but despite their intimate conversation with relaxing attitude, the boarding of such sinister-looking men on the aircraft steadied both their wandering minds. Brett wiped his sweating hands over the clean trousers Mohamid had provided while Alexis froze with shivering fright. The aircraft cabin had offered them both a safe cocoon in which to become familiar. Cruising at 36,000 feet in clear skies with excellent onboard service and comfortable surroundings had certainly done their moral standing no good at all. Now the harsh impact of airport life seemed to be telling Brett to recall his true purpose for being alive, yet he couldn't help himself and turning to Alexis took her hand again. She was particularly tense but managed a brief glimpse of a worried smile as one of the boarded men strode down the cabin's aisle. Her tension increased dramatically as the man approached their seats and she gripped Brett's hand with such compulsion his wedding ring dug deep into his unsuspecting finger. Brett sat quite still, gritting his teeth in sheer agony until the man passed without even a chance glance towards them before Alexis relaxed her grip.

"You must not see 'Control' or his people in everyone who you don't know. Calm down. I know we will be OK," Brett muttered in her ear.

Alexis didn't respond so with all the gentleness he could muster Brett seductively kissed her right ear and allowed his excited tongue to lecherously win back her attention. Brett knew Alexis wanted him to make love to her and despite his turbulent mind attempting to excuse himself from Rebecca, decided he would screw Alexis until her demands were totally satisfied.

She moved away from Brett's probing tongue, turned her head flicking the black hair to one side and said without any doubts, "Brett, how could you say such a thing? These evil bastards have killed two people and for all we know—"

Brett stopped her in mid-sentence with a forceful hand placed over her mouth as the man walked back up the aisle and past their seats only this time he regarded them both clearly out the corner of his eye.

"Alexis for Christ's sake keep your voice down. Although I've just said I think we'll be OK, it doesn't mean to say I don't share your concern, now keep calm. We are a long way from home and I've every intention of getting us both back to where we belong."

Brett had almost whispered these words to Alexis and he didn't expect an answer. He certainly wasn't ready for her next comment but fortunately her tone was equally as quiet.

"I'm not going back to Tangiers until you've made love to me in the best traditions of true dirty bondage."

With that choice comment she stood up and making herself ready to leave the plane, winked a slow, seductive eye at a totally surprised Brett Watson. His face was a picture of total disbelief and he'd been unable to offer an immediate answer. Throughout the flight they talked of love and each other's affections but he'd realised she was coming on to him and even though he'd responded Brett was still a little shocked.

He moved out of his seat and picking up Alexis's black leather holdall trotted off down the huge Airbus to find her. For some reason better known to the authorities all passengers were being disembarked from the two front cabin doors and Alexis had forced her way past all the usual milling people who just seemed to like standing in airplane aisles. With the two tan-coloured suitcases back in their possession Brett and Alexis made their way towards the least congested exit.

The roaring hot afternoon sun hit them both with such incredible force Brett almost tripped but in bumping into Alexis allowed his free hand to quickly fondle her slinky backside. The expression on her face was one of sheer enjoyment but ongoing people pushing to get clear of the plane prevented further developments transpiring for the time being.

They walked across the concrete apron towards a host of uninviting terminal buildings with each of them carrying one of the suitcases. Brett knew this act they were committing was tantamount to smuggling, punishable by a heavy prison sentence, but Alexis was watching him and could tell from his facial expression he was worried.

"Don't concern yourself about getting caught with this stuff."

She pointed to the two cases they were lugging towards the customs hall.

"It's all arranged. We'll sail straight through customs and away into the evil grip of our waiting chaperon," she said.

"How the bloody hell do you know with such cocky certainty, may I ask, madame?" Brett spluttered.

"Mohamid told me so," she said, and gave Brett a most crafty, seductive flutter. He quickened his pace to catch up with her and continued.

"Do you mean to tell me that all this time I've worried myself as to how we are going to get this lot past customs and you already knew it was arranged?"

" Yes," she said with simple delight and continued. "I didn't notice you worrying too much during the last five hours. I thought you were enjoying my body too much."

Her voice trailed off as they entered the customs hall but Brett was stumped for words again as he attempted to remain by her side. She was right, he had enjoyed her body and was intending to enjoy much more but Rebecca's image kept hounding his fertile mind. Brett hadn't convinced his morals to retain a back seat as his lustful mind fought the image of his now limp but longing cock penetrating her silk-like figure. Standing behind her in the customs hall he wanted sex with this woman and despite his love for Rebecca was determined to fuck Alexis. He excused himself by saying it was pure, undiluted lust, low down but preposterously high tone. He could feel his wanting penis stirring deep within his trousers as an elderly customs officer halted them both.

"Do you have anything to declare?" the old man asked.

Both Brett and Alexis drooped their heads as he demanded sight of their passports. Brett rooted around in her black holdall and finding them also felt the cold steel of her revolver. He handed their documents to the officer and yet continued to feel his way around the bag to isolate its other contents. His wallet, credit cards and some incidental junk belonging to Alexis was all he found. The revolver caused him considerable concern but feeling around it whilst still in the bag, noted its safety catch was locked on. They remained standing in that sweltering hall for what seemed like hours. Brett regarded Alexis and although not being able to say anything wanted to ask her if this was also part of Mohamid's planned smooth passage. She seemed totally cool and in command of her emotions yet Brett was uncomfortable, hot and sweat was running down his back more out of fear than as a result of the intensifying heat. If he wanted to check the contents of the suitcases, Brett thought, it would be safer to tell the truth rather than lie but then again who'd believe him? He froze as the customs officer looked him up and down, wishing the floor would open up and swallow him. It seemed to take an age but without hesitation their passports were returned and they continued on their way, passing out of the main terminal building which wasn't particularly impressive.

Alexis took hold of his free arm and said, "There, I told you not to worry. Mohamid can fix anything."

Brett didn't even turn his head and totally ignored her comment. He was petrified, shaking and now to add to his mounting problems torn between two sexy women.

The air outside the airport buildings was hot yet Brett's body felt cooler than while inside. They couldn't see anyone waiting for them due to a large number of coaches taking what appeared to be hordes of holiday makers from recently landed charter flights. Standing around, Brett again felt the vibrations of passion Alexis was transmitting. Her vibrant body, slightly moistened by the intense heat dominated his inner mind but he was totally involved with his own personal turmoil as the coaches in front of them moved away, exposing to their view a large white Mercedes flanked by two men. Brett and Alexis were obviously recognised yet as the two well-dressed men approached them, Alexis tightened her grip on Brett's arm for added support. They halted a little way to their front and without speaking one man drew forward, reaching out for the cases. Brett, not totally sure of his ground took it upon himself to protect what he'd come to accept as their life insurance guarantee and lunged towards the cases. The oncoming gentleman was taken by surprise at the swiftness of Brett's actions but as he straightened himself he opened up his jacket to display a menacing gun. Brett backed off and the man took hold of both cases, never taking his eyes away from Brett, grinning with the amusement of a spoilt child. His partner told them to follow him towards the car and as they climbed in the rear seat, their cases were unceremoniously placed in the boot. The big white Mercedes started and as it drew away from the kerb side the driver leant towards the dashboard, touched a small switch and with a prominent click locked all doors.

Gaining rapid speed Brett and Alexis knew they were trapped only to be released when the two monkeys in front of them saw fit. Alexis moved nearer to Brett but the man riding as a front seat passenger turned around, pointing his large handheld gun towards them. By waving the gun's barrel Alexis was told to leave Brett well alone but he continued to stare at her. His eyes, wandering up and down her twenty-eight-year-old body admired her slender legs, well embraced bosom and long black hair. He was endeavouring to frighten her but even if she was, Alexis didn't let it be known she merely glared at his laughing, round face partially obscured by the revolver.

Brett couldn't take notice of where they were going since he was watching every move the men in front were making. He felt truly annoyed and wanted to hold Alexis very tight to protect her from the evil these two men had in mind.

The big Mercedes followed exactly the same route as it had done much earlier that morning when Christian Beck was their passenger. The two men sat in front of Brett and Alexis started to chat in their native Arabic tongue. Still staring at Alexis, the one man passed a comment to his driver mate which he clearly didn't think either Brett or Alexis would understand.

"I'll fuck the woman and you can have the man!"

The driver just grinned but Alexis objected to both their comment and his manner. She looked at Brett who hadn't understood before saying in her own Arabic dialect, "Over my dead body."

The man who sat pointing the gun at them was plainly shocked at her even understanding him yet alone answering him back and turning around to face the front of the car he muttered, "It can be arranged."

The remainder of their short journey passed without further incident as Brett and Alexis managed to get closer together, enabling them to hold hands. Brett could feel Alexis's hand trembling but by the time the car entered the marina area she was considerably calmer.

Brave Goose towered above the Mercedes as their escorts bundled them out of the car and onto a scorching hot quayside. The brilliance of the afternoon and intense heat almost blinded Brett as Alexis held onto him. Her black holdall dangled from her other hand as they both attempted to absorb the splendour of this prestige, luxury, seagoing masterpiece. With it being such a hot afternoon coupled with a lack of any breeze Brett began to feel his skin opening and rivers of sweat trickle uncomfortably down his well-built, six-foot frame.

Two of the ship's company appeared suitably attired in their impressive white uniform. Brett, Alexis and the two men from the car were all escorted into the ship's rear saloon by the crew but as they entered the chilled, air-conditioned saloon it became apparent powerful people were present. The black glass patio doors were closed behind them and their two tan suitcases were placed onto a large table guarded by Winston Al-Hassan, his wheelchaired father and another crew member.

Brett looked around as his eyes became accustomed to their environment and he could see a formidable array of faces. The two escorts from the airport stood by the patio doors, the two crew members who'd brought them onboard stood right behind Alexis and almost guarding the large highly polished table were the other three men. Brett looked at the austere tan suitcases, nobody spoke and he almost stopped breathing in sheer fright. They were trapped, there was no escape, what was going to happen next? These were Brett Watson's thoughts as he realised he was fucking terrified.

The time was 3.30pm.

CHAPTER 21

Brave Goose. Cabin Number 13.

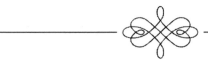

Christian Beck leant heavily against the locked cabin door feeling as if the world had again kicked him in the balls. He regarded the small cabin with an air of disbelief. *How the hell did I get into this ruddy mess?* he kept asking himself with growing aggression. The cabin door and bulkhead felt cold to his naked back yet despite the intense heat outside, Christian felt decidedly shivery.

Brave Goose had an air conditioning system which was particularly effective, resulting in a fridge-like chill being imposed on his frail body and shivering beyond control he began to tremble. He wanted to scream and empty his lungs of life's most precious gift.

Looking down his puny frame, Christian wasn't proud of his physique. Christ only knows what Hans Zenna had seen in him. He wasn't muscular, he didn't even look manly and yet he'd never had any difficulty in finding a lover so long as it was another man. His gay inclinations had often landed him in hot water but this series of events which had led to a big Greek sailor pissing over him was the limit. His now limp penis was diminutive and sore but still dripping with the trace of sperm brought into this world by that bastard, he began to cry.

Christian continued to shiver as he crossed the small cabin. The porthole didn't offer much of a view but as he saw the black plastic bag containing his clothes splash into the sea, he felt the pangs of anger begin to mature. He'd thought his arrival onboard this expensive floating paradise was the start of an upturn in his fortunes, how wrong he'd been. First the searching, then the shower in human waste and now the sight of his own clothes drifting in the sea right outside the porthole beyond his reach proved too much. Christian's eyes narrowed as they issued forth tears of shame, discomfort and hatred.

"I'll get my own back on that bastard Appleton. I'll, I'll... fuck him," he spluttered.

His heaving body rippled in unison with his sobbing outbursts but in reality there was little he could achieve.

Nobody came to his aid as he cried openly for his mother or anybody who'd offer him some comfort. Still snivelling like an impudent child he staggered into the small en-suite bathroom, turned on a hot shower and stood there allowing the scalding water to freely flow over his heaving body.

*

Closing his sore eyes, Christian enjoyed the pain such hot water caused his body. It felt as if he was cleansing his soul but his mind couldn't clear away the hatred he'd germinated. He closed his eyelids; it was nearly two days since he'd slept and during that short time he'd been responsible for many dark deeds. Christian Beck considered himself to be a prince of darkness and although he felt his time on God's earth was now very limited, couldn't imagine Saint Peter opening the heavenly gates for him. The other place was definitely his destination.

The en-suite shower and small cabin had filled with steam as he opened his tired eyes and turning the water off, Christian reached for the clean towels. He rubbed his body dry with little enthusiasm, vowing to become totally celibate as he caressed his own penis. If he lived beyond this ordeal never again would he allow himself to be used.

There was very little room to manoeuvre around the small cabin as Christian came from a damp bathroom in search of something to wear for warming security. He opened the wardrobe, removed a couple of large dry blankets and wrapping them around himself noticed a book wedged in the wardrobe's rear. He reached out, removed it, turned and settled into a corner of the urine-smelling cabin as the bed clothes were still wet with human piss. Christian began to fondle through the pages, it was a past log of *Brave Goose* denoting all her voyages in previous years. He noticed that despite being owned by Arabs, the ship was registered in Piraeus but had only been there once during the lifespan of this log. Christian read on with interest but could feel his tired body demanding sleep. His stomach rumbled with hunger as he recalled the stinking Moroccan who'd presented him with the bomb he'd planted with such devastating effects in the Rembrant as he finally fell into a deep sleep. His puny frame huddled in the corner of that small cabin devoid of all movement. He was totally beat.

*

Christian didn't sleep well. He dreamt of Tangiers, imagining he was wandering around and absorbing all the interesting exotic aromas of that provocative city. However, each street corner held a faded image of the robed man giving him the bomb, the airline stewardess fussing around him en route to Larnaca and the fake money. Normally such dreams would have woken him but he was so tired his body continued to rest.

As his deep sleep moved into a light doze he remembered Hans Zenna, shadowing Brett Watson and the Matos woman as well as recalling a vivid mental picture of Aston Appleton. He was about to fall out with himself again as the cabin door opened but Christian didn't hear Yiannis enter his dormant world and was only made aware of his presence as he kicked his sleeping body awake. At first Christian's eyes wouldn't focus but within an instant he became fully alert. Yiannis stood over him with a broad grin and was bearing fresh clothing.

"Get dressed, bastard. You've been asleep for almost seven hours."

Yiannis didn't say any more as he dropped the clothes on the floor before leaving the cabin and again locking the door behind him.

Christian struggled to his feet, allowing the blankets to fall deckward and regarded his new clothing with suspicion. The light blue suit, white shirt and grey shoes were all good quality. They fitted him like a glove and after washing his face with cold water he started to reload his pockets with his wallet, tickets and other personal possessions.

Twenty more long minutes passed but feeling fresh and alert he peered through the porthole window and saw that same white Mercedes pull up on the quayside. Watching with a renewed interest in life, Christian witnessed the arrival of Brett and Alexis yet felt good after his long sleep despite dreaming so much. The bathroom mirror portrayed a different individual from that he remembered seeing aboard the plane from Tangiers. Christian was ready to make his own killing… given a chance.

It was 3.30pm on Saturday afternoon.

CHAPTER 22

Lenton Parva, 5.00pm Saturday.

As Rebecca and Hans Zenna reached the first-floor landing their stairway climb felt as if it had taken hours, yet the few short minutes had unbalanced them both. After Mohamid Van Jonger had left, both Rebecca and Hans could feel each other's bodies signalling vibrations of sexual acceptance but Rebecca was now having doubts. Hans had kissed her in the hallway in such a fashion she'd weakened to his powerful sexual appetite and yet he'd openly admitted to her his preference up until meeting her had been for men only!

She'd found it difficult to accept he'd never had an orgasm with his penis inside a woman as Hans was without doubt a most attractive object of passion.

Gingerly she took the last few steps along the landing and reaching for the door handle a prominent vision of Brett entered her confused mind. She could see his tall, well-built body looming over her, supporting his loving broad smile. The image wouldn't go away, his youthful appearance was now hounding her mind but as she was about to turn and reject Hans she felt his soft tender touch. For the first time in their two-year marriage Rebecca knew she was about to be shamefully unfaithful. Opening the bedroom door she wondered how Brett would react when inevitably she'd tell him that his loving wife who he'd idolised, had been to bed with another man. Rebecca guessed he'd go apeshit.

Hans followed her into the room, it was not unknown to him as it was here he'd hidden and abducted this incredibly sexy woman only the previous afternoon. As far as Hans was concerned that event only took place in his own mind, paving the way for his next act. He didn't want to hurt Rebecca then or now but had become aware of his own questionable sexuality. She moved around the four-poster bed, uncertain of what she should do but when Hans took her hand with the gentleness of a passionate lover and sat her down on the soft, delicately patterned quilt, Rebecca knew this was it.

He moved over to the Georgian glazed window and drawing the curtains returned to her bedside. Hans smiled at her with a shy boyish grin but since the daylight hours were almost all but gone reached over to turn on the bedside light. The room took on a totally different appearance; its cushioned furnishings with pastel-coloured patterns felt warm and securing. Each part of the four-poster bed's timber frame emanated an air of secluded tranquillity and the thick shag pile carpet made him feel homely, as did the warmth glowing from his newly found love. Inside, however, Hans thought he'd be frightened by the impending act they were about to commit but he felt positive, alert and knew this was going to be a first for him.

Rebecca didn't look at Hans for the duration of his eyes wandering around the room. She considered that perhaps like her he was now having second thoughts but with all his attention now back in focus on Rebecca she knew he meant to carry through the act they'd started downstairs. Her eyes were big and shone as she looked closely at his muscular body still clad in smart but casual clothing. She wanted to rip off his clothes, have a good look at his body and then make him disappear without ever having performed in an act Brett wouldn't forgive her for attending. Rebecca didn't touch Hans but sat and watched with stunned interest.

Purposefully Hans stood right in front of Rebecca and slowly removed his sweater. Throwing it onto the carpet he ran the palms of his hands down his white cotton shirt, stopping short of his trousers and slowly working his way up again, undid all the shirt buttons. The material seductively drifted apart and as he removed the garment his broad, lean chest was exposed covered with a mat of darker hair which matched his eyebrows. Hans stood perfectly still for a few moments, allowing Rebecca to absorb his exposure so far. She looked on with eager anticipation as Hans ran his fingers over the growing bulge contained only by his well-fitted trousers. Serenely he undid the buckle on his belt, released his trouser catch and with painful expression slowly allowed the zip to travel towards its ultimate destination. He peeled down both trousers and underpants in a single action, only briefly moving to remove shoes, socks and deposit the garments aside. Still bent over he moved towards Rebecca and kissed her with incredible seductiveness on her lips. She couldn't respond, she wanted him to stand up right, she wanted to see his whole naked body.

He gazed at her with a certain knowingness and gradually straightened his body until at last he was totally upright. Rebecca looked on with pending excitement. His muscular, strong body was lean, coated with an alluring hairy finish and was powerful. Her eyes averted away from the rest of his body, focusing on his especially large but meaty penis. She could feel herself becoming alarmingly excited as his cock extended to its full solid length. Rebecca continued to stare as Hans moved closer to her. The enormity of his body transfixed her whole form into a demanding sex machine. She moved her face closer to him and rubbed her nose with his enormous cock end. He smelt perfect, she considered, as she placed her delicate hands on his faultless buttocks and pulling him towards her allowed his cock into her mouth. At first Rebecca wondered if she'd choke but realising there were inches left outside her mouth, eased back a little so allowing her tongue to move freely around and embrace his delightful organ.

Hans moaned with sheer delight; his balls twitched with impending glee as Rebecca excited him as no other human being had ever done. The seconds turned into long minutes and Hans although enjoying this undiluted pleasure knew he must respond to her feverish gestures. He moved back, extracting his jumbo-sized penis from Rebecca's mouth but without much success. She grabbed him again, running her busy soft tongue up and down the entire length of his cock before ensnaring one of his balls between her diligent teeth. The sucking effect on his testicle made him begin to hallucinate and as she attempted to wrap her hand around his penis Hans Zenna imagined this feeling to be equivalent of being high on hash. Hans felt he couldn't withstand this torturous pleasure any longer and looking down at Rebecca's bobbing head could see his cock was too big for her tiny hand to encompass its entire girth. He pulled away from her, moved around the bed and approaching Rebecca from behind started to remove her pale cream silk blouse.

Dusk slipped into darkness as her bra fell away, exposing the succulent developed bosom. She could feel his erect cock hard against her naked back as his soft hands teased her aflamed nipples. The sight and feeling of his hairy arms touching her warm creamy skin excited her to the point of total sexual passion. He remained pressed hard against her as the room temperature patently began to rise. The silk bedding was cool to his knees but Hans could feel himself sliding away yet with the ease and sensitivity of a preying lion he slowly but positively moved around to face her beautiful frontage.

He laid her body down over the bed with trembling passion, his heart was pounding and his brow beginning to perspire as he realised this was going to be the most exciting moment in his strange life. Hans removed Rebecca's skirt exposing her succulent, long slender legs; her lace satin underwear shone against the backdrop of her suntanned, clear, sexy skin but his erection was painfully prominent as he seductively removed her skimp panties, throwing them without concern over his shoulder. Rebecca laid there totally naked, throbbing, waiting and absolutely oblivious of her husband.

With powerful arms and gentle touch he leant over the bed, parting her lovely legs with positive reason. Rebecca couldn't help her passion any longer as Hans explored the soft, sweet-smelling part of her body subtended by her long legs. He played with her using his fingers and tongue in perfect harmony as he brought her body to a peak of piercing stimulation. This intoxicating combination carried on for some time as Hans frequently made her climax and ooze her sweet bodily liquid into his mouth with gluttonous satisfaction. He loved it.

Rebecca ran her long, slender fingers through his blond hair, gripping it by the roots as he made her come again and again. He allowed his busy tongue to run up her sensational body, moving softly over her heaving form. She was so wet for him it hurt her pride but his strong, lean, hairy chest filled her entire vision and as Hans suckled her large erect nipples she quivered from head to toe. He manipulated himself over her with an eminent display of true manhood. Rebecca opened her legs with expectant relief but he continued to tease her by stroking his erection across her wetness. Finally with explosive decisiveness Hans slid his solid cock deep inside her and she yelped with utter delight but thought his incision would never end. Hans moved his large cock in and out of her dripping body with the precision of a Swiss watch. They both moaned, rolled, kissed and loved in such a way Hans didn't know was either possible or enjoyable. He played with her earlobe in a moment of brief interlude allowing his cock to remain firmly implanted within her. Their necking and kissing was frenzied but she started to wriggle beneath him to feel the enormity of his large penis. His sizable balls swung against her soft skin as he regained his back and forward motion with excitable ease. Hans made Rebecca reach her orgasm many times but found extraordinary difficulty in maintaining his own climax until she finally demanded his sperm. With one sheer movement Hans raised his chest above her and with arm muscles fully tensed quickened his penetrating body movements. Rebecca whined with undiluted ecstasy as Hans released so much sperm it flooded her, running out over both their interlocked bodies.

They laid totally captivated with each other, not speaking but enjoying the moment. Rebecca had relished his eight and a half inches of pure blissful heaven.

*

Hans rolled off her shaking body and laid at her side. They both stared at the ceiling not daring to speak but deep in individual thought. Finally Rebecca propped herself up and looked at his stunned body, there was no doubt it was quite something. His broad hairy chest which had towered over her was flat and enchanting. His muscular legs were so well shaped she wanted to feel his powerful force again but most interesting of all to her was his still-erect penis, it was fantastic. Hans turned towards her, knowing she was admiring him yet he wasn't sure how he'd react in her continued company but one thing was now evidently clear to him with excessive relief, he wasn't gay anymore. He'd loved in the true sense and kissing her again on those tender lips, she played intently with his wet cock. Hans was far from exhausted despite his pounding heart racing to circulate the adrenalin excited by his newfound understanding. He again approached her with wide eyes and knowing certainty of his ability to satisfy Rebecca's needs. They slid slowly together while laid on their sides until Hans could feel his massive erection sliding over her silky skin. His hand ran down her moist body until it again was exploring her inner warmth. Rebecca closed her eyes with utter complacency but maintained the caressing action of his cock. Her petite hand was dwarfed by this part of his body as she admired him with a welling desire to feel him inside her again.

Their lips met and with startling convulsion their tongues explored each other's tender mouths with eager anticipation. Brazenly she drew him closer to her and with provocative movements Hans teased her dripping body with his large erection. In a fit of desperation to have him again she moved at just the correct moment and his expansive cock forced its way into her. She moaned with sheer pleasure as he moved gently at first and then with quickening motion. Rebecca continued to kiss him in feverish raptures. Her swaying bosom pressed hard against his voluminous chest, his positive motion and her desire to feel his sperm ejaculate within her made Rebecca reach yet another climax. Their bodies were both wet with interlocking perspiration as Hans could no longer control himself and pushing his penis deeper into her than before again issued forth a tide of searing hot life-giving liquid.

They remained locked together with their steaming bodies intertwisted for most of the night before he rolled over on his back, exposing his lovable yet sexy body to her. Rebecca laid at his side watching him drift into a deep sleep; she felt totally satisfied and pulling the silk bedclothes over them both turned off the light prior to trying to sleep herself.

They both slept soundly through the remainder of that passionate night and as dawn broke the rain pelted against their bedroom window, Rebecca woke up on that Sunday morning having almost slept on top of Hans Zenna. Her eyes blinked as she ran her hand through the hair on his chest and became acutely aware of the pain between her legs. Rebecca felt as if she had been ripped in half but recalled their passionate, steamy love making with a cool grin of contentment. Hans still slept but although he looked totally innocent she knew he'd broken his own sexual barrier with fervour. Her wandering hand slithered down his chest and reaching his penis started to caress him yet again. Within a short space of time his body reacted to her manipulations as he started to wake, his cock started to grow and daylight began to filter through the bedroom curtains. Hans opened his eyes and gently smiled at her as she beamed at him. *Christ,* he thought, *she looks ruddy good even first thing in the morning.* He felt like a new man and leaning over Rebecca, kissed her with definite defiance, pulling her towards him. She laid her head on his chest and as he played with her hair Rebecca played with his growing organ.

They talked about their encounter and how the world would react but both of them knew their ordeal was not yet over. Although the bond between them had been strengthened they both knew "Control" still had to be found. As the rain eased Hans began to ask Rebecca about her past yet at first she didn't respond but on realising his interest she drew away from him, sat up and pulling the bedclothes to cover her bosom started to relate her personal history.

Rebecca Watson's Past

Rebecca Watson was born to wealthy parents who lived, worked and grew up themselves in the open countryside of West Derbyshire. She recalled while being a young girl the long walks through the comforting yet rolling green lush farmland criss-crossed with soft-coloured stone walls. The memory of the tiny village in which she'd spent her early childhood still lingered as being a true community with village church, post office, pub, river and narrow bridge all of which would never leave her mind's vision.

Her childhood had been happy and most contented but alas, all this was upturned when her parents sent her away to a prominent local yet private boarding school for young ladies. She'd hated her early years there but the returning image of her loved village life always helped her overcome the most traumatic of events. With school routine well established in her mind Rebecca started to settle in her new environment but unfortunately this was short-lived. A summons to the headmistress always caused the girls a degree of apprehension and she was no different. Standing in front of the sovereign old woman Rebecca listened with disbelief as she related how her parents had died.

It took many years of painful nights before finally Rebecca could accept her parents' death. Never again did she return to her family home which her new guardian's solicitor sold, investing the proceeds in a trust fund established on Rebecca's behalf until reaching the mature age of twenty-one. Her guardians were two sisters, one being very much older than the other, and they had taken considerable pity on the young girl's plight which had been brought to their attention by the elderly headmistress. The two sisters, widowed and childless, brought Rebecca up with the assistance of her parents' estate. They gave her love, respectability, affection and encouraged her throughout her successful schooling.

Rebecca Watson lived with the two sisters in Hampshire and attended the best schools they could secure for her. She passed all examinations with excellence before attending a prominent finishing college for educating ladies high in the Swiss mountains. Here Rebecca learnt the finer points of etiquette and consumer business. She enjoyed her time at the college, learning to ski, learning the finer points of life and came to realise how fortunate she'd been to know the two sisters. Completing her time at this secluded college found Rebecca a grown woman with an inherited fortune, an excellent education but no job. She strived to secure a prominent career but without any major success and it was during a chance conversation at a charity ball in London Rebecca met a group of people looking to appoint a sales manager in their exclusive West End department store. It was whilst working in this field one of her elderly guardians died and Rebecca, feeling saddened by this loss, grew closer to the remaining sister. She purchased a small place for her in Kings Langley while for herself purchased a house in Grovener Mews where she met and fell madly in love with Mr Brett Watson.

Later On Sunday Morning

Hans had listened to her life story with a mixture of sorrow and elation. The rain had stopped but despite remaining closed the curtains permitted daylight to establish itself within the warm, cosy and secure bedroom. Throughout relating her past, Rebecca had played with his penis, making him erect, yearnful and solid. She placed her loving lips on his with a desire to be loved again before throwing the silk bedding away from their bodies onto the thick carpet, running her hands up and down his chest, pawing at the mat of bodily hair. Rebecca herself was again wet for him as she viewed his stiffness with aching languish. Hans knew her body was his but teased her puerile frame until she was no longer able to withstand his advances and grabbed him, pulling Hans on top of her. His cock slid into her as the night before leaving a substantial length exposed between their pubic hairs. She loved his tender movement, gentle yet prominent penetration, and admired his whole dilating frame. They remained interlocked for many enraptured moments before he finally released a stream of hot sperm streaking into her inner body.

They both moaned and groaned but lay quite still in loving embrace until she couldn't stand his weight pressing on her any longer. Her body still not recovered from the previous night was now objecting to this large intrusion again, as Hans rolled over and laid by her side, he knew at last what real passion, love and excitement was, vowing never to sleep with another man again for as long as he lived. Hans and Rebecca both enjoyed themselves to the full and didn't want to greet the remaining day.

Still laid naked on the bed neither of them heard the bedroom door quietly open. They didn't see the shady, uncouth, unshaved and bitter character enter their private moment of passion. As Hans rolled away from Rebecca the uninvited onlooker waited for a few brief moments, raised his aged handgun, aimed with positive intent and squeezed the trigger. The recoil was only slight but as the bullet entered Hans Zenna's temple the effect was devastating. Within a split second of the bullet leaving the gun, Hans was dead and Rebecca not knowing what had happened was splattered with blood. His body lay still yet despite life's exit he was still issuing forth living, life-giving sperm.

The time was 9.00 on Sunday morning.

CHAPTER 23

Lenton Parva. 8.30am, Sunday Morning.

The rain had eased considerably as Aston Appleton began to stir. With startled surprise he opened his eyes and merely gazed at the car's dirty headlining. He remembered leaving the Watsons' household under the impression he'd been drugged and gradually all relative events came back to his cloudy mind. He didn't move but attempted to establish if he'd exposed his identity although still being alive convinced him they'd not suspected.

Aston moved his neck and body from the grotesque position in which he'd been laid only to realise his body was now objecting. He ached all over and his neck was stiff, his back felt crippled, yet moreover his head was thumping with the most tedious of headaches as he painfully straightened himself with the most harrowing disagreeable effects. Aston rubbed the sleep out of his eyes. His mouth was dry and throat was sore, even the car windows were totally steamed up with caustic condensation but it was many moments before he recalled why he'd slept in his car yet still had no concept of the time which had passed. His creased clothes and unshaven face didn't convey him as the noble, zealous entrepreneur he wished to be but were more in keeping with a second-grade tramp.

The rain still drummed on the old Rover's bodywork as Aston

became aware of his acutely uncomfortable situation and looking at his watch, sat mesmerised as if not being able to take in the expensive display which it offered. He regarded his Bulova watch as something of a status symbol but couldn't believe the time it was showing and with his head still pounding he wiped the condensation from one window with his clammy hand. The avenue was deserted as Aston reached over the front seats and turned on his radio just in time to hear the early Sunday morning news broadcast with time check. He turned it off as the noise made his head ache even more but the Bulova watch hadn't been wrong, it was he who'd slept from 10.00am the previous morning to 8.30am that day. Appleton knew he'd not been sleeping well of late but was certain he'd not been that tired, and then remembered his hasty retreat from the Watsons'. The sudden impact of this realisation convinced him beyond all doubt he'd been drugged.

Feeling like death, he opened the car door but the rush of fresh morning air simultaneously took his breath away and knocked him back in his seat. The rain had almost stopped, the sky was beginning to brighten as Aston almost fell out of the car to greet the new day and he stood on the pavement oblivious of the surroundings, surveying his own foolishness. "They must know it's me," he kept mumbling but couldn't understand why they hadn't killed him. Perhaps they considered the drug they'd given him was sufficient, as he smiled to himself with the realisation they'd failed and he could still get what he wanted. Aston considered his plight for some time before making his mind up as to the next move. He removed his old faithful but as yet unused gun from the glove box, slammed the doors closed, stood up to his best height and felt determined to satisfy his inadequate promiscuous ego.

Scanning the quiet surroundings, Aston was ready to make his next move but as he was about to move away from the car, noticed a white plastic-coated sheet of paper wedged under the wiper. He leant over the bonnet, grabbing the document, and was not amused in the slightest to note it was a parking ticket. The anger of past events was brought to a pinnacle by the appreciation of this entwining development which was a very effective record as to his whereabouts. In a fit of rage he removed the paper from its plastic container, ripping it up into tiny bits, throwing them into the gentle breeze. The paper spread like confetti and while marching back towards their house. the dispersion of paper bits resembled Aston Appleton's confused undisciplined mind. He was mad, psychotic and unfit to breathe the same air as other human beings. This man was an animal.

*

Aston walked up the gravel drive to Brett Watson's home with the slinkiness of a beseeched tom cat. He could see the curtains were all still drawn and there was no movement, everything was calm. The gravel was hard yet well set underfoot but nevertheless silence was to be his advantage. Hans Zenna had seen him out of the house yesterday and he'd hoped he would let him in today because it was going to be the last thing that bastard ever did. Aston was planning to kill him on the spot then just vanish but the parking ticket had put pay to that scheme. He now had to create a new idea for his demise which would be swallowed by all possible investigators.

Looming directly in front of him, the large front door looked decidedly awesome as Appleton stopped for a brief moment, turned and surveyed the roadside drive to ensure no witness was present to his current action. The Aston Martin still looked as good as ever despite that score line down one side and he wondered for just a brief moment how Brett and the Matos woman were performing. Grinning with evil thoughts, Aston reached for the door chime but something prevented him from actually touching the button. Instead he tried the door handle and to his sheer astonishment the large door eased open into the cavernous hallway. With pending precision Aston entered and closing the door behind him in absolute silence, skilfully stood, hardly breathing as he listened for the tell-tale signs of their whereabouts.

It wasn't long before Aston's mind comprehended that his envoy and intended hostage were upstairs. He could hear hushed talking and amorous moaning as he followed the noise source. The huge spiral staircase seemed never ending as he climbed but finally standing outside the bedroom door he could hear their groaning. Aston didn't need to see what was going on, the bed was creaking with such a regular pattern he knew Hans Zenna was making love to Rebecca Watson.

Aston Appleton felt rage welling up inside him again. He'd lost Rebecca to that jerk Brett Watson and now she was being screwed by a fucking gay. For a split second he considered if Christian Beck had set him up and all this was a ploy to catch him, ensnaring his own evil plot around his neck, but the photographs of Hans with Christian were too realistic. Hans Zenna was obviously bisexual.

Aston reached for the handle and hesitantly yet quietly opened the door. He slipped into the room just in time to witness Hans rolling away from Rebecca with his cock still erect. They'd obviously enjoyed their love making but Appleton stood in the shadow of the four-poster bed and regarded both their naked silent bodies. She was luscious, he thought, and exactly as the photographs had portrayed, yet Aston could feel his stomach churning as he raised the old hand revolver and fired.

The sound of his gun firing killed the noise of the bullet as it entered Zenna's temple. He lay totally still but his blood had showered Rebecca and the surrounding bedding. As he moved out of the shadows she began to scream blue murder. She looked first at Aston and then at Hans but her naked body quivered with fear as the blood began to run down her silk skin. She hollowed with pulsating terror. Aston moved towards Rebecca and sitting down at her side moved closer, pulling her shaking body towards him. He held her tight but didn't realise the pain he was in until that moment. His own penis was stiff, solid and oozing.

*

They'd remained in the same position for some considerable time as Rebecca sobbed before she found the strength to ask why he'd shot Hans. Her face was drawn, her ash brown hair matted with his blood and her heaving bosom trembled as she spoke in a haughty manner. Aston tried to caress her as she grabbed the bloodstained sheet and cover herself while tears flowed down her almost white cheeks. He couldn't answer to her face so turning away coldly said, "I killed him because I love you. I always have and I always will."

She instantly stopped crying and felt anger instead of sorrow but her thoughts were cluttered with Hans, Brett and now Aston, yet her reactions were less condoling. In a single most positive action Rebecca pushed Aston off her and as he slid onto the floor with a mighty bump, scrambled away from the bed running into the en-suite bathroom.

Turning on the shower, Rebecca stood and watched the water

turn clear from a weak red colour as the searing hot water washed Hans Zenna's blood away from her skin. She was crying not for Hans and certainly not for Aston but for Brett. How she wanted this nightmare to end, how she wanted to feel Brett hold her and how at that moment in time she wanted to be somewhere else. Anywhere would do.

Aston Appleton picked himself up off the shag pile carpet and opening the curtains allowed the full impact of his actions to penetrate his mind as Zenna's body lay on the blood-splattered bed. He knew he must cover the body so acting quickly to rectify, save and maintain control over Rebecca, wrapped the carnaged body without any ceremonious dignity in all available bedding with trembling hands. This was his first murder committed by his own hand and he felt severely exposed.

Trying to regain a degree of decorum he went into Rebecca's bathroom and stood waiting for her to turn the water off before speaking. She stood under the piercing stream of hot water for over an hour yet Aston knew there was nothing he could do but wait and watch her tender liberated body through the opaque glass surrounding the shower cubicle. He drank water to ease his dry throat although brandy would have suited him better while he considered his next action and wondering if it was all worthwhile, finally recalling how Brett had treated him in the past. Aston knew he was too far down the road of revenge to turn back and must go on but more important, he must win.

*

Time passed slowly and Aston was wondering if he should take a look around the house, but as the shower stopped, the doors opened and Rebecca appeared. Naked and dripping wet she just stood there in front of Aston before saying, "Take a good look because this is all you will get. I hate you."

Moving towards the bedroom she reached for a nearby bath sheet and wrapping it around herself ignored Appleton altogether, but the sight of Zenna's wrapped body made her freeze. Aston knew this was the right time to win her back.

"I shot him because he was using you. He was using many people including Brett. This man was evil, crooked, bent and more to the point he was 'Control'."

Rebecca turned and looked at Aston but her glare was so intense he had to turn his face away. Moving over to the window, Aston turned his back on Rebecca while she dressed, not wanting to cause her any further embarrassment especially as he needed her to believe in him.

The early morning rain had stopped and although remaining overcast Aston noticed the paths and roads were drying out yet little activity was evident in the avenue. Appleton stretched but his back still ached and his neck felt twisted, yet other than that he didn't feel any the worse for his long car-borne sleep. He could hear Rebecca getting dressed and spoke to her in as soft a voice as he could manage.

"I know you don't think much of me right at this moment but I'm telling you the truth about him." He pointed to the dormant form of Hans Zenna. "This was 'Control' and I think there is much work to be done to try and locate Brett. Also I'm sure Zenna didn't work alone and so as a precaution I'm staying with you until at least tomorrow morning."

Rebecca didn't appear to hear a single word he'd said, she certainly didn't acknowledge his comments and she'd not shown him any degree of gratitude! Aston started to get a little more irritated as she continued to ignore him and again he tried to break the deadlock barrier.

"Do you understand what I'm saying to you? Because I feel you are in some danger I'm going to stay with you, try to protect you and put myself at risk all because I love…"

He didn't get chance to complete his last sentence before Rebecca turned on him.

"I've no intention of staying in the same house as you, now or ever."

Her voice was sharp and cutting. Aston knew he was in trouble again but wasn't going to let her ruin his entire master plan, his success or his life.

"Where will you go if you don't mind me asking, to your maids house perhaps?" he asked in feverish tone.

"No," she said. "My maid Martha is dead, her body is in the garage."

"Who killed her?" Aston spluttered, oblivious to any other murder having been committed in the house.

"Mr Zenna did," she replied, stopping to stare at his wrapped body.

"There I told you he was 'Control' but you didn't believe me did you. Well I'll tell you something else, madam, yesterday morning when I called round at your invitation he put a drug in my coffee. I hardly had time to reach my car before being totally out for the count. Whatever it was it was strong but not strong enough to kill me as he'd planned. Now do you believe me?"

Aston stood in silence as he waited for an answer. He thought at last he would have convinced her to trust him so enabling him to strive and secure a successful conclusion to his evil strategy. Rebecca didn't stop to look at him, she knew all about the drug in the coffee and this was Aston trying to win her over at Hans Zenna's expense. Again she looked at his wrapped body on the bed and briefly recalled their conversations of the previous day, of Friday night and their frantic love making. She knew Hans was being used as she'd learnt to trust him but the prospect of staying with Aston Appleton made her feel sick. He was a liar, Rebecca knew that, but she'd grave doubts as to how far his involvement truly went in this affair. Rebecca went towards the double wardrobe and pulled out a small suitcase; she opened it and while filling the case with anything which came to hand asked Aston, "How long were you asleep in your car before the drug wore off? I assume you did sleep in the car and didn't try to drive?"

Aston Appleton didn't think about his answer, he was more intent on securing her trust.

"I woke up at about 8.30 this morning," he answered.

Rebecca stopped her packing and turning towards him, placed her hands on her hips, saying, "So you left this house yesterday morning, slept in the car until today then had a brainstorm which concluded in you marching in here, killing him and then saying he was 'Control'. I'd love to hear what evidence you collected between the car and my front door."

Aston knew he'd blundered and felt exposed yet being angry was no good, he'd only himself to blame and knew it. The situation was getting worse, she'd the better of him at present and this he knew must be corrected. Ignoring her past comments Aston continued.

"Since you're not going to Martha's, then where are you going?"

Rebecca had turned her attention back to packing the small case and answered him without faulting.

"I'm going to my mother's."

Aston was quick to respond, almost getting his words caught up together.

"But your mother died years ago when you were small. Brett told me."

"Indeed she did," Rebecca said and continued, "but my mother for all intents and purpose is my remaining ex-guardian."

Aston, surprised by this development and unaware of such a mysterious woman, was again knocked off balance by Rebecca. Edging closer to her and the adjacent dressing table, Aston played with his fingers while asking, "Who is this ex-guardian of yours?"

Rebecca was about to answer him but Aston was behind her and picking up a large vase from the dressing table brought it crashing down on her head. She fell to the floor dragging part of the bedclothes covering Hans Zenna with her as Aston stood in total silence. He knew he'd never see her in the same light as Hans had done but looking over at his body could only focus on his large, limp yet dead penis.

The time was 11.00am Sunday morning.

CHAPTER 24

London. 5.00pm Saturday

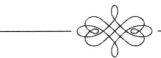

Leaving Lenton Parva the black taxi made its way towards central London. Mohamid Van Jonger was pleased he'd seen Rebecca and although reasonably confident Hans would look after her had a vision of impending doom which concluded in him never seeing Hans again. He tried to put the idea out of his mind. Alexis always told him he tended to be slightly over perspicacious.

Mohamid watched London go past the taxicab window as he sat prim and proper on the rear seat. His light grey suit fitted him to perfection but his own appearance although always relevant, was not foremost in his mind that afternoon.

Before Brett had left Tangiers he'd told Mohamid about the computer codes, the methods. systems and key locations of information contained within Rosco International's office. He'd also told him the easiest way of entry was to collect his set of keys from the antique sideboard in the hallway at Lenton Parva. When he'd arrived at the house a little earlier that afternoon, the frenzied approach of Hans Zenna had given him the cover he'd wanted and without either Rebecca or Hans noticing he slipped Brett's keys into his pocket. Now reflecting on past events Mohamid was supremely aware of the role he was about to play. By having Brett's keys and his authority to enter their office on a legal basis his only worry was if Aston Appleton decided to make an entry. Mohamid felt in his pocket but the Smith and Wesson revolver convinced him his mission was going to be nothing less than successful.

*

From leaving Rebecca and Hans it took the taxi over an hour to reach London Bridge as the late Saturday afternoon traffic had been excessive and the driver had cursed for most of the journey. Pulling up at a convenient location, Mohamid thanked the driver for his patience and duly paid him for his time with a bountiful tip as Mohamid felt he'd served him well since leaving Heathrow earlier that same afternoon. Walking away from the car, Mohamid felt the chilled air of that late September Saturday afternoon.

He recalled Brett saying you could smell the ingress of autumn and for the first time he couldn't argue. Buttoning his jacket, Mohamid picked up his small overnight bag and made his way towards Rosco International's office. People walked past him oblivious of his delicate mission, the traffic continued to thunder along the embankment and the river seemed as if it was the only knowing yet amenable advocate.

It didn't take long before he was standing opposite the office building. The dark stone structure with inset windows was lifeless as traffic continued to stream past its frontage. Mohamid stood and looked, he knew he had to find the top floor and without considering his predicament any further, shivered, crossed the traffic flow and bounded up the steps towards the locked glass doors.

Making his entry look as official as possible proved more difficult than he'd thought, especially since it took a little time to isolate the correct key, yet the brass plaque fixed to one of the glass doors clearly depicting the company name made Mohamid feel more secure. As the latch clicked the door open he literally skipped inside and closing it behind him made sure the lock was firmly secured. Brett had said so long as keys were used in opening all doors the alarm system would remain dormant and Mohamid was determined to keep it that way.

With natural daylight fading fast Mohamid wanted to locate Brett's office for sanctuary and Aston's office for the onslaught as a matter of impending urgency. He didn't use the lift but bounced up the carpeted staircase two at a time until reaching the top landing. Panting a little, he was pleased it was only a three-storey block rather than one of those unprolific concrete skyscrapers and walking along the corridor noted a lack of personal details or distinguishable features until reaching the circular reception lobby. Here the quality of furnishings, decor and ambience changed yet despite the lack of human beings Mohamid felt this was a special place.

He wondered why on his previous trips to London Brett had never invited him here but always met him at a hotel. The domed glass ceiling allowed the last drop of natural daylight to filter through but its dying embers merely reminded him of his purpose.

Walking round the perimeter of this global room Mohamid isolated Aston's office, found Brett's office and sighed with a degree of relief as drawing the curtains he turned on Brett's desktop lamp. It was now dark outside yet Mohamid Van Jonger felt secure as he sat at Brett's leather-topped desk and all owed himself to relax.

Looking around Brett's cocoon of power, Mohamid absorbed the quality of fitments and the atmosphere of the traditional establishment. The tranquillity of this place boosted his understanding of the man but the memory of his destroyed hotel foyer prompted him into action. Standing up, he slipped off his jacket, removed the revolver from his pocket and emptied the computer codes out of his wallet but laying them out on the desk knew he'd a long night ahead of him.

*

Gaining access to the company's financial transactions on the computer proved easy, just as Brett had suggested. The code word was typed in and within a split second the green screen was running their current balance. Mohamid keyed into past proceedings looking for the Moroccan connections and it didn't take him long to find what he'd been looking for. The list of banks complete with account numbers and sums invested, paid or moved made interesting reading yet Van Jonger noted Brett's concern over interest payments, those were listed as having been certified but not paid. By instructing the computer through the function keys Mohamid printed out a schedule of all these transactions, including those which only indicated the money as being certified.

Armed with this information he reclined in Brett's soft leather chair. He knew that at some stage Brett himself would have found these details but it was not evidently clear to Mohamid how the company accountants had missed these non-payments. He could only assume they were either in on this fiddle or Aston Appleton paid in money to cover the debt during investigations. However, the fact was clearly evident, at that moment in time Rosco International was having its funds syphoned and leaving the computer live Mohamid reached over the desk to with draw a sheet of blank note paper from the dispensing tray. Holding it up close to the desktop lamp the clearly embossed initials 'R.I.' shone through just as it had done on his own delivered message. His heart began to beat faster knowing he was now getting closer to the truth but he'd still Aston's office to raid and he began to tremble.

Collecting his thoughts together, Van Jonger made his way from Brett's soft leather desk chair into Aston's office. The street lights of the embankment gave him sufficient light to find his way over to the large desk and drawing the curtains so as not to attract any attention, he turned on the lights.

He was surprised to denote the quality of this room matched that of Brett's but then again he shouldn't have expected any different. The richness of the two rooms were equally matched but somehow this office had a more cutting atmosphere, perhaps it was because Mohamid knew he didn't like the character who used this part of the building.

Routing around the large desk, Mohamid Van Jonger found the safe constructed within its main enclosed support. It was concealed by a series of dummy side drawers and Brett had told him during their long discussions on Friday night he may have difficulty in gaining access but Mohamid wasn't concerned. Now he was faced with the prospect of breaking the code but knowing he must get into the safe, all his senses were telling him that behind the steel door were secrets which would enlighten the world and enable him to plan the revenge for his dead wife.

*

Mohamid Van Jonger was of a cool nature; his level headedness had saved many an innocent person from sure imprisonment within his native Tangiers. As he knelt down in front of Aston Appleton's safe he felt anguish and excitement both at the same time. The room was perfectly still, quiet and despite the noise of traffic outside he could hear his heart beating. Brett had suggested that the combination number wouldn't be any more than six digits and on seeing the safe Mohamid guessed he was right. It had been a long time since he'd done this type of work but he felt the American forces during the war may have taught him something worthwhile other than how to con punters.

Slowly and with his ear fixed close to the combination dial Mohamid started to rotate the knob. Little by little with ever increasing composure he secured the numerical code and just as the atmosphere was beginning to electrify with beads of perspiration forming on his forehead, the safe door clicked open. His trembling hand penetrated the darkness of the steel shell and removing its dubious contents, returned to the sanctuary of Brett's office turning off the light as he went but leaving the safe door ajar.

Mohamid Van Jonger sifted through all the documents he'd stolen from the safe, laying each one out over the lavish carpet as he'd concluded its reading. The missing financial payments of interest from the Moroccan banks tied with his computer data printout and the copies of messages he'd found tied with those in his own possession. He sieved through a wad of photographs highlighting Rebecca and Brett but was astounded to view those of Hans and another man he didn't yet know performing naked acts of utter distressing indecency. These later pictures had "copy" scrawled across them but that didn't deflect his repugnance. There was a list of phone calls made, money paid and what looked to be a master plan.

Mohamid permitted his eager eyes to wander over these documents before opening the remaining pile but he was ripped in half as each sordid detail unfolded before his very eyes. Mumbling in Arabic, Van Jonger was losing his placid nature yet time ticked on and after a brief pause he continued to read the remaining documents.

Untying the pink ribbon of the last bundle Mohamid found himself to be reading about his own past history and his relationship with Brett Watson. He'd gone past being stunned and read on with anger brewing inside his tightening stomach as so much had been gathered about so many people. Mohamid Van Jonger knew from the onset of this affair heroin was the underlying reason but he didn't understand why he or his family, Brett and his family or any of these other people had been involved for as far as he could make out, none were criminals.

Reaching for the last remaining sheet of paper Mohamid's eyes opened wider and wider as he read. It was apparent Aston Appleton was working under a death threat himself and although the document was unsigned, Appleton was not truly "Control". Despite having caused much grief to so many of Mohamid's friends and family it was obvious someone else had also been offended by this creep.

Sitting back in Brett's chair he wondered who else Aston Appleton had offended to create such devastation. Mohamid now with shirt sleeves rolled up prayed Alexis was safe, hoped Allah would secure their freedom and commenced re-reading all the documentation again in the hope he'd establish a cause, a reason and a conclusion to this tragedy.

The time was 6.00am on Sunday morning.

CHAPTER 25

Aboard Brave Goose. Saturday, 3.30pm.

The chilled cabin began to make Brett shiver since it was such a contrast to the searing heat beating down outside on *Brave Goose*. For some time none of those assembled in the saloon made a move or spoke; the atmosphere was rigidly strained yet Alexis turned to Brett and with a shaking act of defiance fumbled to find his hand. She needed support, her terrified body was starting to tremble. The two well-dressed Arabic-looking gentlemen, one seated and one standing by the table on which their suitcases had been presented, were beginning to make her skin creep. She'd been used to dealing with shady characters, God knows Tangiers had enough of them, but there was something about these two which caused her a degree of increasing alarm. Brett was totally out of his depth but was pleased to see from the corner of his eye Alexis still clutching hold of her black leather holdall, at least if they escaped from this mess they'd the means to leave Cyprus… hopefully forever.

Winston Al-Hassan slammed his fist down hard on the magnificent table with such a crack both Brett and Alexis jumped. Unbeknown to them, the other members of the congregation also jumped including Berber Al-Hassan who was clearly not amused by his son's amateur dramatics. Winston moved around the table and stood in front of them both; he didn't flinch, smile or show any emotion whatsoever. His eyes literally penetrated their inner minds as if he was searching to locate their feelings, their deepest of secrets and for any tell-tale evidence of betrayal. Brett couldn't keep up the game and averting his gaze from Winston, exposed Alexis to his full scrutiny but knowing these tactics she responded with admirable ease until after a most gruesome few minutes, he broke his serious frown and began to smile. Instantly the tension in the saloon declined and walking back to his original position adjacent to the table, he clicked his fingers, dismissing the two driver escorts and two of the crew members from their presence.

The room felt more comfortable since only Brett, Alexis, a single crew member, the young Arab and the old man who hadn't moved an inch were the only people present. Brett felt their chance of escape had just been bettered.

It appeared strange in Brett's eyes that such a fastidious vessel of radiating splendour could be run in what seemed to be total silence. Since their arrival on board nobody had spoken, it was as if a vow of muteness had been taken by all those present yet he looked with comforting gaze at the grandeur of the ship's secluded but expensive fitments. Brett knew this was something worthwhile owning and whilst he considered if it was at all possible his wandering thoughts were interrupted as the young Arab finally broke the pointed silence.

"It is understood your trip from Tangiers was not only successful but uneventful and I welcome you aboard *Brave Goose*."

His perfect English shook both Brett and Alexis to their roots as the deep, concentrated, penetrating tone of his voice left no doubt about his powerful involvement. The white robes with colourful headband were crisp with correctness while his clean-shaven bronzed face looked to be that of a young man. Brett was afraid to say anything and failing to secure some positive comment could only nod his head in vague agreement. Alexis didn't flinch but without moving anything other than his lips, the old man instructed Winston in Arabic to get on and stop messing about. She flashed a worried glance towards Brett who'd not understood but Winston had witnessed this act and perceived Alexis could understand Arabic. Her brown face, wild mysterious eyes and shapely figure attracted him as no other woman had ever done. At the age of twenty-six Winston Al-

Hassan had spent most of his life under the shaded wing of his father's past glory. When he'd had his stroke Winston's life was devoted to seeking revenge for his father's health, the loss of their family fortune and the loss of his career prospects in London, but during this time he'd had no measure to fool around as young men do, especially with women. The sight of this unknown goddess made him wonder why he'd never shunned his father's principles and looked at women before but it was with acute embarrassment he admitted to himself he was still a virgin. His father coughed as if to prompt Winston into action.

"Our names are unimportant in this matter and we feel this type of business is best conducted on a most impersonal basis. However, since you've delivered the goods as we'd ordered from our London source, I think a closer examination is now required. Please give me the keys to unlock the cases."

Alexis faltered only briefly; she'd watched Winston and felt a sense of fatal attraction but wasn't sure why yet. Maybe after this whole saga was over she'd have the pleasure of his company in more amiable circumstances. Her hand fished around the holdall until locating the keys, strode over the saloon carpet to the table and held out her hand displaying the two pieces of diminutive ironmongery. Winston leant forward and without taking his eyes away from her gracefully took the offerings, knowing money wouldn't buy her stunning body into his life.

Alexis didn't go back to Brett's side but stood over the two tan-coloured suitcases as Winston fiddled with the locks. They snapped open as Brett joined her and watching as the cases were opened they saw the closely packed lighters hadn't moved. It seemed inconceivable that such innocent-looking objects could contain such a deadly substance.

Alexis looked on but her thoughts were with Mohamid and how he'd been hurt as a small trickle of fluid ran from her eyes. She realised the severity of their actions but Winston saw her fighting back the tears and instantaneously knew she'd suffered great hardship probably under force to deliver these objects of evil. He flashed his eyes towards Brett whose facial expression also purveyed his mind as being elsewhere. Winston Al-Hassan instantly understood these two people had been blackmailed by one means or another to ensure he'd secure his own revengeful spite.

The old man, appreciative of his son's thoughts but dubious of his strategic plan, again mumbled to get on with the proceedings. Winston removed one of the lighters and with the aid of a pair of enlarged nut crackers broke open the plastic casing permitting a white powder to flow onto the table. Licking his finger, he placed it on the spillage, raised it to his lips and tasted a tiny amount. It was good and pure but Winston would never know how expensive.

*

The proving ceremony now complete, Winston instructed the attending crew member to show their "guests" to one of the master cabins. Yiannis stepped forward yet without hesitation proceeded to search their tired bodies for possible weapons. As he finished his task and turned to the black leather holdall, Winston yelled at him to do as he was told without any further delay. Brett and Alexis were both escorted out of the saloon and down the carpeted passage. They passed a small spiral stairway leading to the lower deck before halting abruptly behind their escort at a cabin door marked "Guest Suite". Yiannis opened the door, showed them inside and made his exit, locking it firmly behind him.

Alexis threw her bag onto the king-sized bed, looked at Brett and throwing her arms tightly around him started to weep with increasing intensity. They stood holding each other for many moments, each in deep thought concentrating on their own beloved families.

*

Back in the saloon Berber and Winston Al-Hassan grinned at each other with beaming radiance. The old man didn't think young Winston could have pulled such a stunt but as Winston reminded him the best was yet to come!

As they sat waiting for the drugs' onward customer Berber Al-Hassan spoke to Winston on the lines of taking a wife. He told him he'd witnessed his reaction at seeing the young woman from Tangiers when she'd entered the saloon and confirmed Winston's own view of her stunning beauty. However, he'd worked too diligently to secure this scheme to throw away all its benefits just as they were about to reap financial reward, revenge and success. Failure would only be reflective of his own stupidity all those years ago and the old man begged him not to make a fool of himself as he'd done, if only to pacify the pathos of his dead mother's memory. Winston nodded his head in agreement and sorrowfully stated he'd respect his wishes but instead of killing the two who'd shipped in the drugs, he'd allow them to escape. His father knew why Winston had changed his blueprint but was aware any negative response from himself may have catastrophic effects on his son's judgement. As they heard voices approaching the saloon from the gangway the old man told Winston to make their escape look realistic.

Yiannis entered the cool, sunlit cabin through the black glass patio doors, bringing with him the two dealers who were buying their imported goods. Winston and the old man took their usual posture side by side, thought by thought.

Each of the two cases brought to Cyprus by Brett and Alexis contained six hundred and forty lighters making one thousand two hundred and eighty in total. Winston had calculated from the lighters he'd designed each one would carry at least seventy grams of heroin, providing them with an income of over half a million pounds sterling after the production costs of the lighters had been taken into account.

The two shady characters from the underworld inspected their offerings and after only a few brief words, exchanged the drugs for money. Winston counted as they made their tests yet Berber Al-Hassan was slightly afraid for his son, but didn't allow his eyes to leave their sinister actions. He watched as they coldly and callously conducted a business deal before taking their drugs, well satisfied the purchase was fair. No handshakes took place, no papers were signed, this was the way it was done.

*

The late afternoon sunlight was now fading and in the shadow of a glowing sunset, *Brave Goose* groaned with admiration for her owners. Every part of the ship was perfect, no second-rate equipment would ever garnish this stunning beauty while under the Al-Hassans' ownership. Her proud features stood out against the reddish sky but as the sunset quickly passed darkness encompassed this craftsman's statue of excellence and her self-illuminating form was blessed with seductive pools of twinkling lights.

Inside, the Al-Hassans were enjoying their new source of wealth. The saloon curtains were drawn and although still purveying an air of tranquillity a more homely atmosphere was evident while both men relaxed. Berber Al-Hassan had watched Winston put the pile of Swiss Franc notes into their safe and prepare a package of money in assorted notes for onward transfer. Although not having the use of his body the Berber was that night dancing in his mind the jive of success.

It was a little after 7.30pm on Saturday evening.

CHAPTER 26

Cabin 13 Aboard Brave Goose.

Christian Beck watched Brett Watson and Alexis Matos arrive knowing Aston Appleton's plan was approaching its climax, but he still wasn't convinced that bastard was going to let him live. He knew Aston was basically no good and rotten through to the core, he'd enough proof of that but hoped his own scheming mind could better his personal destiny.

Keeping away from the still-damp bed sodden with urine, Christian parked himself in a less than sumptuous cabin chair. While sat waiting to be called back into the company of the Al-Hassans Christian realised he must be the only person who truly knew "Control's" identity. It crossed his mind this information may have a price and if he could play his cards at the most suitable moment, fancied selling the such information to a number of people, especially Brett Watson and Mohamid Van Jonger. A cruel smirk shot across his face but that was short-lived as recalling the package he'd sent to London via a stewardess, realised it would soon become common knowledge anyway.

Sulking back into oblivion, Christian reckoned he'd have to settle for his original proposal and just pray he lived long enough to see its conclusion. The late afternoon sun had moved around the ship to offer a more intense level of illumination in his drab cabin but the close proximity of the quayside prevented its full penetration. Christian stood up and kneeling on his chair peered out of the small porthole to watch the world go by but was now insatiably bored and tired of being locked up. Things needed to be done, actions had to be carried out and Christian was getting edgy again.

Still leaning against the cabin porthole, he witnessed the arrival of a large black American car of a marque he didn't recognise and two men blundered out wearing catalogue-type clothing with rather stupid hats. They approached the ship's gangway, disappearing from his vision but within a few seconds he could hear their heavy footsteps on the deck above him. Christian gathered their business with the Al-Hassans was all contained within a bulging black briefcase he saw chained to one of the men's wrists. He didn't show too much concern; after all, since meeting Aston Appleton he'd witnessed many events and on reflection he'd rather not know. Scanning what he could see of the quayside, nothing else moved, the world view offered by the porthole was dormant.

Returning to the stinking, damp bed Christian rescued a dry pillow and placing it on his chair resumed his vigilant watch of all comings and goings. His knees started to object to the hard surface of the chair but the pillow softened their protest.

He remained propped against the bulkhead for some considerable time, allowing his mind to drift from past to present and back again knowing that since he was locked up, there was nothing he could actively pursue. While considering his plight of fate footsteps on the deck above grew louder and passing over his head, he recognised them as being the men from the American car. A few long seconds staggered past before they came into his view again on the quayside. The bulging briefcase had been replaced by two tan-coloured suitcases and as the men placed them in the car's boot, they surreptitiously surveyed their surroundings before madly getting in the car and driving away at great speed. As the big car moved out of his sight its creative dust cloud obscured his line of vision to such a degree Christian gave up his vigil and returned to face the darkening cabin.

Bored and fed up, he wandered into his en-suite bathroom. The mirror still portrayed his light blue suit as being smart and combing his hair, he heard the cabin door unlock. Christian's heart jumped; at

144

last there was to be some action.

*

Quite some time had passed since the departure of the American car with its two odd-looking occupants and the unlocking of his cabin door, yet nevertheless the sight of Yiannis made him feel particularly apprehensive. This was a man he didn't care to trust but at that present time he'd have conveyed the same thought about any man.

Yiannis grinned, showing his perfect white teeth, and still dressed in the ship's uniform ushered him along the corridor, up the small spiral stairway and into that grand saloon. The stench of his own cabin must have been horrendous as the sweet aroma of previously undetected herbs greeted his swaying nostrils. The soft lighting and tranquil setting of his new surroundings offered Christian an undiluted boost to his dented ego but standing just inside the saloon doorway he waited for his next disaster to formulate, yet was surprised by Winston Al-Hassan walking over to greet him.

"I'm so sorry for having kept you waiting but preparations had to be made before your departure could be secured. I trust you've caught up with your sleep and Yiannis has suitably served your needs."

Christian didn't know how to answer him without putting himself to shame and with the big Greek sailor still standing in the room he'd decided to just acknowledge Al-Hassan's comment. Winston continued.

"I think you must agree your new suit of clothing looks far better on you than your old... shall we say overalls."

Christian nodded, not daring to answer him back just in case he was sentenced to another twelve-hour stint in that urine-filled cabin. The old Arab's eyes watched Christian but as before didn't show any sign of expression.

Winston took his arm and led him to that highly polished table where the black briefcase he'd seen the two men from the American car bring in, laid.

"It is my understanding you are aware the case contains a substantial sum of money and your Mr Appleton has instructed you on how to dispose of its contents."

"That's correct," Christian mumbled.

"Well," Winston continued, "I'm sure you wouldn't mind signing this document for me. It's merely a formality to acknowledge receipt of the money."

Christian looked slightly isolated as basically he'd no idea what the briefcase contained. His facial expression must have shown his concern because Winston unlocked the catches, slipped the locks and lifted the lid exposing a host of varied coloured bank notes. This display of such trust secured Christian Beck's signature on the document and so released the case of money into his trust.

Winston clipped the security chain to Christian's wrist, locked the case, gave him the keys and wished him luck. Walking down the gangway of *Brave Goose*, he turned and marvelled at its enormity but couldn't help noticing Alexis and Brett Watson with their noses pressed hard against a cabin window watching him drift off into the night.

*

The air was warm yet it felt refreshing to him after his extended period of being confined within that small cabin. Christian walked down the quayside away from the splendour of *Brave Goose* and towards a pulsating nightlife enjoyed by Larnaca's marina jet-setting population.

Feeling good and as if life could now be rescued, Christian wandered amongst the crowds of happy, carefree people out to enjoy themselves. The music, bright lights and roadside cafés offered him a sense of security he'd not felt since leaving London. Still chained to his wrist, the briefcase given to him by Winston Al-Hassan did more than fill him with security, it made him want to laugh out loud as this contained his future but as yet that evil bastard Appleton didn't know. Smirking with a sinister grin, he decided he'd give anything to see the look on Appleton's face once he came to appreciate what he was about to lose.

Christian's plan for self-preservation could now be put into action as for all intents and purpose he was a free man. Continuing to walk through the crowds of people milling around, not noticing how they were looking at him, Christian Beck laughed to himself but didn't care to know their thoughts, he was just happy to be alive, free and rich.

Reaching the central taxi rank Beck climbed into a car, instructed the driver to go directly to the airport and rooted inside his jacket pocket to locate his next but crucial airline ticket. The cut of his new jacket felt good, matching his own personal feelings, and he knew he could now achieve a respectable goal.

Finding the remaining two tickets, the passing street lights offered enough light for him to determine which one was to be used next. Replacing the London-bound ticket in his pocket Christian played for the remainder of the short journey with the voucher for tonight's flight. His mind was full of crazy ideas as to how he'd spend Appleton's money but their arrival at Larnaca Airport departure terminal brought him back into line.

The airport was reasonably busy but not overpowering and as he checked in, his Swiss Air flight to Geneva was called. Christian made his way quickly through the formalities and with a sense of impending fulfilment almost ran across the concrete apron, bouncing up the aircraft stairway and boarding the DC 9 jet with only minutes to spare. He'd planned to be at the airport in good time but due to his delayed departure from *Brave Goose*, this had been cut very fine.

The jet engines started to whine as the flight crew prepared for their taxi movements and cabin staff darted around making the aircraft secure for flight before announcing the usual pre-flight safety procedures. Christian took notice this time, feeling he'd more to lose should anything go wrong, a vast change in attitude from his flight into Cyprus earlier that same day.

Loaded with only a sprinkling of passengers, the Swiss Air DC 9 gave a short lurch before finally leaving the terminal gate. The plane made its way over the bumpy taxiway to its holding point just short of the runway and after a brief pause, eased onto the wide long stretch of man-made grey ribbon. Finally, as the two powerful engines were opened up the roar filled its passenger compartment and they quickly built up speed. Runway lights, terminal buildings and flickering lights from adjacent buildings sped past his window seat with increasing rapidity before he felt the nose of the plane lift into the warm Mediterranean night. Christian Beck was airborne again, happy and wealthy... or so he thought.

The time was 10.30pm on Saturday evening.

CHAPTER 27

The Guest Suite, Brave Goose.

The late afternoon sunlight was streaming into their cabin through its tinted glass window as Alexis released her weeping embrace on Brett's sturdy frame. She sighed with relief and apprehension knowing their lethal imported goods were no longer a part of them, yet being a prisoner was none too inspiring despite the majestic surroundings of their cabin.

Turning away from Brett's youthful well-built body, she walked towards the bed, sat and stared at him with eyes of utter impetuosity. Alexis knew that while they had the heroin they were safe but now she didn't care to think of the immediate future and her smooth, brown, lovable features appeared to drain quite visibly of colour as Brett only half watching her considered their next move.

The cabin was sumptuous with rich furnishings, cut glass, expensive fabrics and a lavish soft pile carpet. The en-suite bathroom contained a circular, maroon, sunken bath surrounded with gold ornaments, large urns of herbs and was entirely enveloped by mirrors set at slightly differing angles. Each of the light fittings seemed to have been placed so as to highlight another part of the body in an opposing yet equally revealing mirror. The scented cabin and opulent air of privilege began from their early entry to unnerve them both.

They hardly spoke but for some time merely took in the all-embracing effects of their current predicament.

Brett strode up and down the cabin trying to avoid Alexis yet formulate in his own mind a plan of escape but Alexis watched him wishing he'd just hold her again as they'd done when first locked in that cabin. Brushing the remaining effects of her tears away, Alexis stood up and reaching Brett's designated path blocked his way. For a few moments of hesitant longing they just stared at each other in fearsome chastity before she moved towards him, flicking the long black hair away from her unblemished face. Brett's cautious nature prevented him from going to her but she advanced on him with a sense of need. Her mysterious eyes still damp with tears didn't penetrate his mind as trying to kiss him, Brett moved slightly away and without looking at her, spoke in a soft gentle tone.

"Not here, not in this place, I want everything to be right."

Alexis knew she'd not been rejected but was aware of Brett's nervous state and although being jittery herself thought an act of love may inspire confidence in them both. She reached for his hand in soothing firmness and together they went over towards a fitted sofa directly under the cabin window. Kneeling on the plush cradle of cushions they both peered towards the outside world just in time to witness the arrival of a large black American car on the dusty quayside. Brett and Alexis watched as the two men approached, totally unaware of Christian Beck doing exactly the same thing from a small cabin directly below them. The two men passed their cabin window, never noticing their plight but Brett, observing a briefcase, knew this was part of "Control's" plan. The total silence seemed to be reflective of their status with Alexis considering Mohamid and Rebecca, while Brett was only considering himself with Alexis and in so doing permitted an image of Mohamid to enter his mind, how he wanted to love her but she was Mohamid's "second wife" and Brett recognised the problem yet still couldn't imagine not screwing her. He didn't want to imagine Mohamid finding them out.

Their individual thoughts continued to flourish on these lines until the two men reappeared, passing their cabin window and heading back to the black car complete with their two cases brought in from Tangiers. Brett and Alexis turned, looked and gripped each other's hand a little harder but turning back continued to watch the car disappear towards Larnaca.

The deflation of the moment was almost unbearable. They both expected more than an obvious quiet exchange but it made them both aware of their now increased vulnerability. Faced with a less than favourable position Brett broke the silence and although knowing part of her involvement, still wasn't clear of her total story. Mohamid had spoken briefly of the instructions Alexis had received at Heathrow but now he wanted to know the whole truth and why she'd been so aggressive.

Historical. Friday Morning At Heathrow Airport

The Royal Air Maroc jet landed at Heathrow a little before its scheduled time but during the flight Alexis had tried to collect her thoughts together, yet without any degree of compaction since for most of the two-and-a-half-hour flight she worried about Mohamid; their secret was now no longer sacrosanct. He'd worked so hard to build the Rembrant and her own life into respectability yet the thought of being rejected, ridiculed and expelled from Moroccan society filled her with an intention to succeed no matter what the cost.

Leaving the aircraft with bitter determination, Alexis Matos cleared the formalities, never allowing the small security locker key sent by "Control" to leave her hand. Terminal two was larger than she'd remembered but it had been some years since her last visit to England. With painful ease she located the banks of airport security lockers, isolated the guilty one and in a fit of doggedness opened the small steel door. As the locker's contents came into view Alexis could see nothing particularly sinister. She removed the package, found a seat in a quiet part of the concourse and started to reveal its contents.

The typed instructions were clear and precise, the bundle of money was fresh and new and the .38 revolver was far from a child's toy, but as her brain accepted the fact it was a real gun her long slender fingers let go of the cold steel and it fell back into the package. She'd not been ready for such a presentation and quickly looked about to make sure nobody had seen the sinister article her trembling hand had touched.

With shaking undertones of hatred and beads of perspiration forming on her perfect forehead she began to read the accompanying message.

Now you have arrived read these instructions with care, follow them in each detail and you will secure your own life and that of Mohamid Van Jonger.

Go to the Royal Air Maroc information desk and tell them your name. In turn they will present you with a set of keys for a Transit van which has been hired on your behalf. Inside the van you'll find two pairs of overalls and two pairs of training shoes. It is essential you and Mr Watson wear these garments on your return journey to Heathrow as they will ensure your free passage through the airport formalities and you will wear the airline's security passes which are currently located on the van's dashboard. At exactly 5.00pm today you will be at Mr Brett Watson's house in Lenton Parva to secure his return to the Rembrant Hotel. All that is necessary for you to do, is to press the door chime and my man Hans Zenna will let you in. Zenna will have already abducted Rebecca Watson but you must maintain a superior quality as he is weak and gay! Rebecca Watson is a two-timing bitch so dominate, frighten and demand her attentions.

Alexis was now feeling most disturbed; her black leather clothing felt hard against her damp skin as she began to appreciate her role in this affair. Her thoughts of Mohamid and their lives being ruined brought Alexis back to reality; this was no dream but a true nightmare as she continued to read on, unaware of the increasing number of people milling around her.

Once you have gained access to the house you will wait for Brett Watson to return. When he makes his entry use the enclosed revolver to secure your mission.

At 6.00pm you will ring the number at the top of this message and report to me before you start back to Heathrow with Brett. Use surgical tape to keep them both from talking if it is necessary but instil the fear of God into them all.

Hans Zenna will remain with the Watson woman at Lenton Parva until I've achieved my goal and then I'll decide how to dispose of them but make damn sure you've Brett Watson's passport and credit cards in your possession. Watch him with the eye of an eagle as he's an evil man not fit to live on this earth, but make sure he drives the van back to the airport. Displaying your passes, use the enclosed map of the airport to drive directly through the staff service gate of terminal two and go without faulting to gate 41. There you will find the R.A.M jet waiting for your arrival. As airline employees, leave the van at the aircraft steps and board it, taking your revolver with you.

As a precaution you will notice the gun has no bullets within its chamber, your ability to frighten and overpower the aforementioned people is all you need. Succeed and you will return to normal, fail and you along with Mohamid Van Jonger will die a death of gruesome devastation.

"Control"

Alexis re-read the entire message again to make sure she'd understood its full implications. She daren't go to the police for fear of hurting her beloved Mohamid but sat totally frightened for many moments before folding the typed message and slipping it back into the package felt perspiration trickling down her steaming body.

*

Alexis Matos manoeuvred the almost new van out and away from Heathrow's intense traffic towards the exclusive residential area of Lenton Parva. She'd not driven in any other country before except Morocco and was decidedly uncomfortable, yet the time was only just one o'clock and she couldn't determine how to spend the next four arduous hours. Driving with full concentration following the map "Control" had prepared, Alexis noticed she was passing a large park and with an instinct only displayed by a woman, she turned off the main road. Halting the van at the first convenient place Alexis took stock of her shaking body, opened the van door and breathed the delightful warm September air.

Her mind was full of apprehension peppered in bitterness but with growing hatred she left the van and walked in this peaceful place. The mature trees all displayed a host of rich brown, red and yellow as they turned from deep summer greens. The grass was dry but soft underfoot and the sound of squabbling ducks on a nearby lake made her understand why England was loved so much by so many.

She walked, totally unaware of her destination, enjoying the afternoon sunshine as at last Alexis began to unwind. The tension which had built up inside had made her crave for food but she did not want to eat, she couldn't, and continuing on her stroll began to recall how Mohamid had spoken of this Brett Watson.

She couldn't recall him saying anything bad about the Watsons, in fact it was just the opposite, but in view of the threats against her and Mohamid, Alexis Matos knew that although she must obey "Control", she felt there was a missing link.

Returning to the van, she was aware of her tension growing again and starting its engine, turned away from the park en route to Lenton Parva. It was 4.30pm.

Back In The Guest Suite Aboard Brave Goose.

During the time in which Alexis had revealed the contents of her instruction, Brett had watched Christian Beck leave the ship with unconcerned interest. He'd been totally absorbed in the events Alexis had related but as she concluded her dialogue Brett felt the trickle of sweet tears running down his tired face. They held onto each other, comforting their painful but secure relationship. Each was now considering their future or if their lives would end here.

The time was 9.30 on Saturday evening.

CHAPTER 28

The Escape

Winston Al-Hassan left his elderly father neatly tucked up in bed as he closed the cabin door. His mind was racing with schemes as to how Brett and Alexis could escape without them knowing the act was fixed, yet striding back into the main saloon he was unaware of how the tension was building up inside himself again. Tomorrow and Monday were going to be busy days for both himself and his old father but they both knew all their efforts would be well worthwhile. A glimmer of a smile shot across Winston's face as he considered how they'd cheated Aston Appleton but the most amusing part of all being he didn't know, yet.

Going out through the black patio glass doors Winston drank in the warm evening air whilst wandering with some discomfort around the aft deck of *Brave Goose*. He sat in a wicker chair and while staring across the marina an idea struck him like thunder. With the same sinister grin appearing across his brown face Winston Al-Hassan stood up walked down the deck past Alexis and Brett's cabin window before alighting onto the dusty quayside. Stars filled the night sky like shimmering sequins yet Winston didn't take any notice. The quayside lights flickered a dancing light on the dark surface sufficient to permit his captives an illuminated view of his pending actions.

Towards the stern of *Brave Goose* and on the opposing wharfside was a small stone-built warehouse once used by local fishermen when the now plush marina was a working port. Winston deliberately meandered across to its broken down door and whistling, gently slipped inside.

It was pitch black yet he knew Yiannis kept his powerful motorcycle in there throughout the time he was actually working onboard the ship. With something approaching brute force Winston located the machine and kicking up its stand moved the heavy cycle out into the night air. Yiannis was a strong man, although a little simple in Winston's mind, yet his loyalty had always been prominent in the family bosom and he now considered how Yiannis would react once he'd found out his only true love had been stolen. Winston knew he could never admit to having been involved. The massive Honda Goldwing took him some considerable time to move into a situation which would tempt his captives away from *Brave Goose* but with surrendering exertion the 1,500cc machine was left standing in front of the white Mercedes still parked on the quayside. Looking delightfully sinister against the white backdrop of the car, the black bike sat in readiness under the scented night sky bathed in demure lighting.

Standing to admire his handiwork, Winston felt about his person for the bike's key. He inserted it in the ignition, turned around and went back onboard *Brave Goose*. Climbing the gangway, a lower deck porthole was well illuminated and Winston could see some of the crew playing cards in a smoke-filled atmosphere. Amongst them, Yiannis was holding a prominent position, he was without doubt their equivalent to a union leader and Winston knew the other crew members feared his hunky size yet shaking his head a little he continued up the gangway only to be met by the ship's Captain. Stephanos Constandinos was a precise man who liked his charge to be in nothing less than perfect condition and treated *Brave Goose* as if it was his own. He was not a big man, in fact rather the opposite, but his style of shipboard management suited the Al-Hassans. His manner was not dissimilar to a Victorian butler, seen but never heard yet all the crew respected him, even Yiannis.

Captain Constandinos greeted Winston and reported everything to be in order but his flashing Greek eye, which as a rule didn't miss anything, noticed the black motorcycle standing in conspicuous fashion against the white Mercedes. Winston watched his vigilant stare and diverted his attention by requesting information on the following day's sea conditions. The Captain instantly forestalled his concern over the bike and hoping for a day at sea scurried off to prepare his charts. Winston knew there would be no such voyage but played on his Captain's desire to put *Brave Goose* back on the high seas.

During the course of their brief conversation Winston began to worry if his plan would work. He had to conclude his efforts as quickly as possible but in order for everything to succeed he'd changed his mind about engineering a fake escape to literally kicking them off his ship. This change had been brought about by his faithful Captain's attentive glare towards the big Honda bike.

Quickly, Winston Al-Hassan made his way through the lavish saloon and down the carpeted corridor towards the guest suite, unlocked the door and with dart-like speed almost fell over the threshold. Closing it behind him, he was met by two very startled people who'd obviously been watching his every move on the grubby quayside as Brett and Alexis clambered away from the sofa with naked surprise. Facing Winston, they became aware of his emerging concern.

Young and dynamic although he was, Winston Al-Hassan had during the short time he'd known Alexis Matos fallen for her, and couldn't bear to see her in danger. He knew that by formulating her escape he'd have to let Brett Watson go with her yet in so doing could lose Alexis forever. He couldn't harm either of them and by now knew he didn't want to but it was still of paramount importance to win the whole game over Aston Appleton, but their deaths no longer were a feature of the plan.

Standing in front of them, Winston reached for Alexis's hand, raised it to his lips and kissed it with all the inner warmth his churning body could muster. He didn't want to let go, he wanted her badly and his virginity needed to be broken. Alexis Matos would have been his perfect partner, he thought. The lengthy fondling of her hand made Alexis feel uneasy but Brett was more shocked than worried. He'd not considered an approach from these people quite in this manner yet was aware of piercing undertones and as her hand slipped back to her side Winston's deep penetrating voice whispered to them both, "Can you ride a motorcycle?"

They both looked blankly at each other before Brett responded, "No."

Alexis suddenly felt the urge to be free again and cut in with a dominant voice, "I can drive one."

Winston had never taken his eyes away from her and after her response, smiled. His clean shaven powerful face beamed at her as he drew closer to Alexis, ignoring Brett altogether. He continued his unprepared speech.

"You see that large bike on the quayside, take it and escape while you can."

They stood transfixed. Both Brett and Alexis had watched Winston move the huge bike out of the old warehouse but didn't associate their escape with this man's conspicuous assistance. Winston with goaded tone asked if they needed money and without them responding thrust a wad of new Swiss Francs into Brett's hand. He went towards the cabin door, dimmed the lights and checking the corridor, opened the door wider for them. Brett and Alexis couldn't believe this was happening but Winston's menacing tone telling them to go brought instant reaction. Brett Watson passed through into the corridor, turned to make sure Alexis was behind him and was a little surprised to say the least as he saw Winston kissing her with captivated emotion. He pushed Alexis away from him and dragging her black holdall she followed Brett who stormed through the saloon onto the aft deck and like a prowling cat down the gangway, over the quayside and onto the waiting Honda motorbike.

With the black, distinctive, two-wheel powerhouse between them, they stared at each other knowing each had been offended by the other but the sound of a closing door aboard *Brave Goose* united their spirits. Alexis, lifting her full dress up to her waist, climbed on the wide machine while Brett eased his way over the seat behind her and securing the holdall made himself ready for a ride he was never going to forget. Alexis started the engine, kicked up the bike's stand and engaged the gears, allowing the huge machine to purr down the dusty and hard grey quay towards the glaring lights of Larnaca. Despite feeling unsure of herself on such a machine her balance was almost perfect. Once past the ship she turned on the bike's lights and was enthralled by the vast array of dials; it was very different to anything she'd ever ridden.

*

Captain Stephanos Constandinos saw the Honda Goldwing slide quietly past his ship and knowing how Yiannis liked to take liberties, darted down to the crew's quarters to find out where he'd gone without his consent. Racing towards that part of the vessel his surprise overpowered him as entering the crew's main dinning cabin, Yiannis was still there playing cards. In spluttered tones of concern he related his findings but before he'd finished Yiannis was up and bounding out of the cabin in a state of eruption cleared the table of cards, drink and food. He leaped over the quayside towards the old stone warehouse and seeing his precious motorcycle had gone issued forth a host of marauding Greek at the top of his voice. The tranquil setting of Brave Goose was overturned in a matter of seconds as lights were turned on, voices yelled, doors banged and finally three of his crewmates raced over to him. One man waved the keys of the Mercedes in his hand and without regard for the others piled in, started it up and screamed off in search of the two escaped foreigners.

It had only been a matter of a few moments from the Honda bike leaving before the white Mercedes had taken chase but despite having watched these events, Winston hoped he'd given Alexis a head start. For the first time in his life Winston Al-Hassan had felt real love, had reacted, and now wished he'd gone with them, yet he doubted if he'd ever see her again. Returning to his own suite of cabins he sat on the sumptuous bed wishing thoughts of a jealous yet benign lover.

*

Alexis was now coming to terms with the huge machine. She found its triple discs, dual-piston callipers and proportioning valve made the massive cycle easier to handle than she'd expected. Exploring the other instruments, Alexis found the bike had a five-speed gearbox, cruise control and a computer, but she didn't think of using any of them since maintaining balance and speed were her primary concerns.

The warm evening air seemed a little cool to them both as the bike picked up speed. Her long black hair flicked Brett's face with uncomfortable regularity but he was more concerned for their safety. They passed the port area and swish cafés along the Phinikoudhes Boulevard, not taking notice of passers-by or other traffic. Their destination had to be the airport as it was their only real way out back to their beloved families.

Turning off the main boulevard and into Zenon Kitieos Street, Alexis was aware of a fast car closing behind them but it was not until it drew a little closer she realised it was that distinctive white Mercedes from *Brave Goose*. She yelled to Brett behind her who in turning to see for himself almost made her crash the powerhouse of a machine. He didn't speak but fiddling around in the black holdall located the gun in readiness; he understood this to be big trouble. Neither of them spoke again as they watched the prominent vehicle get closer, they didn't even wonder about Winston Al-Hassan's motives as they were both shit scared.

With the white Merc almost on top of them the traffic seemed to have eased and Alexis opened up the bike's throttle. With a screaming of rubber the big Honda leapt forward at a frightening pace, leaving the car and Brett's stomach far behind. The bike increased its speed but gradually so did the Mercedes and Alexis presumed the only way to lose them was in the maze of narrow adjoining streets. She braked. Brett's stomach caught up and promptly overtook them as her braking action had been hard, and as they turned into Kitkis Street, the car was still on their tail having again caught up. She turned almost straight away again into Kirnon Street but the car followed. It was as if the white Mercedes was stuck to them but Brett could hear their engine screaming as they tried to keep up with Alexis weaving her way in and out of the street jungle. Turning again into the old town and passing the church of St Lazarus, the streets became considerably narrower. She sped down them with lights flashing and the horn making a most piercing racket but the car followed although not with so much speed; they were having specific problems negotiating the tight corners. People jumped out of their way, old men hollered at them for disrupting the peace, yet still the chase continued. Becoming darker and narrower as they progressed away from the more fashionable sections of town, the streets were beginning to help them as Alexis felt she'd really begun to understand this exciting Honda.

Brett was thrown from side to side, feeling every bump and once or twice thought he'd be thrown clear. His head was pounding, it felt like being in a spin dryer as again Alexis turned and accelerated past a small open market. The Mercedes didn't quite make the turn and slamming into the stalls brought produce raining down all over the road. They didn't stop but merely accelerated away to a host of abusive comments from local people and leaving the street in a total shambles. Yiannis was screaming at the driver to catch them yet not to damage his precious motorcycle but the driver ignored his plea, putting his foot hard down on the accelerator.

Alexis watched the car's headlights catch them up again so braking fiercely turned into a long but empty cobblestoned marketplace. Her turn was so abrupt Brett couldn't hold on to the gun, the bag and the bike all at the same time. Closing his eyes to avoid his pending sickness the .38 revolver slid off into the darkness as leaving the turn she applied the accelerator yet again.

Spinning like a child's top the Mercedes spun into the marketplace and with a screeching of brakes regained its composure to set up the chase yet again. Alexis dodged late-night walkers and choosing the narrowest exit made her speedy getaway but not to be outdone the car gave chase with Yiannis still screaming. Shooting out of the marketplace like a greased bullet the Honda Goldwing was pursued by the Mercedes and as they entered the narrow street the car's driver knew he'd made an error of judgement. Once into the street it narrowed dramatically to only a meagre three and a half feet wide. The Mercedes couldn't brake in time, couldn't turn and with a screaming of stone against metal became well and truly jammed between the buildings in a shower of flying sparks and broken glass.

The noise died down and silence fell to this sleepy part of Larnaca as the occupants of the car realised how they'd been tricked. Being so badly squashed the doors wouldn't open and the roof had been pinched together with such force a metallic pyramid had sprouted. Well and truly encased like sardines, the Greek crew sat dazed and bewildered. There was nothing left for them to do except watch the motorcycle disappear into the night and an old man seated on his balcony return to reading the paper after a brief moment of excitement.

With splintered glass all around them, they slowly started to remove themselves through what was once the rear window and walking away from the scene of such embarrassment they started to argue amongst themselves. The only audible comment concerned Yiannis and his fucking motorbike.

*

Alexis didn't ease her driving determination after the Mercedes had come to such a grinding halt but made all haste towards the airport. Brett was petrified and had been since first sitting on that machine. He vowed never to sit on one of these things again for as long as he lived but the sight of the airport terminal buildings gave him fresh hope for a more cultivated existence.

Not bothering to park the bike, Alexis could see a number of aircraft sat on the concrete apron and intended to board one of them. Roaring up to the terminal doors the bike mounted the pavement and came to a juddering halt. She kicked out the stand, eased the machine over and alighted looking decidedly smug but Brett had almost frozen with fear and attempting to follow her lead, fell his full length onto the hard paving slabs. She picked him up, dusted him down and giving him that seductive smile dragged him into the terminal. Alexis checked out the destination board and seeing the only flight heading west was to Athens, made her way over to the Olympic Airways desk with Brett in tow.

There were spare seats onboard so purchasing two tickets with some of Winston's money, they headed for the departure lounge as their flight was given its final call.

Brett and Alexis didn't hesitate about leaving Aphrodite's Island since they both knew Athens would offer something they both wanted. As the Boeing 747 raced down the runway, reached V2 and soared away from Cypriot soil they took each other's hands, gently kissed each other and promptly slept for the flight's duration. Sunday would bring passion never known before.

The time was 00.01 Sunday morning.

CHAPTER 29

Christian Beck

Once the Swiss Air flight was truly on its designated route the Captain announced the scheduled arrival time would be maintained and their cruising height was 27,000 feet. Christian Beck felt such relief he almost dropped into a deep doze but with the black briefcase stuffed full of money held close to him, considered his contentment with raptures of certainty and reaching for the in-flight magazine tried to fight his sleeping desire.

The meagre sprinkling of passengers ensured the cabin staff had an easy time that night and were content to chat amongst themselves until serving a rather tasty evening meal. Christian consumed his dinner with the gusto of a man possessed. For the first time since leaving London he'd felt absolutely ravenous and didn't leave a single scrap. In view of the pending day ahead Christian didn't partake of any alcohol but once the meal service was concluded and cleared away, adjusted his window seat into a reclining position and endeavoured to catch a little sleep. The cabin was warm, comfortable and with dimmed lights the DC 9 aircraft powered its way over Greece on route to its home destination.

*

At precisely 2.00am on that Sunday morning the aircraft made a gentle landing at Geneva Airport and it was only the engines having reverse thrust applied which woke Beck. He was instantly alert and collecting himself together watched the airport terminal lights come into view. As the plane came to a halt and other passengers started towards the exit Christian felt more than important, he felt like a tower of human power and walking through the deserted customs hall he knew this was it, his own brand of revenge was about to be implemented.

At such an early hour of the morning very little activity was evident outside the airport building but a single awaiting taxi provided Christian with all the inspiration he needed. Walking towards the Opel car he became aware of the night's coolness and refreshing air, it being a far cry from the humid heat of Tangiers or Cyprus. The car's driver half asleep reverted to full attention as Beck approached and seeing he was carrying no luggage conceded to drive him to the Hotel Angleterre in Lucerne.

Seated or rather slumped in the back seat, Christian watched the lights meander past as they made their way along the lakeside. Leaving some of the more densely populated areas behind he could see lights reflecting like dancing fireflies in the lake slightly overshadowed by a glowing full moon. Little to no traffic passed them during their journey and the only human life Christian saw revolved around street cleaners.

Pulling up outside the hotel Beck paid the driver with some of Al-Hassan's money, climbed out and watched the taxi's rear lights disappear into the night. Standing alone, he listened to the silence before turning towards the quaint balcony-ridden building and as he entered the hotel with apprehension, was delighted to see how receptive the night porter proved to be. Christian hired a smallish single room overlooking the lake, signed the register and made his way towards his new sanctuary.

Turning on the light, he noted how tastefully the room was decorated. It had a low ceiling and an air of simple cleanliness with a large window shuttered by louver doors. Walking over towards them he opened the old metal catch, drew the shutters aside and pushed the glass doors open allowing the sweet, fresh night air into his lungs. Leaving the doors wide open, Christian went towards the bed, stripped off and hanging his new light blue suit on a hanger crawled into bed. Flicking the light off, he drifted into a deep sleep with the briefcase tucked in closely at his side. He dreamt of his past, of Hans Zenna and throughout the remainder of the night sported an enormous erection.

*

It was after 9.45am on that clear, warm Sunday morning when Christian was awoken by the passing traffic and general street noise but strong sunlight flooded into the room as he blinked before finally reaching full alertness. He moved his hand and locating the briefcase managed a shy, weak smile only witnessed by himself. Turning over, he gazed at the low ceiling and remembering the impact the room had made on him as he'd entered earlier, felt pleased to see it was equally pleasant in daylight. Christian lay still for a short while before his hand worked its way down his body and feeling his limp penis started to caress himself. With incredible ease his cock grew to its full length and masturbating with indulgent pleasure, reached the point of no return. Sperm flowed freely onto the bedclothes as he thought again of Hans. Yet unbeknown to him, this was to be the last sexual pleasure he'd ever encounter.

After taking a shower and having a shave using the courtesy toilet pack supplied by the hotel he dressed, grabbed the briefcase and went down to the lobby. The whole place had a most serene atmosphere and although filled with blooming fresh flowers still felt as it had done on his arrival, of ordered cleanliness.

He purposefully made his way through this ordered environment out to the hotel's roadside restaurant and making himself comfortable at a table away from the other guests, Christian took stock of his surroundings. The restaurant was open air although covered by a large multicoloured awning which had obviously been exposed to some intense natural sunlight by its faded appearance. The white linen tablecloth was clean, heavily starched, matched only by the napkins and set with weighty cutlery. Christian's attention was drawn away from the hotel past a bed of full-coloured geraniums separating the hotel from the footpath and road. Over towards the lake a paddle steamer was making heavy swishing noises as it docked, allowing its passengers to alight and then with a rupturing blast on its horn moved away towards its next lakeside destination.

The morning was hot and crisp yet this place seemed almost too perfect for someone of his calibre. Christian's mind was not on his current predicament but miles away thinking of what his future had in store.

A rather large, round gentleman approached his table and introducing himself, Christian Beck realised this was Aston Appleton's banker. He glanced at his watch – it was nearly 11.00am, this was the time for him to create his own fortune.

Bo Perroud was not a reputable Swiss banker but the only one Aston could find who'd even consider working on a Sunday morning. It was part of his scheme for Christian to hand the money over to Perroud, obtain a receipt and then attempt to make his way back to London. As an added precaution Aston had instructed Bo Perroud to telex a copy of the transaction to him at the earliest possible moment since he knew Beck would never be seen in London again.

Placing his enormous fat backside in a chair next to Christian, the two men hardly spoke at first as an attentive waiter brought coffee to their table, but the banker declined in drinking the sweet black liquid. Instead he reached into his jacket pocket, retrieved a tatty receipt voucher booklet and suggested they conclude the business in hand.

Beck had been watching Bo Perroud with concern. He was certainly overweight, his suit didn't really fit and sweat was running down his flabby but boyish face. He wondered how Appleton had trapped this man into such a shady deal yet knew not to ask and with a grunt of anticipation, Beck cleared his throat, announcing there was a change to Aston's original brief. The banker stared blankly at him, not passing any comment so Christian continued.

"The money contained in this briefcase," he said, pointing at the black case on the floor by his side. "It is to be put into my own account which I trust you will open straight away. Should anything happen to me the only two people who can draw on the account are my parents. Their names and address are written down for you here."

Christian passed Bo a plain sheet of white paper with the information written in bold, strong letters across its entire width. The banker snatched the paper from Beck, wiped his forehead with a less than clean handkerchief before stating he knew nothing of this change. Christian spoke firmly, telling him Aston was a busy man, didn't have time to contact the bank and entrusted himself to make all necessary arrangements. Still the banker was not convinced, suggesting that their transaction should be delayed until he'd spoken to Appleton himself, but Christian was getting annoyed and knowing he must succeed, banged his remaining airline ticket on the table.

"This is my flight ticket back to London. The take-off time is 2.30 this afternoon and I intend to be onboard having concluded Aston's business."

Christian was going to continue but thought better of it as the greedy banker now appeared to be convinced it was now or never. With a suggestive nod the briefcase was handed over. Bo Perroud counted the money, totally oblivious of people watching from a respectful distance, signed a receipt form, told Beck his new account number and was gone.

Christian watched the fat banker disappear into the crowd of people milling around the ferry boat mooring while he withdrew a stubby cigar and lighting it, absorbed the sweet, tasty smoke into his inner body. At long last he was rich to the point of it being painful and calling a nearby waiter to his table Christian ordered a bottle of champagne. He intended to celebrate his newfound fortune even though he knew Aston wouldn't settle until he'd been made to answer for his actions.

The midday sun was scorching hot as Christian sipped the ice-cold nectar. His cigar was almost finished but he watched the passing procession of people wandering back and forth along the tranquil lakeside. At regular intervals a lake steamer would appear, exchange its passengers and head on to the next stop while a gentle breeze made the colourful geraniums bob and dance with impending excitement. The whole scene was totally peaceful and coupled with the drowsing effect of his champagne, Christian really did feel the world had at last been good to him.

He could have remained at that place forever but time ticked on and he knew he must be onboard that flight back to London. The sight of Aston Appleton's face would be a picture when he realised what evil trick he'd played but after all, it was only as evil as Appleton himself had been. Groaning with satisfaction, Christian lifted his weedy frame from the table and entering the hotel reception paid his bill with some of the money he'd removed from the Al-Hassans' briefcase. He noticed the clerk looking at the crumpled notes but didn't attach any importance to her actions once she'd accepted the money. Calling a taxi, he thanked the clerk for a most enjoyable although brief stay and concluded by saying he hoped one day to return.

He walked out from under the faded awning as the taxi approached and clambering into the rear seat. he instructed the driver to go directly to Geneva Airport. Christian watched the passing lake with a growing love for that part of the world, knowing it was beautiful, clean, hot and for him successful, the epitome of everything he now wanted in life.

As the car raced towards the airport Christian's mind started to become unsettled and he wished he'd the guts to remain there but knew it was necessary to return to that awful city of London. Even so, he'd had this feeling before and then felt uncomfortable but now was feeling most uneasy to the point of breaking out in a running sweat. His blue suit felt clammy, his hands were sticky and his mind turned like the wheels of an active water mill. The return journey to the airport appeared to be over in an instant as the car pulled up outside the departure hall and with regret Christian made his way towards the rows of check-in desks.

His ticket that afternoon was for an economy-class passage non-stop to London on a relatively new and highly cherished airline. The check in desk of United European Express was buzzing with activity and brightly-clad, exotic young women fussed their prospective clients like bees around honey but Christian wasn't impressed. He wanted a low-profile departure, not a carnival, yet selecting the least populated desk he waited his turn to check in and was delighted to secure a window seat just in front of the starboard wing's leading edge. Unbeknown to Christian, this seat was above cargo hold C and at that same moment was being loaded with sealed containers specially designed for that type of plane. United European had overcome the aftermath of one of their aircraft crashing and were again on a rushing tidal wave of success.

Their latest aircraft were the pride of Europe; larger than the ageing 747s these had five engines, four slung under the wings and one mounted in the tail. The huge, cavernous Fairway 800 was parked directly under the main international departure lounge as Christian waited patiently for his flight to be called. He'd cleared the usual customs formalities with considerable ease yet standing at the large expanse of tinted glass overlooking the airport complex, he felt deep rumbling butterflies develop in his stomach. The intense sunlight flowing into the lounge was matched by a steady stream of tears running down Christian's face while he was unaware of the flight being called.

Surging people pushing towards the loading gate of the United European Express flight brought him back to his senses and hearing the flight called for a final time he made his way towards the ramp. With most of its passengers onboard the Fairway 800 looked like a packed auditorium as he took his allocated seat. The cabin crew made themselves busy with preparing the plane for flight and Christian, not taking much notice, tightly buckled himself into his seat. Loaded with a full complement of passengers and cargo the massive aircraft moved towards the taxiway system.

With engines roaring, United European Express flight UE 429 forced its huge bulk down the long concrete runway and as it reached the point of no return lifted away into the hot afternoon air. Christian grabbed the armrest of his seat during those early moments of that flight with such intensity his knuckles went white and climbing away from Geneva the Fairway 800 made a course change to put itself on a corrected heading for London. Christian felt the sudden awareness of danger but it was too late. Continuing its climb under full power on now its designated course the massive aircraft was ripped in half by a severe explosion. Christian Beck didn't know anything, didn't feel anything but died instantly along with all his remaining fellow passengers.

The bomb placed in cargo hold C under Aston Appleton's instruction had performed its duty to perfection. Wreckage from the aircraft fell over a wide area of the French Alps but fortunately no one on the ground was killed and many passengers were covered, never to be found, while due to the severity of the blast others couldn't be identified.

It was a disaster of enormous proportions created by an evil man to destroy another of his kind who was puny, insignificant and a total guttersnipe, but how he'd still cared for his parents. Appleton's final key to life had started to turn, his own end was in sight.

*

Returning to his flat in Geneva, Bo Perroud opened the black briefcase he'd accepted from Christian Beck but on inspecting the varied notes realised they were all fakes. His fat, sweaty body trembled as he became aware moment by moment of the consequences and sat for most of the remaining afternoon considering which course of action should be taken.

Reaching for his best French brandy, he gulped the first quarter of the bottle before having sufficient courage to draft the telex to Aston Appleton. The brief note took him ages to prepare yet once it was concluded he sat staring into heavenly space. With an explosion of passing wind from his lower body Bo Perroud knew he must send the message and to be totally truthful yet tomorrow would be early enough. He devoured the remaining brandy, collapsed on the floor and snored his way through the night like a great beached white whale, totally unaware of the airline disaster now being splattered over all news broadcasts. Life for him was sweet if not short.

CHAPTER 30

Old Athens City

Touching down at Athens Airport, the Olympic Airways 747 trundled along the maze of taxiways before reaching its designated unloading ramp. Eager passengers concerned with their own welfare passed through the varied formalities while Brett and Alexis meandered along at a much slower pace. They slept heavily during the one-and-a-half-hour flight but felt the presence of other human beings had cramped their style.

Wiping traces of sleep away from their eyes they walked through long airport corridors towards a still-active city. The time was a little after 2.30am on that Sunday morning as they finally made a slow entry into yet another hot but dark night.

Brett had little interest in his current surroundings yet had managed to check the departure time of aircraft leaving for London and while studying this timetable he'd again become aware of Alexis sending signals of passionate fancy. She'd stood at his side with pending purpose as they read in silence but according to Brett the next direct service was not until 2.00am the following day. Sighing with a degree of contented relief, it was not within the next few hours he turned towards Alexis, took her hand and together they moved with growing excitement towards a city which would offer them a haven for love. Alexis didn't feel apprehensive, she knew Brett wanted her but she'd no intention of falling in love with him as her mind had been smitten with another. Brett had told her many times over the past two days how he loved Rebecca and worried for her but Alexis was aware of his craving for a fling of passionate embrace without strings. She intended to be his fling, his mistress for a night, his lover and his night of rampant sex.

Leaving the airport behind them, they called a taxi, instructing its driver to find them a small hotel with excellence as its norm within the oldest part of Athens. Initially the driver was unable to comprehend their request but again they told him of their requirements and with nodding head he produced a broad grin of zealous envy.

Their journey into the ancient city of masters took only a short while but both Brett and Alexis felt inspired by the sights passing the car window despite the late hour. Large ocean liners were lit by quivering lights in Piraeus Harbour; the modern city was still alive with nocturnal people enjoying the hot, late summer night, While heading towards their destination the Acropolis overpowered all monuments by its stunning beauty illuminated to perfection. They sat in the back of the car holding hands with loving intent as the driver nosed his taxi into Plaka. Brett was hot with desire to love Alexis while she almost trembled at the thought of his naked body touching hers.

Turning away from the Acropolis the taxi made its way through the narrow streets lined with old stone buildings and whitewashed houses neatly laid out like cake icing. Negotiating his way within the endless labyrinth of slender streets, the driver cursed under his breath but persevered until like the dawning of a new day entered with a sigh of relief, a small tree-lined square of impeccable proportions. The twinkling old-fashioned street lights cast warming shadows over the cobbled road as Brett decided this place must have been the inspiration for life itself. Shuddering to a halt, both Brett and Alexis began to comprehend how utterly exhausted they felt but without so much as a word, knew they'd arrived in a special place.

Clambering onto the sidewalk, the hot air filled their shattered lungs and becoming aware of the night's humidity glanced around their new environment. A café situated within the central part of the enclosed square was still buzzing with people enjoying the atmosphere, seductive music and total ambience of that night. The whole scene reminded Brett of a forgotten fairy tale acted out within the drawing room of past excellence.

Alexis, still clutching her black leather holdall reached out for Brett's hot, sticky hand with a desire to hold him tight. She could feel him trembling a little yet knew it was not through fright but willing apprehension. Gently, her long slender fingers gripped his firm hand and edging towards the graceful whitewashed hotel, Brett began to walk with her. It was a harmonious-looking building attractively decorated with brass plates, wrought-iron balconies, bowls of multicoloured plants and baskets of fuchsias supporting astronomic blooms radiating a stunning fragrance.

Together they climbed the old red brick steps and entered the secluded world only offered by a handful of hotels throughout the world. The Hotel Omega was a genuine jewel within a city full of stunning monuments and expensive desires yet with marbled floors, skin rugs and a cooling atmosphere of seclusion they made their way through the lobby to a potted tree ridden reception desk. Met by a matronly woman of large proportion who they later found out to be the owner's wife, Brett hired a double room overlooking the graceful square they'd just admired as the woman eyed them both with evil scepticism but not wishing to turn trade away, took them via a creaking old stairway to their allocated room. The whole hotel was decorated in much the same worldly fashion as the lobby and entering their room the old woman was clearly pleased she was a part of the establishment. Waving her flabby arms like the sails of a windmill she acquainted her guests with the room before wishing them both a restful night.

The room was an attic feature with twin, double opening, floor to low ceiling windows. A small yet prominent wrought-iron balcony ran the entire length of their room and was cluttered with stone pitchers full of flowering red begonias. As Alexis opened both windows the hot night air rolled into their room bearing the sweet aromas of that fragrant city and she inspected their small yet lavish bathroom equipped in white porcelain with ordered rose petals painted around each item's perimeter. The soft white bath sheets hung loosely in neat rows and complimented the lines of jars filled with scented creams. She returned to the bedroom to find Brett standing by the open windows breathing in the languishing flavour only offered by such a city of gods and looking totally bewildered by his distant expression yet tired appearance, Alexis visually inspected the imposing timber framed bed. The sheer size of this mattress arose heavenly inspiration as she began to feel wet for his body.

With a seductive series of movements she wormed her way to his side, lingering for a brief moment while Brett was able to catch the distant aroma of her fading perfume. His mind had been elsewhere thinking of Rebecca, Lenton Parva and all the events of the past two days. During the space of forty-eight hours his whole organised world had been turned upside down and inside out, yet the pinnacle of current circumstance was being highlighted by Alexis herself. He loved one woman, wanted sex with another but was too tired to fight any more as Alexis peeled away his shirt, exposing his lean muscular, dark, hairy chest. She muttered a series of short expressions in Arabic of which Brett was only able to understand the gist but knew it related to the forgiveness of Allah. Leaning towards him, she ran her fingers through the matt finish of his chest and kissed him with inspiring passion before turning away towards the bathroom. She wanted to prepare her body, her mind and her soul, for tonight he was to be hers.

With Alexis out of sight Brett couldn't forget how Mohamid Van Jonger had looked at her and how he'd feel knowing they were about to commit such a mortal sin against the Muslim faith. Brett looked at himself in a full-length wall-mounted mirror adjacent to the bed, shook his head and went to draw the net curtains across the open windows.

Brett's head was full of cluttered inspiration as he lay down on the large, inviting, blissful bed still wearing his trousers but bare chested and without further ado drifted into a deep heavy sleep.

Alexis appeared from the bathroom and making her grand entrance to rapturous overtones of snoring felt rather deflated but not totally surprised. Her naked, smooth brown skin glistened with scented creams and oils she'd found in the bathroom while her long black hair was swept around to one side of her perfect face as she stood with legs slightly apart and hands firmly planted on her hips. She'd taken time to prepare her succulent body for his pleasure but her nakedness couldn't wake him.

Gliding around the bed Alexis bent over him and started to remove his trousers, underwear and shoes but felt herself becoming excited by the free-flowing motion of her well-proportioned bosom. Brett's well-built frame filled her vision as she exposed his entire youthful, six-foot, masculine body before she could feel herself reaching the point of orgasm just by looking at him. Alexis fingered his limp penis, explored his meaty balls and ran her fingers over every part of him before laying down at his side.

Alexis Matos couldn't sleep for fear of Brett waking and her not being ready for him but in fondling her body she located the tender point which excelled her inward desire to climax. Playing with her own form, she expelled a stream of excitable fluid before reaching the point of no return. Alexis made herself come before she too drifted into a deep sleep harbouring thoughts of Brett Watson's cock.

*

The hours sauntered past as night became dawn and dawn became another full-blooded day, yet still Brett and Alexis slept. Outside their serene room of unexplored sex, Greek Sunday life continued as normal. The usual banter, chit chat and daily commotion grew until a nearby church pealed its traditional midday bells, startling most if not all the surrounding area.

Brett stirred at the sound of church bells ringing but Alexis was already awake, alert and ready to pounce on her prey as soon as he woke. A gentle warm breeze was blowing the net curtains towards their bed with seductive suggestion followed by mouth-watering aromas of food being roasted in the square's café. It was a hot day again outside but still cloistered within the charming attic room Alexis could again feel her own temperature soar. She peeled back the thin cotton sheet covering them both and exposed their nakedness to the new day but with cat-like inclination Alexis Matos started to caress Brett's chest. It was time for him to wake up, it was time for her to enjoy his body and by the love of her god she intended to do just that.

Teasing his nipples with her tongue and stroking his penis with her left hand, Brett began to wake in more than just one way. His eyes flickered open and his cock grew while she was already wet for him with excitement. Her longing moment arrived with a start as he regained his full composure, realised she had already enjoyed playing

174

with him and knew there was nowhere for him to go.

Stretching his powerful body, Brett Watson's penis grew to its full size and while she lingered over him, he reached for her well-developed brown tits. Her cat-like stance excited him more and seeing her naked reflection in the mirror, he dragged her towards him. Giggling with pleasure Alexis allowed Brett to run his long tongue around her bosom, his hand to play amidst her pubic hair and his solid cock to stroke her soft belly.

The warm breeze continued to waft the net curtains but they were both now so involved with each other the rest of the world didn't matter. She placed her moist lips over his and explored the innermost parts of his mouth while Brett almost had to fight to secure a degree of action in this movement. Alexis dominated him and he knew he'd just have to lie there and take it, all of it, for this was something so totally different.

With awe-inspiring certainty Alexis moved her attentions away from his lips and running her tongue down the pelt of hair on his chest, concentrated on his manly organ. In so doing she kneeled astride his chest and pushing her wetness towards him Brett allowed his fingers and soft tongue to explore deep inside her. She was wet to the point of saturation and his concentrated action wouldn't have made the entry of his cock into her any easier than it was already. Alexis wanted it, wanted him and was showing she meant to get it.

These fanciful moments of passion continued for many hours as their bodies began to run with sweat and they explored each other until no stone was left unturned. It was without doubt heated, explosive passion.

Alexis slid off his body and going to the bathroom winked at Brett who lay naked, stiff and in her eyes so sexy. She'd only been gone a few moments before returning with a large pot of clear, slightly scented jelly and as she unscrewed the cap Brett sat up but only had time to see his own dripping penis before she pushed him down again. Dominating the entire action, Alexis dipped her long slender fingers into the pot, withdrew a mass of the clear jelly and proceeded to rub his whole naked, excited torso. Her hands slid over his solid hairy chest, teased his balls, ran up and down his strong legs and finally became totally engrossed in the massage of his erect penis. Brett's hardness was made all the more solid by watching her perform on his body through the mirror but somehow it made this exotic series of events feel considerably more sexy. Alexis didn't allow her efforts to diminish, she again reached for the jelly and rubbing more of the clear substance up and down his cock placed her tender lips around his moist dripping flesh. She gently tantalised him with her tongue while allowing her jelly-ridden fingers to slide in and out of his backside. The pleasure this gave Brett was unsurpassed by anything he'd ever felt before and caused him to forget his wife, Mohamid and channel all his efforts into loving Alexis.

As their moment of passion continued to raise both their temperatures the hot afternoon air ridden with tasteful aromas of cooking filtered past the gently swaying net curtains. Brett was so taken with Alexis and she with him they didn't care about anything else except their own lustful aspirations.

With his body now beginning to perspire through the scented jelly covering him, Brett offered the same massage treatment to Alexis. Her tender brown skin glistened with imminent excitement as he plagued her nipples, caressed her supple belly, stroked her tender legs and finally titillated her female explosion. They both knew such exasperating foreplay couldn't continue for much longer and pushing him away from her, turned over and kneeling like a dog on heat made suggestive motions to Brett. His utter elation caused him pain but entering her from behind his cock felt twice its actual size. At first he moved with sedated intent attempting to make the event last forever but catching a glimpse of themselves in the mirror just made him feel more beddable. Reaching forward with both hands Brett held onto her well-formed bosoms and pulling himself deeper into her she winced with intensive pleasure.

Sweat began to drip from his forehead, his body oozed with warm, sticky yet scented perspiration as he could no longer contain or control his feelings. With total unison Alexis again reached her climax as Brett shot into her inner body a fountain of hot, amorous sperm.

They remained lovingly interlocked for some time, just feeling their two bodies rubbing against each other. Brett didn't lose his massive erection but continued to pump his long cock into her mouth-watering body as she pulled away from him, turned over and they made love again in a more traditional caring manner before drifting into a light sleep totally contented.

*

Early afternoon coasted into late afternoon and Brett woke with a stunning start. He didn't feel any remorse for what he'd done, in fact he knew more about life now than he'd ever dreamed was possible. Still fluttering in the breeze he watched the net curtains play before turning his attentions back to Alexis. She was sound asleep but as music from the café outside their hotel became audible to him, Brett began to wonder about the dreams she would now always be able to cultivate. Peter Sarstedt's song began to take on a new meaning for him which would last forever as making his way towards the shower Brett turned again and looked at Alexis as the song continued.

"Where do you go to my lovely, when you're alone in your bed. Tell me the thoughts that surround you. I want to get inside your head…"

CHAPTER 31

Athens On Saturday, Late Afternoon.

Brett Watson turned on the shower and standing under the cool flow of lavish water washed his entire body. The scented jelly Alexis had smeared over him eased away from his taunt skin while dried sperm dissolved into nothing. Brett had enjoyed his encounter with that shapely brown goddess but now yearned to be back with Rebecca and although not feeling guilty wished he'd tried to contact his loving wife. His thoughts turned away from recent actions of passion as he considered how Mohamid was getting along with their formulated plan. As the cool water washed over his refreshed body Brett knew the past few days had changed his outlook, changed his life and more prominently increased a better awareness in life, but knew when he did eventually return to Rosco International, the company would now have to change to suit a newfound worldly wealth.

Standing with his back to the shower door Brett didn't hear Alexis enter behind him but felt her sticky hands begin to manipulate his firm buttocks. He knew it was over, their passion had been nothing more than a lustful revenge against "Control" and turning to face Alexis realised she felt the same vibrations.

They showered together admiring each other's dripping body but never offered to touch or hinder each other again.

While waiting for Alexis to dress Brett stood on the open balcony overlooking that neat pretty square. Again, he was permitting his mind to wander but in a vague attempt to rectify his sense of wellbeing watched a pair of dancing white butterflies play in an upward spiral, until the breeze caught them and they were blown out of his sight. He felt a degree of sadness, loneliness and deflation but knew very soon his questions would be answered.

Alexis came and stood by his side; her perfume was strong and harmonious with the occasion but she gingerly took Brett's hand, offering a slight smile before they went down into the hotel's lobby. The receptionist glared at them both with knowing disgust but they took no notice as making their way into the cobbled square they began to stroll through the pretty narrow streets of old Athens.

Little was said as wandering around the maze of irregular roads time passed quicker than they imagined. It was strange them both wanting to talk about their afternoon of love making but holding hands was the best they could achieve. Their wanderings brought them back to the square which contained their hotel and now feeling pangs of hunger, drew up two chairs at a vacant table. Refreshing glasses of ouzo and lemonade were brought filled with ice as they both came to terms with each other's actions yet the relaxed atmosphere created within the café's lush surroundings made each of them aware of the need to talk.

Alexis started the conversation with Brett joining in at opportune moments but it wasn't long before they were both laughing, yet Brett still seemed distant to Alexis. With searching eyes she asked him outright what was really bothering him.

"I should have tried to contact Rebecca," he said in muted tones of guilt.

Alexis, however, stressed to him that Mohamid had specifically said not to try such a move as it could endanger their creative, delicately planned attack on "Control". He nodded his head in agreement but she knew there was something else and waited with bated breath to learn his real concern. It wasn't long before he'd opened his heart to her. She sat and listened to Brett's concerned comments as to the way in which his values of life had changed but more importantly to his regret at having made love to Mohamid's "second wife".

Alexis had never considered this point as a worry since she knew it wasn't true but listened nonetheless. Once Brett had concluded his speech of concern she knew this was the time and the place to fill in the blanks Mohamid had deliberately left out relative to their relationship.

He couldn't believe what she'd told him but was most relieved despite being slightly annoyed Mohamid hadn't considered him totally trustworthy with such information. Alexis Matos sniggered as her foxy decorous nature again became apparent but she longed for her return to Tangiers, to her only home and find a solution for a problem which was now haunting her. She told Brett of her desire for Winston Al-Hassan, to marry him and make Mohamid a grandfather before finally climbing to the uppermost pinnacle of Moroccan social life.

Brett took in all these details with growing interest and couldn't help but offer a smirk of pleasurable satisfaction at himself being off the hook. She playfully offered to slap his face in retaliation but food was brought to their table and devouring it became considerably more important than their general banter.

As evening began to draw its darkened blanket over old Athens they concluded a delightful dinner of smoked fish, salad and avgolemono soup all dutifully washed down with a bottle of less than brilliant white wine. They talked, laughed and enjoyed each other's company as the coloured lights hidden within the surrounding eucalyptus trees started to flicker, announcing the arrival of yet another night.

Brett and Alexis were happy to remain at the café until it was almost time for them to depart from that pastoral place. With deep regrets on one hand and pending excitement on the other they paid for their dinner before going over to the hotel, paid the bill and stopping a passing taxi were on their way back home.

It was a little after midnight as they checked in for the British Airways flight back to London but with no baggage except a black holdall, the formalities were swift.

The departure lounge was hot, sweaty, and crowded as Brett made his excuse to visit the gents. He knew Alexis was watching him so with avid gusto entered the WC only to leave again as soon as she'd turned her back. Almost running towards the nearby rows of public phones he dialled his own home number and it rang many times before being answered. Brett could hardly speak as he heard Aston Appleton's voice booming down the line. That bastard, he thought, was with his beloved Rebecca and Brett Watson knew straight away it was Aston who was "Control". He started to shake and knew he must kill him before Appleton caused any more damage, yet was totally unaware of Alexis standing directly behind him.

She knew Brett wouldn't be able to resist attempting to ring Rebecca despite Mohamid's instructions but nevertheless Alexis envied him far too much to be angry. Her gentle voice eased his immediate pain and as he related his findings she was reminded of their pending duties.

Together they sat waiting for the London flight to be called both in absolute silence, dripping with sweat and both very apprehensive.

It was 1.30 on Monday morning as Aston Appleton's life drew into its final day.

CHAPTER 32

Mohamid Van Jonger. London.

Sunday morning announced its arrival with a dim daylight finding its way around the heavy curtains of Brett's office. Mohamid Van Jonger hadn't slept a wink during that long night but had spent the whole time studying the vast array of documents still laid out before him. He'd read and re-read them many times in a vain attempt to isolate Aston Appleton's dominating influence but as time had ticked past the overall picture had become more clouded with his own interpretation of the facts.

He stood up and moving towards the curtained window, drew the heavy material back permitting natural daylight to overpower the now insignificant illumination offered by electric lights. It was a dull morning with rain falling from grey skies yet stretching his tired body away from the window, Mohamid knew he must sleep at some time but didn't really feel inclined to throw away this most valuable opportunity.

He stood for a short while in something of a trance watching the sparse early morning traffic trundle down the embankment while the Thames was muddy, grey and utterly unimpressive, yet it still seemed to offer him a degree of satisfying encouragement. Glaring directly at its steady flow of uninterrupted succession, its tranquillity helped him formulate his own ideas on how to pass the next twenty-four hours. He knew it was well out of the question for him to roam this powerful city as his presence was meant to be on a very low-profile ticket. If by some unfortunate error Appleton was to spot him Mohamid knew his advantage would be blown and they'd never secure Aston to his cross of death. The rain didn't appear to ease at all and moving away, he turned off the lights in Brett's homely office. Van Jonger remembered he'd left Appleton's office with the curtains drawn and not wishing to attract any attention to that building, had to return them to their original position. He wasn't keen on entering that room again yet it was a necessary evil.

Opening Brett's office door the circular reception lobby with glass ceiling dome was still neat and business like, just the way he'd remembered it from yesterday evening when he'd first arrived. It was a strange sensation being there all alone, but it had never bothered him until that moment. Suddenly Mohamid wanted his wife's company; they'd gone through a great many trials and tribulations during their married life but with the realisation she was dead, he began to feel anger steaming up his real sense of reason.

Spinning his five foot six inch lean body towards Aston's office door, the image of his wife pinned to the floor wouldn't leave him and he considered the delayed shock of her death was only now beginning to affect his normally level headed nature. Mohamid wanted instant revenge but for Brett's sake and out of respect for Alexis, knew he must wait until the appropriate moment.

Entering Aston's office a strange smell met his twitching nostrils which he'd not noticed the previous night. Making his way towards the window he drew back the curtains, noticed the safe was still open and although grinning to himself couldn't hide his interest in that smell. He knew he'd smelt it before but couldn't quite isolate it at first and then like a clap of thunder understood it to be heroin.

Mohamid Van Jonger knew the drug was involved, he'd handled those lighters, sent his Alexis with Brett to Cyprus even though that move was under considerable duress but didn't consider that evil substance could be present in such a bastion of English society. Feeling a little weak kneed he sat at the desk proudly prominent within that sinister room and looked himself up and down. The light grey suit trousers were still well pressed, his rolled up shirt sleeves felt tight on his arms and overall he felt a degree of revelation about his own inner character.

Mohamid didn't take any particular care in his search for that devilish fine white powder. He knew it was there, he wanted to find it and during his search it crossed his mind how he could use the drug himself once it was found. He searched every possible hiding place, some twice without any success, but still he didn't give up hope.

Sitting with his head implanted within his hands he again looked around the now untidy chaotic room. Books and papers were strewn around the floor, it looked as if it had been ransacked yet Mohamid wasn't satisfied he'd been beaten. With methodical precision the elderly man started his search again but as he did so, not a single book, box or file went unchecked. Progressing his search Mohamid returned the various files and books to some type of order back on the shelves since his enhanced plan deep set with in his mind, required Appleton's office to appear untouched in readiness for that evil man's return to work on Monday morning. Surprise was still their key to secure this creep's downfall.

Moving around the office Van Jonger again drew a blank and started to become angry with himself. He knew the drug was there, he could smell it like a sixth sense but parking his tired body in Appleton's desk chair, he surveyed the richness of the fitments. An ordered appearance had again returned to that room and the rain outside had stopped as sunlight was now brightening up the whole day. Turning in his chair Mohamid noticed the Thames had taken on a different appearance and with light rays flickering on the steady flow of water, he again focused his anger back into that room of discontent.

The safe door was still slightly open yet despite knowing its contents were spread over the lavish carpet in Brett's office next door he felt the need to make sure it was really empty, like Old Mother Hubbard's cupboard the safe was bare, cold to the touch and austere to the eye as Mohamid's attention was drawn to a pair of drawers located directly under the large desktop. He'd searched their contents before but there was one element about them he'd not checked, it was his last hope.

Unlike previous occasions he removed both drawers from their runners and placed them on top of the desk. It was like a breath of fresh air as Mohamid Van Jonger realised Appleton's hiding place.

One drawer was considerably deeper than the other even though their external dimensions matched and placing the one drawer back under the desk, he emptied the contents of the other not taking any notice of the trinkets he'd turned out. With a sharp knife he eased out the drawer's false bottom and as if knowing, intense rays of sunlight shone at that instant onto a most macabre collection of syringes, small packets of white powder and various instruments of drug administration. Mohamid couldn't smile, couldn't laugh but felt disgusted with his findings. Aston Appleton was a drug junkie and Brett Watson didn't know.

*

Removing all the drug and its related accessories from the drawer, Mohamid returned to Brett's own sanctuary, yet before so doing made sure Appleton's den of mischief was left in the same manner and state he'd found it the previous evening.

The well-being of Brett Watson's working environment gave Mohamid a sense of security as he placed the drug and syringes on the leather-topped desk next to his own Smith and Wesson revolver. With a sigh of painful relief Van Jonger sat down staring at his findings, the vast array of paper laid out over the floor and played with his well-groomed beard. Mohamid's sun-blessed face looked grey with hatred while his black-grey hair seemed whiter than it had done two days before, yet he could only really think of Alexis and the Rembrant Hotel. It was nearly 3.00pm on that Sunday afternoon as he realised it had taken almost twenty-four hours to truly hate Aston Appleton.

CHAPTER 33

Mohamid Van Jonger. Sunday Evening.

From finding Aston's collection of heroin Mohamid Van Jonger had allowed his mental state to run wild with matchless hatred. He had recalled his wife's death so many times since finding the drug he couldn't control or co-ordinate his emotions any longer. Brett's office was still awash with papers laid out in neat piles over the floor as he'd methodically read each document so many times. He now knew the role this bastard had played but still couldn't determine who was controlling Appleton. Someone or some group had a real hold on this fucking maniac and although not knowing their identity realised, that would soon become clear. However, whilst waiting for that information to come to light he'd have to bide his time and channel his thoughts into a positive approach.

The majority of his afternoon had been spent brooding over the events fired at him over the past couple of days yet he was tired and hungry but couldn't succumb to satisfying either of these desires. It was his own form of punishment for his past involvement in lucrative deals which Mohamid now felt Allah was making him answer for, yet he hoped after this ordeal was concluded his account with Allah would be paid up in full and he could return to running his hotel with the beautiful Alexis at his side for comforting support.

Time slipped past and the late September sunlight was fading as the river began to take on a cooling effect relative to its prominent surroundings. Mohamid lifted himself out of Brett's chair with painful precision and slowly moving around the office began to collect all the documents from the floor. He formed a series of neat piles on the desk, each relating to one of the players in this dangerous game. Little did he know two of these impoverished pawns had been killed without any regard for the human form but Mohamid only knew of his wife and Martha's death yet strangely felt as though others would have to follow before long.

Next Van Jonger turned his attention to the austere array of drug related equipment. It had been many years since he'd seen such a sleazy, sombre collection of death-inspiring instrumentation. Many people had made vast fortunes whilst buying, selling or administrating this fine white powder yet Mohamid felt disgust at their activities and was determined to join the ranks of those who acted to suppress such destructive forms of human exploitation.

He carefully opened the packets of heroin and emptying their contents onto a clean sheet of paper started to split the pile of white powder into six smaller heaps. Each of the piles was then mixed with a solution of diamorphine until the powder was totally in suspension. Mohamid took six syringes from the desk and filling them to capacity with the lethal solution, marked each one with a person's name. Brett Watson, Rebecca Watson, Alexis Matos and Mohamid Van Jonger's name took care of the first four but the remaining two were nameless for the time being. Mohamid had taken an assumption to heart concerning the last two dripping syringes. He thought deep down Aston Appleton's own blackmailers would arrive on the scene as he feared they wouldn't be able to resist a hand in his downfall. Van Jonger still had no idea who they were or even if it was just one person but sensed the dawning of Monday would answer his searching questions.

*

Darkness had once again drawn its black veil over England's capital city as Mohamid turned on Brett's desktop lamp. He'd arranged this morbid selection of syringes close to the piles of documents removed from Aston's safe and although feeling relieved to a point could detect his own apprehension germinating like the seeds of a viper's egg.

As the evening matured into night Mohamid Van Jonger sat and stared at the collection of evidence in front of him. His mind was blank as his hands gripped the desk from outstretched arms, he knew he could no longer remain awake.

Pulling himself closer towards the desk Mohamid folded his arms, placed them on the leather top and lowering his head onto the arm-formed cradle, instantly fell into a deep sleep, dreaming throughout the night of his pending revenge. Monday was going to be a day he'd never forget.

The time was 11.55pm on Sunday night.

CHAPTER 34

The Al-Hassans. Saturday Night.

Winston Al-Hassan watched how well Alexis had handled the massive Honda Goldwing as she'd manoeuvred away from the ship down the quayside and on into Larnaca. He was full of admiration for that woman and wished he was in Brett's position, as he longed to hold her succulent tender body if only for a moment. Winston could still taste the sweetness of her lips from that brief kiss they'd stolen from each other as he'd almost thrown them off *Brave Goose*. Winston Al-Hassan knew she was the woman he wanted to spend the rest of his life with but doubted if he'd ever see her again. Thinking almost aloud he decided once this affair with Appleton was over he'd make a concentrated effort to locate her, hopefully marry her and settle down as a whole man rather than carry on being a rich virgin.

Winston had also witnessed the frenzied departure of Yiannis and his fellow shipmates in the white Mercedes. He'd almost prayed they'd not catch the fast motorcycle but was aware he'd have to wait and see if they'd secured a safe departure from Cyprus or if Yiannis was to get the better of them.

After the car had made its speedy exit from the quayside an eerie silence descended over the luxurious ship. There was no life on board except his sleeping father and the ship's Captain plotting a proposed passage for the next day but as Winston entered the Captain's quarters he announced there was a change in plan. Sunday wouldn't see *Brave Goose* at sea but instead he and his old father had to travel to London in readiness for an early meeting on Monday morning. Captain Constandinos was clearly more than disappointed and slammed down his pencil with obvious anger while staring at Winston before suggesting he should make their travel arrangements.

Stephanos Constandinos had come to the conclusion he was nothing more than the Al-Hassans' personal secretary. *Brave Goose* hadn't been to sea in months and both he and his crew were sick of being tied up in the marina yet they carried out their shipboard duties as normal, ran the engines every day and generally didn't complain but things seemed to be getting more static all the time. Stephanos knew the old Berber did not like being housed onboard the ship but it was Winston's steading influence which ensured their well-paid jobs.

It was known, however, that Winston wanted to be a high flyer in London while old man Al-Hassan dearly wished to return to his former glory as a Berber in his native Morocco. In the meantime each crew member had to accept the rules forced upon them but they all felt things were about to change. Each man was sceptical, uncomfortable and apprehensive which moulded the Captain's reasoning in allowing his crew certain otherwise amoral concessions like having the local ladies of harlotry in their cabins.

The Captain, accepting this latest development, assigned himself to formulate a timetable to move the old Berber while Winston strolled back along the deck to his own quarters. It was a little after midnight and glancing up the wharf he saw his crew returning from their chase without Alexis, Brett or Yiannis. His heart jumped, seeing they'd failed to secure the capture of their fugitives but on asking where Yiannis had gone, received a host of derogatory comments.

"He's still looking for that bloody motorcycle, sir," said one man while another told Winston how the Mercedes had been wrecked.

Winston Al-Hassan didn't really care, he was glad Alexis had made her escape and entering his own cabin laughed to himself with cautious passion.

He stripped off his robes, showered, climbed into bed thinking of Alexis and nothing else but as the night lingered Winston still couldn't sleep for thinking about her. The more he thought the more he became obsessed until finally supporting a sturdy erection closed his eyes, formed an image of her naked body in his mind and masturbated himself until sperm covered his chest.

Winston eventually drifted into an uncomfortable sleep having torn his foreskin but wasn't aware of his own blood mixing with the sperm he'd enjoyed producing, until the morning.

*

Sunday morning dawned for Winston Al-Hassan at 9.30am when Yiannis entered the cabin complete with fresh white uniform and carrying his morning coffee. Instantly he asked Yiannis what had happened the previous night but only attained a more than potted version of events. He was only concerned about his blasted motorcycle having been found at the airport undamaged which was more than could be said for the Mercedes. The noise of a tow truck outside averted their attention and seeing the car, Winston gasped in horror at the damage. Yiannis on the other hand was gasping at something else. He'd seen the blood on Winston's bedding but he himself had more important things on his mind.

After taking a long refreshing shower Winston dressed in yet another white Arabic robe and adorning it with coloured braid, made his way towards the aft deck to take a light breakfast. His father was already seated with his wheelchair at the table and being fed by one of the ship's crew while basking in the hot morning sunlight. The freshness of that morning had already left the atmosphere humid as the heat of yet another powerful day began to take hold. Winston greeted his father with a broad, leering gawp but the old Berber was not totally amused. He dismissed his male attendant and in a low tone of ill humour told Winston his release of Alexis may have been a fatal mistake. The young man chose to take little to no notice; after all, it was he who was in love not the old crustacean.

Breakfast was concluded in silence with the Berber still grabbing at his past glory and young Winston thinking of nothing else but that really sexy lady, who even in her absence had damaged his vestal penis.

With the sun growing to its full strength the appearance of Captain Constandinos eased the silent tension which was festering in the mind of both father and son. In a duly rehearsed ceremony he announced a car was now waiting to transport them both to the airport but upon the Berber's own instruction, Yiannis was also to travel with them as his personal valet. This brash young sailor who always seemed to be in trouble with the authorities was the Berber's favourite and he knew Yiannis would look after him while his ever powerful son strode to assert his manhood.

Winston knew better than to argue with his father and since Yiannis was a strong man, assumed his own attendant duties would be only trivial. As they rose to depart the Captain pushed the wheelchair towards the gangway but having done this operation many times and knowing how the Berber hated being bumped around, took great care with his charge.

The quayside was as dusty as ever but the rented blue limousine was clean and impressive. Yiannis had loaded their luggage into its boot and standing by the open rear door helped to secure the old man and his wheelchair into position. Within a few brief moments they'd left the tranquillity and splendour of *Brave Goose* behind them as their car was driven through Larnaca.

The pink flamingos still padded the salt flats with their slender long legs but Winston wasn't concerned or even interested in viewing a sight he'd seen so many times before. It was now almost midday as with increasing intensity the sun's heat opened his skin and permitted a small yet uncomfortable trickle of perspiration to run down his forehead.

Feeling his own stomach churn with pending excitement they approached the airport building and instead of having to suffer the usual indignities of air travel, were whisked straight to the steps of an awaiting private Lear jet.

Yiannis always admired the Al-Hassans' style but even he wasn't ready for this. Never having flown before, he found the size of the Lear to be a little unbalancing especially when compared to a nearby commercial Boeing.

Captain Constandinos had done them proud. There was no messing around, no aggravation and as they took their seats the crew fixed Berber Al-Hassan's wheelchair to the floor before moving towards the flight deck.

Winston watched the activities surrounding the Lear jet, the old

Berber channelled his mind towards the events which lay ahead and Yiannis sat petrified as he watched their crew prepare the small jet for take-off. With its twin engines roaring the plane leapt forward and rapidly made its way towards the runway. The two Al-Hassans didn't flinch but Yiannis was so scared he could feel his bowels knotting up. His hands tightly gripped the armrest as reaching the runway engine noise filled the small cabin and the jet roared towards its point of no return. In only a few brief seconds its nose lifted skywards and the Lear was airborne, powering its way in the afternoon sky while Yiannis was green with fear.

*

Throughout the five-hour flight each man maintained his own private thoughts, developing anxieties beyond the normal grounds of compassion. Only the crew spoke but they too were aware of an atmosphere within the polished, elegant cocoon which unnerved their normally professional manner.

It was with their utter relief the Lear touched down at Heathrow and its cargo of strange men departed for other pastures. The time had just turned 5.30 on that cooling Sunday afternoon.

CHAPTER 35

Lenton Parva. 11.00am On Sunday Morning.

Aston Appleton inspected the bedroom but seeing his two victims lying in a varied array of positions, began to feel panic flourish throughout his entire diminutive body. The small pieces of a once elaborate vase lay scattered around the thick pile carpet but more disturbing was Rebecca's limp form spread out like a prostrate starfish. Aston hated himself for such a spur of the moment action but knew he'd not convinced her of his total sincerity, she was planning to leave him yet Appleton couldn't allow that to happen since it was necessary for Rebecca to remain at Lenton Parva for his sinister scheme to succeed.

She lay on the floor partially covered by the bedding he'd attempted to cover Hans Zenna's body with but the blood-saturated sheet was pulled tight between them. His eyes followed the deep red stains leading towards Zenna's body but only his lower legs remained covered; his face was plastered in blood and the bedding beneath his head oozed with a soggy mixture of blood and the contents of his skull. The smell was beginning to filter towards his twitching nose as he viewed the rest of Zenna's perfect form. His broad chest covered in hair was smeared in blood while his limp cock still dripping with sperm lay dormant like an extinct volcano having produced its last eruption. Aston Appleton would have made love with Rebecca but knew he'd blown all his chances of that ever transpiring, she clearly didn't trust him or love him and if he admitted the truth to himself, knew she never had. Still gawping at Zenna's cock the realisation that his now limp flesh had penetrated the only woman he'd ever wanted made him feel all the more angry.

He wanted to touch that part of Zenna's body and then smell the innermost juices of Rebecca's form which he'd never enjoyed despite his efforts. In a fit of pure hatred he left the bedroom, ran down the huge spiral staircase to the kitchen and grabbing the sharpest knife he could find went back upstairs to the scene of his own disaster. Wielding the sharp blade in his right hand, he grabbed Hans Zenna's limp penis with his left hand, pulled at the flesh and with a single swift action severed his dormant cock from the rest of that dead body. Blood began to stream over the lower parts of his torso but Appleton still wasn't satisfied. He sank the knife into Zenna's stomach, upper legs and slashing at the dead man's balls began to feel his own life ebbing away like a rushing tide.

For a few brief moments he stood and glared at the mutilated body which lay in front of him before laughing out aloud with riveting raptures of untold jealousy. His own clothing was speckled in blood like pepper dust.

As the September sunlight brightened up the room through the still-closed curtains. Aston became aware of the withdrawal effects suffered through not maintaining his regular fix of heroin. He knew he'd left his main source hidden in a drawer at Rosco International's office but considered an alternative outlet with favourable response. The approaching effect of not having a smoke concealed about him began to send shivers up his feeble spine but in closing his eyes for a brief moment, he managed to regain control of his decaying emotions.

Batting his eyelids like a sleeping puppy, Aston Appleton re-focused his vision on Rebecca Watson. He'd thrown her to the wind and although hating her for marrying Brett, having sex with Hans Zenna and rejecting himself, still couldn't harm her luscious body. He considered what to do with her but knew full well it could only involve severely restricting her movements. Finally with his mind made up he descended the staircase, went through the hallway and opening the front door walked down the gravel drive into a still avenue towards his car. He'd remembered a length of old rope contained within his beat up Rover's boot, it would have to do as he needed to act quickly and time was running out fast.

Rummaging through years of accumulated rubbish he located the frayed, tatty length of fibrous rope and bundling it together, dragging part of it on the ground, Aston made his way back inside the house. The spiral stairway seemed to increase in size every time he went up or down and this time it seemed never ending.

He tried to quicken his pace but felt as if his legs wouldn't make the next step upwards. He knew what he needed but was desperately attempting to avoid his own admission to being a drug addict and that was also Brett Watson's fault in his opinion.

Reaching the airy landing offered him a brief glimpse of success and locating a rather sizable wooden chair, dragged it over towards the balustrade. Pushing the chair's back tight up to the timber railings which over looked the hallway, Aston re-entered that bedroom of carnage.

Rebecca was still flat out but the smell radiating from Zenna's body was beginning to grow and forcing his thin arms under Rebecca's armpits, he began to drag her away from the four-poster bed. She was considerably heavier than he'd imagined could be possible but was aware she must be held as his captive if only as a reasonable insurance policy. Aston pulled with all his mustered strength as sweat began to trickle down his distorted face. Through the doorway and along the landing they staggered until reaching the chair and rope he'd left ready to secure her by. Rebecca's weight was crippling him yet he had to lift her into that chair and feeling slightly nauseous laid her down, moved around her front re-securing his arms in readiness to lift her again. He was tired, a little scared but most of all in need of a fix to preserve his dying strength. With a series of awkward jerks Aston Appleton had Rebecca seated even though she looked most uncomfortable.

Relief filled his shattered, thirty-four-year-old, withered, drawn, stooping body as he stood back and again admired her. Rebecca's ash brown hair lay in a bedraggled mess over that delightful face while her well-developed bosom still protruded with tantalising intent through her thin clothing. Appleton continued with his plan and reaching for the rope commenced wrapping it around her, the chair and the timber balustrade. Once it was finally secured and he was satisfied she couldn't move Aston returned to the bedroom, ripped away a section of that bloodstained bedding and returning to Rebecca, tied the gag over her lustful mouth.

He now felt he could relax to a point but felt his neck and back were still aching from having slept for so long in his old Rover the previous day. His creased clothing was ridden with the pungent smell of his own body odour while his unshaven face felt rough and dirty. The lethargic effect he'd felt earlier had left him feeling slightly sick but Aston's main requirement at that moment was his favourite but lethal drug dosage.

Returning to the bedroom for a last time he retrieved his old revolver, had a final look around and winced at the carnage he'd created. Hans Zenna's body stank and reaching for the segregated penis Aston placed it like a dead frog into a nearby glass ashtray, grinning as he left the room, closing the door behind him and walking towards Rebecca. He'd decided to place that ashtray complete with its sordid contents on the floor directly in front of her as a reminder of a painful betrayal.

*

Making his way down the staircase again, Aston elected to take a look around the Watson household hoping he'd find something of major interest to himself. He'd thought of carrying out a detailed search some hours before but had discarded the idea hoping he'd win Rebecca's heart.

Aston searched through the entire ground floor of that house emptying drawers, cupboards, files and boxes everything he could find but even in Brett's study couldn't locate a shred of documentation which was of any importance. Basically he didn't know what to look for but just hoped something would turn up and after spending many hours shifting through their home. Aston felt he'd again been cheated by the Watsons, yet before leaving helped himself to Brett's car keys. He was almost laughing out aloud as he climbed in Brett's own status symbol of success, started the car's powerful engine, engaged the first gear and roared away down the avenue known as Lenton Parva.

Aston Appleton had left behind him his old worn out Rover, Hans Zenna's mutilated body and Rebecca Watson, alive, tied up but unconscious. Aston's evil life was almost over.

CHAPTER 36

Rebecca Watson And Aston Appleton

Rebecca Watson

The sound of their door slamming and the Aston Martin roaring away brought Rebecca Watson back to life. Her head pounded with a pain she'd never experienced before and as she regained her momentum for life, realised she was gaged and bound. Her inability to move horrified her now trembling body but in focusing those tender eyes she saw the ashtray placed on the carpet before her. It took Rebecca many moments to comprehend its disgusting contents but as she came to understand her eyes filled with the tears of hatred, shock and sorrow.

She recalled with a clouded memory the events of that morning but wasn't sure in her own mind how much time had passed since. Rebecca remembered Appleton's frayed advances, his sneaky comments, his shooting of Hans but that was all. Waking up tied, bound and gagged viewing what she knew to be Hans Zenna's penis surrounded in blood contained by the ashtray did nothing for her. She longed for Brett to come home, to forgive, love and hold her as he'd done so many times before. Rebecca wanted to leave Lenton

Parva and start a new life away from all this bloodshed, away from that evil bastard Appleton who she now knew to be "Control" beyond all reasonable doubt. She cried tears of failure, passion, hatred and love but could do nothing except look at the macabre contents of that ashtray as she heard the lounge grandfather clock strike 4.00pm.

Aston Appleton

Aston Appleton had never driven Brett's Aston Martin before and initially found it to be a demanding vehicle but fell in love with its superb interior. The plush leather and walnut adorned his eyes while its aroma filled his spinning head with pictures of grandeur, prestige and status.

"At last," he muttered to himself. "I've begun my takeover in earnest. The rest will follow but I can't ease off until that bastard Watson is finally out of my life forever and everything he owns becomes mine."

Appleton eased his foot down a little harder on the accelerator. The car responded and in no time at all was speeding towards central London at speeds in excess of 120 miles per hour. Aston was loving himself beyond all reason considering he'd every right to be pleased and chose to forget about Hans Zenna; after all, his purpose in life was now concluded.

The Sunday afternoon traffic was light, even sparse, but the sun had left the sky and it was now dull, grey and generally uninspiring as he continued to drive. He steered the car with considerable satisfaction past Rosco International's office and grinned at the thought of Brett's empire becoming his own. The building was dark and empty but Monday morning would bring about some lightening changes, or so he thought.

During the course of his drive from Lenton Parva Aston had attempted not to think about his body's craving for the heroin it was demanding but alas, the bells of demand were now pealing with intense resolve. He had to have a fix since he was getting desperate but with just a few short miles to go, began to sweat and tremble. He drove the car harder yet was unable to maintain any true constant speed but finally and almost sobbing with growing pain, arrived at his destination wishing he'd gone to his office instead of a casual supplier. He'd put using the supply from his desk out of his mind some hours earlier after considering the risk involved in making an entry to that building at such a strange time. Moreover, there was another reason why he'd chosen to visit his supply source, he wanted to order another batch and that couldn't be done by phone.

Aston parked the car outside a row of pleasant-looking terraced houses located near the Royal Albert dock, turned off its engine and moving his shivering body proceeded towards the least attractive dwelling. The long, narrow garden footpath wound its way through a maze of small shrubs which clearly needed tending but Aston had no interest, to him they were something other people wasted their time attempting to cultivate.

Reaching out he pushed his stubby finger at the door bell and pressed it with vigour. Inside, the shrill sound of bells continuously ringing began to annoy the occupant immensely as she hurried down the narrow steep stairs. She'd every intention of giving that idiot who'd never taken their finger off the button a large chunk of verbal abuse but on opening the solid front door, Molly Soon was met by the vision of a very scruffy Aston Appleton.

"Well, well, well, what do we have here?" she mumbled in tones of patronising amusement.

"Molly, I need your help. Can I come in?" he spluttered.

Molly Soon threw open the door but before allowing him inside glanced up and down the street yet saw nothing to cause her any concern except the expensive-looking car parked in front of her wild garden. The car registered money in her mind but after that initial moment she stored such knowledge for future developments.

Aston pushed his way past and standing in the hall waited for her closing the door. She wondered what the hell this fucking jerk wanted this time and especially so late on her sacred Sunday afternoon. It was now nearly 5.30 and this type of intrusion didn't go down well.

Molly turned around and wearing stockings with arrows pointing towards her knickers, led the way into a small tacky lounge demanding to know what it was he wanted.

"I need a fix. I am desperate," Aston whispered.

"What the shit have you done with the last lot? I only let you have it on Wednesday. Don't tell me, you've sold it to make a quick profit I suppose."

Her face was beginning to twist and reform into some sort of gargoyle but she continued.

"That reminds me, you still owe for all the dope I've already supplied."

Aston didn't let her finish before he was on the defensive with imaginary daggers drawn.

"I'll pay you double the price we agreed. I've got the means but I need a fix right now. For crying out loud, you bitch, I need it."

The tone of Appleton's voice stunned her for a split second. She'd done business with him before, he'd always paid and never let her down but this time she felt threatened. Going five days with no income from this fart worried her but there was something else and she couldn't quite put her finger on the reason for this discomfort.

"Ok, OK," she yelled, "but prove you can afford such an inflated price. Are you rich all of a sudden?"

Aston glared at her. His unshaven face was drawn and felt stale but if it would get him the fix he need, then she'd have to know some of the plan or at least the result even if it wasn't quite secured as yet.

He slumped into an easy chair, making an adjacent pet cat shriek with startlement. Appleton told of his taking over the top position in Rosco International's organisation, his newly acquired Aston Martin, the house in Lenton Parva and a fortune which had been Brett Watson's.

Molly Soon listened to him rabbit on and although not liking Aston Appleton suddenly realised a way out of the poverty trap she was always fighting. She also realised something else, something far more personal and something with incredible prospects.

*

Molly was only twenty seven but she'd been around to say the least. In her early years she had worked the streets as a prostitute but after having met some men who'd hit and hurt her, she'd turned to pushing drugs but only to people who could pay. Molly had never been married, never loved or cared for any other human being which tied with Appleton's own character.

Her five foot five inch frame was totally out of proportion. She had a large bust, large backside and massive nose which coupled with her spotty face, red hair and foul manner didn't make her attractive to many men. She'd always been poor – even the drug sales hadn't made her much money – yet she still had delusions of being rich, secure and more important of late, pregnant.

She couldn't remember her parents since her mother died whilst giving birth to Molly and not knowing who her father was ensured her childhood days were spent being passed from one home to another until at the age of fourteen, she escaped from the social system and took to the open streets. It was there she really learnt to hate people and her hot temper flourished.

It was only by chance she'd arrived at the small terraced house near the Royal Albert dock and at first Molly was pleased to have a permanent place even though it was only rented but now since Appleton was playing in to her hands she'd other ideas. How she was going to make the male world suffer though this bastard was only known to herself but sooner or later he'd find out.

*

Aston Appleton concluded his snivelling speech concerning his newfound wealth as Molly inwardly laughed at him and offered him yet another type of deal.

She swayed her odd-shaped body in front of him with promiscuous intent before shedding the tacky blouse which covered her enlarged bosom. Appleton wasn't impressed and Molly knew he'd no interest in having sex with her but she'd all the bargaining cards on her side. Moving around the small, dingy living room, she stopped by an oversized chest of drawers which dominated a complete wall. A loose-fitting drawer was duly opened and reaching inside it she withdrew a clean white heroin smoke. Aston jumped to his shaking feet but couldn't grab the cigarette from her before she'd pulled it out of his reach and her large nose quivered while giving him a sinister smirk of satisfaction. Molly knew he was desperate to the point of no return and intended to make the best of this rather bazaar situation.

Miss Soon held the heroin-infested smoke well above her head, slowly backed away from Aston towards the door and like a lamb to the slaughter he followed her upstairs never taking his eyes away from that evil tube of white paper. They reached Molly's bedroom and it was there she offered her terms which were not negotiable. In return for sex he could have the heroin he so badly wanted and she'd also forget about the money he owed but Appleton didn't really pay any attention to her knife-edged words, at that time he would have agreed to anything.

Molly gave him the drug he so badly needed and as he lit up inhaling the putrid smoke, she removed all his clothing. The thought of having intercourse with this mouse of a man didn't really turn her on but the bargaining facility this situation offered made her yearn to feel his cock inside her.

He stood there limp and lifeless while she stripped the remaining cheap clothing from her body. Aston clearly wasn't excited but while he continued to smoke and fill the room with the blue lingering haze, she set about his manly parts.

It seemed to take an age before Aston Appleton's body reacted to the attention it was getting. She led him to the unmade bed and forcing him to lie down, proceeded to climb on top of his withered body. Still he continued to smoke while she rode his crooked penis until as the last dregs of his fix filtered away, she felt him release a pathetic trickle of sperm. She hoped to all the evil gods within the world his futile efforts would reward her.

*

The small three-quarter bed housed both Molly and Aston that night in a type of uncomfortable unison. Only Aston slept. Molly's mind churned with the desire to become pregnant and screw the bastard for every fucking penny he'd acquired. She wanted money, power and to leave the sordid type of life she'd learnt to exist within. At last she too dropped into a deep sleep but it was dawn and he was already starting to awaken.

The dawn dragged itself into yet another full-blooded Monday morning as Aston Appleton realised his actions of the previous day. He lay there thinking of Rebecca, Hans Zenna, Christian Beck and all the other people he'd used to secure his own goals but in attempting to move to a fresh position felt Molly tucked tightly in beside him. It was a strange sensation which he didn't like and that in itself shook him back to reality.

Sliding out of the bed, Aston knew he'd had sex with Molly but couldn't recall all the details and nursing a thick head started to dress himself as quickly as possible. Leaving the bedroom, sneaking downstairs and out into that wild garden he made his way towards the car. Aston was suffering from a heavy hangover but nevertheless was sane enough to know he'd have to deal with Molly Soon in the same way he'd dealt with the others who'd used him.

Clambering into the luxury car, he started it up and made his way towards his own apartment within the Dock Lands complex. It was during this short journey he discovered he'd left his old revolver in Molly's bedroom but it was too late, he knew he couldn't go back at that moment since there were other pressing things he must attend to, yet later he'd make that bitch suffer.

Throughout the last few days Aston Appleton had tried to forget the death threat which he was under but like a cold winter wind it came back to the forefront of his mind. He'd never been able to work out who it was who'd forced him to show his true colourless character or even what they'd really wanted but he knew their demands had used up all his own capital and some of that belonging to Rosco International.

Pulling into his car park he left the Aston Martin with a degree of swelling pride and entering his apartment, made straight for the shower. It was delightful to his abused body, feeling the hot water wash away the previous days' grime and he hoped some of the memories he now fostered as well.

Armed with a fresh set of clothing and clean-shaven face, Aston surveyed his own image of self-induced importance. His dark grey pin-striped attire was in marked contrast to the grubby blood-peppered clothing he'd left Molly's bedroom in only a short while before.

Strolling around the living quarters while listening to an array of messages now being delivered by his answerphone. Aston Appleton's ears picked up as he heard Christian Beck's voice. The message was generally very distorted but since Aston didn't have any further need for Beck he didn't really care. Christian had phoned Aston's apartment twice during the last twenty-four hours as he'd been instructed to do but on both occasions the answerphone had taken the calls, not Appleton himself, since he'd been attempting to avert the failure of his plan by destroying Hans Zenna. Now the whole saga was moving to a close but Aston was looking forward to running Rosco International and having lashings of money for himself. The letter box flipped open and seeing the morning paper arrive, he went to pick up the folded bundle. Glancing at the minor front-page stories his eye reverted to the main news item of the day. Aston was shocked at the photographs of the Fairway 800's wreckage spread out over the French Alps. The horror of this accident filled his pathetic body with shivering thoughts as he read on to discover the reporter suggesting many British, French and Swiss were aboard the fated airliner but the only name mentioned was that of Christian Beck.

Aston Appleton's mind flipped. He only just heard that man's voice on the answerphone and now he'd read Beck died yesterday. It was too much for him to accept as he realised at that moment in time what an evil bastard he really was since he'd only agreed with his blackmailers to Christian's quiet death, not mass carnage. Appleton instantly perceived this to be a display of his blackmailers' power to secure their winnings. He also knew if the authorities ever traced a lead, it would have been calculated to point directly towards himself.

He threw the paper down to the floor and could feel tears of fear building up inside his shaking body. Never before had Aston Appleton felt frightened but now for the first time in his life he was shit scared. It was a natural progression from his fear, for him to realise he'd never really enjoy the newfound wealth he'd spoke to Molly Soon about. Aston didn't worry about Brett Watson's return; after all, if that's the way they destroyed Beck, Brett wouldn't stand a chance but what would they do to him? Aston was petrified.

Still with his withered body trembling he checked his Bulova watch and seeing it was a little after eight o 'clock on that fatal Monday morning, left his apartment for the office. Brett's beautiful

Aston Martin eased its way towards the City of London but the traffic was heavy and Appleton knew he wouldn't be seated in his new elevated position until after 9.00am.

Unbeknown to Aston this was to be his final journey in a life he'd abused and taken for granted.

CHAPTER 37

Mohamid Van Jonger. London.

Mohamid slept through the night like a new-born baby but instead of waking refreshed and ready to attack the next day, he'd not been able to stop dreaming which had only made him feel uncomfortable. His active mind had gone into flashback mode recalling his childhood in the dirty, narrow back streets of Tangiers. Those disagreeable years seemed to have occurred centuries before but to him they seemed like only yesterday. He could vividly see the image of his parents standing before him while he stood there in a scruffy caftan with no shoes on his dirty feet. Van Jonger continued to sleep but his heavy dreaming caused him to sweat and shake as he recalled the birth of Alexis, how her mother had died and the price he'd paid for so long. His mind wandered through the years he'd supported the young Alexis, the ease in which his wife had accepted her presence in their lives and the formation of their hotel into being one of the best in North Africa.

Mohamid continued to sleep in a most unsatisfactory manner but he'd been so tired, it seemed foolish but that was the prime reason for his uneasy night. Mohamid slept with his head in his folded arms until as his dreams reached the explosion which had killed his wife, he woke instantly.

*

Monday morning met Mohamid Van Jonger with the impact of a thunder bolt. He'd slept longer than he expected but as Mohamid started to straighten his body commencing with his neck, arms and then legs, he began to worry about the events he'd planned for that morning.

Moving himself out of Brett's chair he felt dirty, his shirt sleeves were still rolled up and his grey suit trousers looked worse for wear but noticing the time as being nearly 6.30am felt the need for prayer. Walking around the office Mohamid approached the centre of this plush room and kneeling on the floor, faced his holy city of Mecca. Slowly he bowed his head, raised himself up and then bowed again but this time remained with his head touching the carpeted floor. Mohamid Van Jonger remained there for many moments talking in Arabic at great speed, praying for his forgiveness and all the time hoping Allah would show him the way forward as he'd done so many times in the past.

Eventually and feeling much stronger he concluded his praying ritual, stood up, reached his full height and moving out of the office into that circular reception room attempted to locate a bathroom. He tried all the doors leading from that now naturally well illuminated place but as usual it was the last door which gave him success.

Armed with his small but expensive-looking overnight case he'd brought from Tangiers, Mohamid entered the small but basic washroom. He splashed water over his face, shaved what little was not covered by beard and changed into a new crisp white caftan. Mohamid tidied his hair and straightening himself pushed the suit trousers into his bag before emerging out of the bathroom back into that light-ridden reception lobby.

Considering the events which lay ahead of him, Van Jonger made his way back to Brett's office but as he stood in front of the desk his eyes became transfixed on the pile of documentary evidence against Appleton.

It was a clear morning outside and as the sun settled into a steady climb in the sky, it looked to be one of those September mornings for which England was famed but nevertheless Mohamid still had the final preparations to conclude. He arranged six chairs in such a way they were not visible from the open door until people were actually in the room. Next Mohamid returned to Appleton's office and just easing the door open, he reached his hand around it, withdrew the key from the lock, closed the door and locked it from the outside. Holding tightly onto the key Mohamid scurried back to Brett's office and placing it on the pile of evidence against Aston, picked up his Smith and Wesson revolver and sat waiting in Brett's chair of power.

At the large leather-topped desk Mohamid Van Jonger sat in readiness for his master plan to come together but having relied heavily on his suspicions coming to fruition, was convinced they'd now bear him the fruit of sweet revenge.

It was 8.30am and Mohamid knew it would soon all be over for better or worse as his body tensioned in readiness.

CHAPTER 38

The Al-Hassans. Sunday Evening. London.

Armed with one of those damn airport baggage trolleys which can't make up its mind which way to go, Yiannis followed the Al-Hassans through the complex of customs and arrival halls at Heathrow. He hadn't been informed of the duration of their stay in London but guessed it would only be for a couple of days. Yiannis had hated the flight from Larnaca yet in order to retain his sanity tried to forget about their passage home. This was his first visit to London and he hoped the Al-Hassans would allow him some free time to explore the nightlife he'd heard so much about. In the meantime his prime function was to serve the two men who'd brought him.

Winston was pushing the old man's wheelchair as if he was transporting a highly breakable and especially valuable antique. The crowded airport clearly offended Winston but arriving at the main terminal doors, the relief on his face was evident as a hired chauffeur appeared to transport them into central London.

Winston Al-Hassan didn't expect anything less of Captain Constandinos's organisational ability but nevertheless he made a mental note to thank him for not throwing them all as prey to hordes of eager taxi drivers.

The young driver, who was clearly under most stringent

instructions to treat them with care and respect, drove the spacious car into London at a steady speed. Time was definitely on their side as the volume of Saturday evening traffic increased and their progress was slowed. Yiannis sat in the front seat alongside their driver but although watching every move, kept one eye on his passing surroundings. He knew London to be a big city but didn't expect the speed of life to be so dramatically different from that of Cyprus. Everybody seemed to be in a such hurry and couldn't afford the time to observe any of life's niceties.

Deeper into London they drove until without any warning the car pulled off the main road and almost instantly stopped outside a hotel. As if like clockwork and having been rehearsed the driver skipped out, opened the boot, removed their cases and almost stood to attention while hotel staff opened their doors. Yiannis was not used to being treated as if he was someone very special but enjoyed their attention. In the meantime, bell boys appeared to carry their cases and whilst taking over the duty of pushing the Berber's wheelchair from Winston, Yiannis made his way into that elegant hotel's foyer.

Winston attended to the formalities while Yiannis, the Berber and their cases were taken directly to a suite of rooms. Each man was shown their respective quarters which consisted of a well-furnished bedroom with en-suite bathroom all connected to a rather large and spacious lounge.

It was many moments before the staff of this exotic hotel left them in peace but before they did so Winston ordered dinner to be served within their own surroundings rather than make use of the restaurant.

Old man Al-Hassan was glad Yiannis had come a long and since he'd nothing left to achieve that day told him to prepare his room for bed straight after they'd all eaten. Yiannis had never eaten at the Al-Hassans' table and although he usually enjoyed his food wasn't really looking forward to that meal, he wanted to get out and about in this exciting new city.

As Sunday evening gathered maturity darkness cloaked their large suite and turning on the lights Winston became aware of the room's soft, warming colours. He'd hated their journey into London and at that moment in time wanted to be very much alone. London, Winston considered should have been his city yet looking towards his elderly father became aware yet again of the real purpose for their visit.

A full evening meal was delivered to their suite, laid out and admired yet each man had other, more important things on his mind. The meal was hardly touched with Yiannis frightened of making a fool out of himself, Berber Al-Hassan being too tired and Winston being concerned over actually meeting Aston Appleton.

At the first available opportunity the old man made his excuses, demanding Yiannis should take him to the bedroom, prepare him and put him to bed. Like a shot Yiannis stood up and moved the Berber to his desired location, undressed him, put him to bed and within the space of some thirty minutes was out on the streets of that fascinating city.

Winston Al-Hassan had also been pleased like Yiannis when the old man had retired to bed for it gave him those moments he needed to secure his own peace of mind. Throughout their short dinner he'd felt very apprehensive and despite his father's inability to move, knew he also felt the same way. Winston had felt pity towards Yiannis for having been caught up in their scheming plan but his presence seemed to pacify his father so having concluded his duties, Winston let Yiannis go out on the town.

The confusion which reigned in Winston's mind became apparent to himself once he'd been left on his own for only a short while. His hands started to shake, his body trembled and a thin film of perspiration formed across his forehead as the culmination of many months' planning and preparation were about to reap reward.

Knowing he couldn't sleep, Winston chose to walk in the cool night air and leaving the hotel still dressed in his flowing white robes, started a nocturnal stroll which was to last him many arduous hours.

*

Yiannis had found himself unsurpassed nightly activity around Soho. He drank, sang and became involved with other Greeks who led him into their own style of drunken debauchery until he could no longer keep up. With eyes glazed and legs wobbling he made his way back to the hotel broke, drunk and very much worse for wear but his night out in London was one he'd never forget. Yiannis had really enjoyed himself beyond all doubt!

Sneaking back into their hotel suite, the sobering influence of the Al-Hassans hit him like a stone wall. His drunkenness drifted away from his inner soul as he recalled from his fading mind the apprehension the morning held for his masters. He knew it was something of a delicate nature which had secured their visit to London but wasn't aware of the historical background for which the Al-Hassans were now seeking their revenge. Yiannis clambered onto his bed and instantly dropped into a heavy sleep knowing full well Monday morning would be a time in his life which would never be repeated.

*

Winston continued to wander along the tree-lined roads and although a gentle but cool breeze made his flowing robes trail behind him, his mind was elsewhere. He would have loved to visit old acquaintances he'd made many years before but couldn't muster up sufficient enthusiasm. Instead he drifted past the fancy showrooms filled with expensive products and lit with seductive lighting as his mind continued to undress Alexis Matos. Winston couldn't get that woman out of his system, she now meant everything to him but his head was spinning with thoughts of Appleton's death, finding Alexis, losing his virginity and working again in London. He continued walking unaware of anything around him as the windmills of his inner thoughts merely tangled up his whole identity. How he wanted his life to be simple, clear cut and free just made him angry but Winston knew the breaking of daylight would at least clear part of his confused mental state. He didn't know of the surprise which was in store for him.

*

As Monday morning crept into Winston Al-Hassan's life he returned to the hotel and taking a long, hot shower came to terms with the events that day would impress upon them all. His father's revenge would soon be complete but his own life would maintain a clear emptiness until he'd found Alexis and screwed her.

Calling from the bathroom, Winston summed Yiannis to awake and dress the old Berber in readiness for the event, while he dressed in a fresh white robe adorned with colourful braid of Arabic extraction. Yiannis felt limp and slow. His head thumped as a result of the large intake of alcohol he'd consumed the previous night but nevertheless knew he had a duty to perform. Waking Winston's father was always an easy job as he was a light sleeper but washing and dressing him became more difficult as the years passed. With a surge of limited energy Yiannis had the old man dressed as Winston would have wanted and wheeling him towards their breakfast table concluded he looked every bit the Berber. His robes were tidy and folded to perfection around his wheelchair, his withered body adorned with the chains of his ancient office despite having been deposed and his glazed eyes although still looking awkward were filled with excitement. The eighty-six-year-old man was as ready as he'd ever be to meet and destroy the man who'd almost killed him.

They sat and ate breakfast in a strong silence, Winston not caring to offer any conversation while Yiannis being too busy feeding the old man, remembered his station in their lives.

Time passed slowly but finally it was the hour for them to depart. The young chauffeur appeared on the scene as if by magic and loading the car, they left for Rosco International's office. Nothing was said except by their fire-filled eyes. The time was 8.30am Monday morning.

CHAPTER 39

Geneva. Monday Morning.

Bo Perroud had been awakened by the traffic passing his dingy living accommodation. He felt dreadful but seeing the empty bottle of brandy knew he'd only himself to blame. His head thumped and his fat stomach rumbled as he recalled the meeting with Christian Beck. Through his small puffed eyes Bo could clearly make out the black briefcase containing the fake money Christian had given him and to one side the message he'd prepared for Aston Appleton.

Slowly he dragged himself to his feet. His mouth felt rancid, dry and as if it were full of sawdust but knew that was the result of drinking a full bottle of brandy. He moved over to the briefcase, picked up the fake money and just looked at it in sheer disgust knowing someone was pulling the wool over somebody else's eyes with this little lot. Bo Perroud picked up his prepared telex and ringing the telephone company dictated the message he wanted to send to Aston Appleton.

Completing the task in hand Bo parked his great fat backside on an adjacent chair, reached out for his brandy decanter and started drinking again. With sweat pouring from his flabby brow Bo Perroud drank himself unconscious, never to wake or smell the clear air of dawn again. He died as he always was, a failed man.

London

Mrs Alice McDonnald slid the key into the lock and turning it, pushed open the door to Rebecca Watson's small perfumery shop but as she entered the aroma of seductive fragrances made her nostrils twitch. She loved that shop and even more so adored Rebecca herself, having every reason as it was she along with her now dead sister who'd brought Rebecca up once the small girl's parents had died.

When Rebecca had introduced Alice to Brett she'd been so delighted the pleasure of Rebecca's happiness had made her cry. Alice was a caring person and even though she now worked for Rebecca as undermanager still felt very protective.

With Brett returning home from Tangiers on Friday Alice didn't expect to see Rebecca on Saturday at all. She was, however, a little surprised she hadn't rung to make sure everything was in order but then again they were in love and that was really far more important.

Moving around the shop, her tweed suit flowed and followed her swaying hips as she turned on the showcase lights, picked up the mail and checked her watch. It was nearly 8.45am and for the first time in many years she suddenly felt as if there was something wrong since normally Rebecca was at the shop long before this time, especially on a Monday. Alice McDonnald continued with her routine, making the store ready to receive customers but all the time her mind allowed disturbing thoughts to flourish. At last she could stand the worry no longer and reaching for the phone dialled the Watsons' home number. Brett and Rebecca were all the family she'd left in the world and Alice loved them both dearly. There was no answer; she phoned the police as tears began to stream down her made-up face, not knowing quite what to say.

This was the start of something new in Alice McDonnald's life, a time she was going to relish but as yet she didn't understand or know why.

CHAPTER 40

Brett Watson And Alexis Matos

The British Airways Boeing 757 made a perfect touchdown at Heathrow but as it made its long taxi way to the mass of airport terminals, both Brett and Alexis could feel their individual apprehensions grow. Their flight from Athens had been totally uneventful yet despite having spent the previous afternoon in raptures of long embrace, the relationship which seemed to have adorned their inner lustful desires had turned into a cool respect. Each had passed superficial comments but neither had directly brought their individual thoughts to the surface. Reality of daybreak had certainly put their pillow talk and sexual desire into a mummified corner of no return.

As the aircraft drew to a halt both Brett and Alexis were on their feet, much to the cabin staff's disapproval, and waiting for the door to be opened passed a last knowing glance which effectively signified the flickering candle of passion's last glimpse of life.

Making their way through the terminal building Brett raced ahead of Alexis, who although only carrying her black holdall found it difficult to keep up with him. She yelled at him to slow down and for a moment he waited for her but then continued on his way with considerable haste. Attempting not to run, Brett Watson walked as quickly as he could through the main doors and stopping a passing taxi almost caused a fight with other people who'd queued for some time as Alexis Matos caught him up. Brett pushed her inside and climbing in behind her slammed the door closed to torrents of verbal abuse from that typical of British traditions, the queue they'd left behind.

It was 5.20 on that Monday morning as their Austin taxicab left the airport underpass and started its journey towards Lenton Parva. Alexis had wanted to go directly to Mohamid but Brett took no notice and for the first time since they'd met, dominated her. She watched him out of the corner of her eye and although wishing he was Winston Al-Hassan, still felt a little love for him but knew she could never show that side of her affection again. Brett's love for Rebecca was deeply entrenched within his heart despite his lustful yet highly toned afternoon of sexual passion with Alexis.

The taxi sped its way towards his beloved Rebecca and throughout their journey Brett sat on the edge of his seat, urging the driver to go faster. His mind was all keyed up to seeing his wife again but more importantly to securing Aston's downfall. Brett had thought long and hard as to which method he should adopt to put Appleton out of their lives forever and shooting him was always his favourite idea but a long, slow death would have a more enjoyable impact. Brett couldn't make up his mind and decided to make a choice after he'd heard Appleton's story but with his mind churning over the events of the past few days, he eventually settled down to enjoy the remainder of the trip. He was almost home again and that meant a great deal to him yet as for Alexis, she didn't rate in his favour ever again.

Alexis on the other hand had given some thought to Brett and considered Rebecca a most fortunate woman, but other than wanting to be with Mohamid again she could feel her body trembling with passion for Winston Al-Hassan. She carried an image of him deeply set within her mind and although he was cloaked in his white robes she was enjoying herself mentally undressing him. From that point in time Alexis never really considered Brett Watson again, he was now just another string to her past bow of life.

With Brett still urging the driver to increase his speed the taxi spun into Lenton Parva, travelled down the avenue for a short distance before screeching to a halt behind a beat up old Rover. Brett left Alexis to pay the driver as he shot out of the car and seeing

Aston Appleton's old car instantly increased his already steaming anger. She joined him on the pavement but his itchy attitude shook her and grabbing her arm, Brett dragged Alexis towards the house.

The gravel drive only housed Rebecca's XR3 as Brett realised Appleton had probably left his old Rover and taken his own prestigious Aston Martin.

"That fucking snivelling little two-faced bastard," Brett yelled but reaching the front door found it to be locked and having no key, another dilemma was forced upon him.

Pushing past Alexis who followed him like a lost sheep, Brett went to one of the smaller leaded windows at the side of the house. He gazed around, picked up a rock from the garden and threw it at the glass. The window shattered with a resounding crash but before the flying glass had time to settle, Brett was almost through the gaping hole. Once inside he opened the window properly and with blood trickling from his cut fingers pulled Alexis in behind him.

The house was quiet yet Brett had a sense of impending doom and followed by Alexis, he made his way out of the drawing room into the hall. Everywhere he looked things had been turned inside out and upside down while papers, books and files were strewn about the entire place. Brett could see someone had been looking for something guessing it was his "friendly" partner, Aston Appleton.

Standing in the hallway by the spiral staircase they stood and listened but it was only a faint sobbing noise they heard coming from upstairs. Brett bounded up towards the landing two steps at a time until reaching the top he froze in sheer dismay. Rebecca was trussed up like a Sunday turkey, bound, gagged and frightened just as Aston had left her.

As Alexis appeared Brett was removing the gag from his wife's sumptuous lips yet Rebecca couldn't speak for being so delighted at seeing her beloved Brett again. She gasped for breath while tears of joy ran down her pale, drawn cheeks as Brett continued to untie her and when the last binding fell away, Rebecca rose from her chair of despair, hugging him with such force he also had to fight for his breath. Alexis looked on and feeling their emotion began to cry herself as the lounge grandfather clock struck 6.30am.

Rebecca Watson

Rebecca had been tied to the chair since 4.00pm that Sunday afternoon unable to move, speak, yell or even cry properly. In fact she'd had to control her breathing just to secure her very survival but the most frightening element of all was not knowing when she'd be released or when Brett would come back, if ever at all.

She'd reflected on her past life with special emphasis on the time since Hans Zenna had abducted her in the shower on Friday afternoon. Rebecca regretted having slept with Zenna despite having enjoyed it at the time but the sight of his once proud cock surrounded in blood contained by the ashtray made her feel sick, guilty and depressed.

She had not really slept at all that night, it was merely a series of cat naps strung together with spontaneous sobbing sessions. Rebecca hated that house and everything in it but as the night dragged on she fell out with herself many times before feeling so weak she eventually thought dying might be an easy answer to all her problems.

Dawn broke over Lenton Parva on that Monday morning but by this time her confused state of mind had settled down to a steady series of thoughts. Rebecca had decided to tell Brett everything, confess and suggest her future was in his hands yet suddenly she was frightened again, but the thought of her small shop with Alice McDonnald brought some sanity into her mind.

She dozed again for what Rebecca considered to be a much longer period of time but was awoken by the sound of breaking glass downstairs. Being unable to move she remained in perfect silence for many moments yet when she felt the presence of others in the house, she tried to make herself known. Rebecca Watson was aware her futile efforts at shouting were only being transmitted as a faint mumble but hearing the stairs creak she knew someone was coming. Her eyes caught sight of Brett mounting the landing and all of a sudden she felt like a child again. Rebecca wanted Brett to love, hold and remain with her forever. He was the best thing she'd ever known.

CHAPTER 41

Lenton Parva, Monday Morning.

As Brett and Rebecca embraced with tantalising awareness, Alexis began to feel like a dispensable spare part at a wedding. She coughed as to clear her throat but nothing prevented their close embrace from faltering. Turning away to hide her evident embarrassment, she heard Rebecca question Brett as to the motives and behaviour of Alexis Matos.

Brett was clear and precise as to the role Alexis had played but as he called her over towards them, Rebecca was not convinced. The two women glared at each other with painful resentment before Alexis finally broke the ice.

"You're a very lucky woman to have this man, he loves you beyond the earth's end," she sighed in her warm but soft Arabic-tainted English.

Rebecca looked towards Brett, reached for his arm and offered him a gentle smile. She still had something to tell him but this was not the time or the place.

As if by some magnetic force all three of them glanced down at the same time. The ashtray was prominent on the floor and as Rebecca informed them of its contents. Alexis dived off into the bedroom.

The four-poster bed stood proud and prominent within her sight but Hans Zenna's body was something different. As soon as she'd opened the door a nauseating smell engulfed her tender nostrils and with Brett right behind her she was forced to make an entry. The body of Hans Zenna turned their stomachs as Alexis took a closer look before vomiting, while Brett didn't want to believe the pain his Rebecca had suffered during their whistle-stop enforced tour of the Mediterranean. A strange silence fell over them all but Rebecca felt she had to say something and in a weak monotone voice whispered.

"Aston Appleton did it. He is the 'Control' you've been searching for. That evil thing of a man killed Hans, tied me up and has caused so much grief it hurts me to think that it was I who called him a friend. Brett I've been such a fool…"

Rebecca's voice trailed off as she began to sob and leaning towards Brett, they looked at each other knowing now they were back together Aston Appleton's death was the top concern in their lives.

Brett glanced around their bedroom as he saw Rebecca's partly filled suitcase before his eyes again focused on Zenna's body, the crumpled sheets, scattered clothing and finally he started to put together a mental picture of the preceding events. Rebecca had been too paranoid over Hans for his liking but he knew he'd nothing to be holy about as he stood next to his wife on the one hand and the woman he'd screwed in Athens on the other. Brett's heart sank as he realised sooner or later he'd have to confess to Rebecca but considered it should be done another day, in another place.

*

A short period of time passed as they each attempted to freshen up their tired bodies. Rebecca made coffee as Brett and Alexis joined her in the now untidy kitchen. The whole house was a mess, they all felt tense but most of all each had a secret confession to add to the general confusion.

At precisely 7.50am they all made their way out on to the gravel drive and into Rebecca's XR3 but as Brett drove away from their once grand house, he didn't wish to return and recall the carnage their house had witnessed.

Monday morning traffic into London was usually quite heavy and that day was no exception. Brett, who normally drove with due care and attention, made the car work hard. He dodged, weaved, accelerated and forced his way towards Rosco International's office at the expense of his passengers' stomachs. He had always enjoyed his work but today he really didn't care about the company, his only concern was Aston Appleton and how he could make that fucking murdering bastard pay for his actions.

The car sped on with increasing ease until they finally arrived at that sombre destination. Brett stopped the car with a screaming of objecting tyres as they slid into the company car park and with a quick thinking move, hid the car out of sight.

Grinning with evil anticipation, he escorted his two ladies inside the building, totally unaware of Mohamid Van Jonger's death plan brewing ahead of them.

CHAPTER 42

Rosco International's Office, London. The Arrival.

The clear, crisp air of that morning made the old river and its surroundings look sturdy and sovereign as easing its way into the cloudless morning sky the sun picked out prominent colours, sharp lines and seductive shadows. London was coming back to life after the weekend with thousands of carbon-copy people pouring into those few square miles they considered to be heaven but Mohamid Van Jonger couldn't have cared less. He was only interested in those who he'd laid his auditorium in readiness for. Sitting in Brett's chair Mohamid looked every bit the self-made millionaire he really was, his sun-blessed face with smallish well-trimmed beard looked decidedly sinister and the flowing crisp white caftan folded neatly around his body created an air of total superpower.

The room was still and quiet but the piles of paper stacked methodically on the leather-topped desk coupled with the syringes indicated a resounding event was about to take place. Remaining absolutely motionless, Mohamid continued to permit his mind to run over the strategic scheme he'd developed to secure Appleton's downfall. The time was drawing close for him to join that elite club of legal executioners but without any warning the telex machine located near the office window sprang into life. Mohamid's heart missed a beat, he wasn't ready for such an unexpected intrusion into his now ordered existence. Turning his lean frame towards the machine he watched as it printed the message sent from Bo Perroud. Once the chattering of the type had concluded, Mohamid removed the thin, flimsy paper and read the bold words with a frowning smile of satisfaction. He re-read the telex again before adding it to the pile of evidence he'd found against Aston Appleton. The time was now 8.45am.

*

The minutes ticked past but as Mohamid arranged himself behind the desk yet again, he heard rapid footsteps approaching. He'd heard other people moving around as they turned into work but hadn't considered them as being a threat and sliding his hand onto the revolver Mohamid eased it up with positive intent, pointing it at the doorway. Now he was ready for anything.

Within a split second of the gun's cold steel being pointed towards the door, it was thrown open only to reveal Brett, Rebecca and Alexis standing there in utter bemusement. Motioning them to come in and close the door, Mohamid was delighted to see they were all in reasonable health and in respect of Brett and Alexis, back safe and sound.

Starting to chatter at the same time, they all had a story to tell but Mohamid recognised time was short and he must maintain order. Rapidly he raised his arms whilst still sat and demanding silence told them very quickly he'd gained all the evidence they needed to send Appleton to his death. Mohamid pointed at the pile of documents and the syringes he'd prepared but the others were only half listening to him. They'd not appreciated the gravity of Van Jonger's scheming mind but were still involved within their own personal relief. Still remaining seated, Mohamid's manner began to draw their attention to the seriousness of events which were about to befall them all and like sheep waiting for a shepherd, they each looked to Van Jonger for help but Mohamid had no intention of allowing his mind to become cluttered with private relief at being back with his friends. The joy of their reunion would come later.

With a stern but steady voice Mohamid Van Jonger instructed them to be seated in his make shift auditorium. Alexis who was delighted to see Mohamid could judge from the tone of his voice and manner he had serious notions in his mind and this was not the place to show her affections for him.

Looking slightly worse for wear, tired and scruffy they seated themselves as Mohamid had demanded with Rebecca and Alexis each side of Brett. They waited in an uncomfortable silence and as Rebecca gripped tightly onto Brett's hand he looked around his office with very mixed feelings. Before this latest train of events struck him down Brett had loved that place and his job but now he no longer wanted to be a part of this institution. All that mattered in his life now was Rebecca and he hoped she'd forgive him for his night of passion in Athens. Brett Watson had made a decision as to his future, it was radical but he felt it would be for the best.

The awkward silence which rained around them was broken along with their individual tensions as the telephone on the leather-topped desk rang with an ear-piercing alarm. Van Jonger reached for the receiver and putting it to his ear, listened with frowning expression. His only comment was to send them in and not to disturb them until he told Brett's secretary otherwise.

Reaching for his Smith and Wesson revolver again, Mohamid pointed the barrel towards the door as he'd done when Brett had arrived with his two ladies. Slowly the door eased open and for a split second nobody made an entrance. The silence became electrifying as the tension within the room rose and they each held their beating hearts in suspension. Finally the wheelchaired old man was pushed into the office and as his escort passed through the open door it was closed firmly behind them. It was now 9.00am.

*

The Berber of Marrakesh and his son Winston Al-Hassan stood there totally awestruck but reflected the thoughts of the already seated onlookers. Clad in their white flowing robes adorned with colourful braid they clearly didn't know how to respond to this confrontation. Both Al-Hassans had only expected an interview with that bastard Appleton but deep down they perceived these people also had revenge in mind.

Still pointing the revolver at them, Mohamid could feel his heart beginning to shake as he came to terms with the latest arrivals. Both the Berber and Mohamid recognised each other despite their advancing years, while Alexis allowed her emotion to travel beyond a fresh peak at being in the company of Winston yet again. Brett on the other hand couldn't determine why they were here at all, he thought the Al-Hassans were just middle men of a superior type and should still be aboard *Brave Goose*. Rebecca sensed an increasing tension build within the office but had no idea why.

Mohamid glared at the old man; after all, it was he who'd forced him all those years ago into an unnegotiable agreement concerning their daughter, who was the mother of Alexis Matos. Little did the Berber know Alexis was his very own granddaughter.

The two men never spoke as each one dragged up the past within their own mind but again, time was pressing and Mohamid wanted the floor cleared in readiness for Appleton's entry. Turning his eyes away from Berber Al-Hassan, Mohamid Van Jonger spoke in Arabic to the young man telling him to join the others in his growing audience and watched as they moved towards the chairs. The Al-Hassans seemed distant from the others within this growing sect but Mohamid noticed the furtive glances which were being passed between Alexis and Winston. He hoped to Allah these two young people hadn't any ideas of starting something they would regret, especially since they were related. Mohamid knew he'd have to tell Alexis who they really were and why she must not mix with them but his mind cleared itself away from her as he realised it was the Al-Hassans who were again causing his family grief. They were the ones who'd sent that blackmail letter to Appleton and there were many questions Mohamid wanted to fire at his now captive group of mixed people but they would have to wait for a few moments longer.

Seeing the door handle move, Van Jonger quickly redirected his revolver towards it and for the first time stood up. As he gained his full height Mohamid could feel the hackles on the back of his neck stand to attention as Aston Appleton strode into the room with a cocky confidence displayed only by a successful trickster. The grin his weather-beaten face supported was instantly wiped clean as he faced Van Jonger with his steel grey gun while behind him the door slammed shut, firmly sealing his escape route.

Aston Appleton stood like a child before his headmaster and turning a little he saw all those who he'd used and hated over so many years. His feeble body began to wither at the knees as he realised they'd all worked against him. Mohamid moved away from the chair he'd occupied for so long and pointed towards it. Appleton moved and sat down in a dazed state of mind. He'd no idea what was going to happen next.

The time was 9.15am.

CHAPTER 43

New Scotland Yard, London. Early Monday Morning.

Detective Inspector Dan Sung turned into work very early that morning. He was a single man and lived for his job, nothing else seemed to matter in his life these days and he considered the time for him to assess the quality of his private life would come to him in later years, but in the meantime police work ruled his every thought.

*

Dan was born and brought up in Hong Kong, being of hard working stock with parents who'd joined that thriving city from the poor farming communities of China. His parents had worked hard to maintain some sort of reasonable lifestyle with his mother working as a cleaner and his father as a dock hand. They'd lived on a small, old, broken down houseboat which continually leaked and was generally not fit for human inhabitation. Dan, however, recalled those early years of his life as happy days until he came to terms with the value of money.

He was determined to break the bonds of those ragtime conditions which he'd grown to hate as the years passed on and Dan became old enough to understand the better things in life. It was during his late teens Dan Sung began to comprehend the quality life could give him but he found it very difficult to escape from the bonds of his floating shanty town upbringing.

Finally, after many years of painful searching and determination he joined the Hong Kong police force. With an uphill battle ahead of him Dan gave the force everything he could, attempting to make a successful career for himself. He eventually left his floating birthplace of poverty and clawing his way up the ladder of promotion Dan became a leading figure with in that infamous city of right and wrong.

As Dan's years of experience developed he became increasingly involved in preventing the movement of drugs but a series of most unfortunate events led him towards the web of Triad misdeeds. It was whilst investigating one of the many Triad-related crimes he found his life coming under increasing threat.

It was with great regret Dan Sung took the advice of his masters and moved to England with the intention of becoming a low-profile copper. The strain of his last years in Hong Kong had taken their toll and Dan had witnessed many gruesome crimes of heart-searching pain but they'd never left the vision of his mind. He often woke up in the middle of the night in a cold sweat as again he recalled every vivid, disgusting detail.

New Scotland Yard provided Dan with the breathing space he'd needed to rebuild his life into an orderly existence, albeit a long way from his beloved Hong Kong.

*

At the age of forty-two the pace and times of life had changed dramatically as Dan Sung adapted to a different type of police work. He'd never been involved with a woman, as part of him still wanted to honour his parental traditions and one day return to marry in Hong Kong itself. The type of work he'd undertaken in London was very different to that he was brought up to understand in both culture and content but Dan considered this to be just part of life's very rich and varied tapestry.

*

However, as he sat at his desk that morning he unwrapped the package which lay before him with his name scrawled across it but the plain brown envelope he ripped open contained elements of a crime he'd only ever seen in his birthplace. Slowly, Dan Sung removed the note book, the four fifty-pound notes which he instantly took to be fakes and a series of typewritten notes. Detective Inspector Sung read all the painfully written documentation which lay before him and started to feel those pangs of apprehension fill his ordered mind again; it had been a long time since he'd read such damning evidence so accurately laid down against a single man. Dan re-read the note book's contents again before he realised the writer was afraid of death but knew deep down he'd never have the opportunity to directly uphold the law and bring his employer to justice. Dan was horrified by the note book and more so by the typewritten notes. The man called Aston Appleton to which most of the writing referred was evil and it shone through all his readings. The writer mentioned sexual activities of a less than delicate manner, the placing of a bomb in a Tangiers hotel and many more sinister deeds.

Feeling the blood begin to pump around his brain with quickening speed, Dan Sung grabbed his jacket and almost running out of the building snatched a copy of the morning paper from an adjacent news stand. He commandeered an idle marked police car, yelling at the constable to drive him directly to Rosco International's office on the Embankment. The note book had been quite clear about Appleton's involvement and the writer had made observations Dan himself wasn't entirely sure were incorrect.

Speeding through the morning traffic with sirens wailing, Dan opened the paper he'd brought with him. It was a ploy he'd learnt to use when attempting to convey himself as a composed, collected policeman. Any calmness he could have mustered instantly left him as reading the headlines Dan Sung read the name Christian Beck as one of those killed onboard that fated Fairway 800 jet airliner. It was the same person's name which adorned the note book he'd been reading only a few minutes before. Dan, horrified by the loss of so many innocent lives, suddenly became aware the loss was no accident, it was murder and made his Triad chasing days look insignificant. Reaching for his gun Dan felt his hand shaking, his forehead beginning to sweat and his heart thump. It was all starting again.

CHAPTER 44

The Complete Revenge

Aston Appleton sat in Brett Watson's chair, the leather-topped desk spread out in front of him like a sea of barren hatred broken only by the pile of papers stacked on one side, the sinister syringes lingering like rolling white horses and small but incidental ornaments which Brett had collected littered its leading edge. The room was silent, there was no movement, no motion but an atmosphere of increasing tension broken only by a tape recorder's motor running at an even speed. Outside the office window the morning traffic surged up and down the Embankment in the crisp September morning sunlight but inside Aston's head, things were far from clear. He was fucking petrified and perceived he'd good reason to be concerned. His head pounding with theories, escape plans and ways of talking himself out of this horrendous situation but never before had he been faced with so many who'd so much against him.

The silence continued to reign supreme as Appleton's body began to shake, break into a cold sweat and acknowledge this was a situation he'd never planned. It became clear to him Mohamid Van Jonger was really enjoying himself as Aston glanced around the room. He looked at each and every face in turn as they all continued to stare at him with deep, penetrating, revengeful eyes. Appleton could see

Rebecca holding Brett's hand, she'd clearly been crying and he wished to hell he'd killed her at the same time as Zenna had died. He knew why he hadn't, it was his own lustful crazy mind which had prevented him and now he again regretted his wish to lure her into his own bed. Brett Watson's face looked drawn and tired but Aston couldn't help despise the man with all that remained of his aching heart. It had been a part of the deal for the Al-Hassans to have killed Brett and then seeing him sat glaring with knowing eyes made him feel angry and betrayed. Appleton's gaze moved onto Alexis Matos; she was every bit the stunning beauty her photograph had portrayed. Her involvement had been as a direct result of Mohamid's demanding youth and at the time Aston had enjoyed using her as a lever against Van Jonger. The young Arab sat next to Alexis was not really known to Aston but he presupposed it was Winston Al-Hassan, his very own blackmailer.

Aston Appleton had tried to use all those who he'd hated and admired to secure the demands the Al-Hassans had placed on him and at the same time gain from their unfortunate past lives himself. Winston looked to be a young man who had much to learn in the world as he thought of their money which should by now have been placed in his very own Swiss bank account. Aston also quickly recalled how Christian Beck had died and realised this young, innocent-looking man was no second-rate crook but a real master, yet still didn't understand why they'd forced him into moving the drugs around the Mediterranean.

Beside young Winston, Aston recognised the old man as being the Berber he'd done business with all those years before. Appleton recalled their deals in United European Express shares, the money the Al-Hassans had lost and the vast gains he himself had secured. Old man Al-Hassan looked different now. He'd never moved and Aston felt a cold shiver run up his lifeless spine. Somehow the old man's distant gaze answered his questions. It was the Al-Hassans who'd controlled him right from the beginning of this saga, that he knew, but the underlying reason was attached to the Berber himself. Aston's mind became increasingly blurred with apprehension as the tension built up inside his body.

Still nobody had moved or spoken and shifting his searching vision over to Mohamid, wished the floor would open up and swallow him since there was nowhere for him to hide, he was on trial. Van Jonger looked the part of a judge but Aston understood his meagre part of defendant would be conducted without the benefit of English law being consulted. He was a dead man and he knew it as urine began to trickle down his inner leg.

Mohamid had calculatingly allowed silence to rule for those tender moments while each individual present could reflect on the past few days, the strain which had been inflicted and view the scorpion who'd created such evil in their lives.

Moving towards the desk, Mohamid heard the door being opened and turning with rage germinating inside him, saw Detective Inspector Dan Sung slide into the atmosphere ridden room. Van Jonger was fuming, anger was written across his face but Dan calmed him by offering the plain brown envelope he'd received that same morning. Mohamid removed its contents, reading the evidence as quickly as he could before the two men introduced themselves to each other. Van Jonger didn't know quite how to react but as was his manner. Dan Sung took the lead.

"I gather this pile of paper relates to more of the same," he said pointing to the stacked documents on the desk.

Mohamid glared at him but his blank expression and worried face was sufficient for Dan to understand he'd interrupted a kangaroo court hearing. Detective Inspector Sung caught hold of Mohamid's arm and taking him to one side out of ear shot of the others, spoke in soft but firm tone.

"Which is the man called Appleton?"

Mohamid a little taken back by the Detective Inspector's approach answered in equally soft but disturbed tone.

"The one sat at the desk, shaking."

Dan Sung nodded his thinning hair, quickly glanced at the other occupants and then turned back to Mohamid.

"I gather these people have all been offended by this man in a similar manner but have survived his treacherous actions and are now seeking their own type of revenge."

Mohamid just stared at him not knowing if the Inspector would call a halt to his finely tuned death plan. His concern obviously registered with Dan Sung as he took Mohamid's hand, shook it hard and mumbled to him.

"Talk to me when it's all over. I was brought up to deal with this type of crime and know the law courts will not uphold the revenge which you all seek. I am the only copper who knows about this and I would like it to remain that way. Do you understand?"

He shot a brief smile towards Mohamid before leaving the room with that impending sense of excitement still growing in his stomach and wished he could have stayed; he had a true dislike for Aston Appleton the mass murderer. As the door closed firmly behind the detective, Appleton's heart sank to a new low; he was now really alone in every possible way. The others had watched the brief encounter with Dan Sung but they'd no idea what was going to happen next. Mohamid Van Jonger was master of this macabre ceremony.

Waiting with eager anticipation Mohamid's audience watched as he gathered his full height, cleared his throat and launched his pointed attack on a pulsating Appleton.

"Aston Appleton, I, Mohamid Van Jonger, charge you with fraud of your company funds, embezzlement, drug running, blackmailing, the bombing of my hotel, the murder of my wife, the death of Martha the Watsons' maid and conspiring to take control of Rosco International by deception. I also charge you with the murder of Christian Beck, the crew and passengers of the aircraft which blew up yesterday and of being not fit to breathe the same air as good people."

The room remained silent as Appleton listened to the charges Mohamid levied against him. He started to shift about in his chair. His manner was uncomfortable but before he could say anything Rebecca Watson spoke up, unable to maintain her silence any longer.

"He shot Hans Zenna in my bedroom, cut off his penis and then mutilated his body almost beyond recognition. He tied and left me for hours. This man is evil, the devil, a seraph of Satan himself."

She started to cry but Brett put his powerful arm around her sobbing body and attempted to offer comfort. Winston Al-Hassan stood up, glanced down at the Watsons in close embrace before adding to the list of charges being thrown at Appleton.

"I charge you, Aston Appleton, with the loss of my family fortune and for my father's heart attack which as you can see has left him crippled. You ruined my career, my life and caused many painful years of torment. We also feel you are not fit to share the same air as the rest of us."

Winston sat down and reached for his father's hand to at least offer a small token of comfort. The old man was proud of his son yet tears trickled down his lined cheeks, as he too realised Winston had suffered.

Again the room fell silent but Aston felt hatred for all these people. Without even looking at any of them he took a hold of himself and spluttered, "I don't give a damn what any of you say. None of you can prove anything. I've got the money from that so-called drug run to which you refer but I was blackmailed into doing it. You can all go to fucking hell, I don't care. I am rich, powerful and will get even with every bloody one of you."

Appleton raised his eyebrows and checked the response his speech had secured. Brett jumped to his feet and started to hurl abuse at Aston but Mohamid put him firmly back in line. Aston was grinning with pleasure, he knew he'd just scored a fatal hit on a tender nerve which he thought would shake that smooth-talking shit. Aston decided to continue while he had the opportunity and really rub salt into the already open wound.

"You stole from me, Brett Watson. You stole my girl in that restaurant, you married her, you stole my company, everything I ever did you stole it from me. I've hated your bad guts for years right from university. I think you're nothing more than a rotten barrel of stale frog shit."

The hatred of Aston's speech was powerful but again Mohamid stepped in with as much diplomacy as he could muster given the nature of Aston's onslaught.

"I find you the most distasteful man I've ever known. You insult my friends, my family and mankind. How do you plead against all these charges?"

Appleton glared at Mohamid, stood up and in a brash tone yelled at him, "Why don't you all just fuck off? You've no real proof except the cock and bull rubbish you've all spat out."

Mohamid was getting hot under his caftan, the others in the office began to tense up yet outside the clear sky had become heavily overcast as if a storm was about to break.

Walking towards the desk, Mohamid gave Aston the telex which had arrived earlier that morning. He read it and then read it again. Mohamid told him to read it out aloud but he couldn't and as the contents of the message sank into his brain, so the colour drained from his face altogether. The money from the drug sale had been channelled into Beck's account and with him being dead, Aston understood he was broke.

While Aston Appleton was still off balance Mohamid struck with the venom of a rattlesnake. He displayed the various notes people had received from him giving such sordid instructions which had caused so much grief and highlighting the watermark he'd found tying Aston back against the company, Mohamid could feel his revenge growing hard. He gave Appleton copies of diaries, notes of meetings, copies of photographs and everything he'd found in Aston's safe but lastly Mohamid offered him Christian Beck's note book brought in by Detective Inspector Dan Sung.

Aston Appleton sat bewildered by the tide of evidence put before him. He was outraged but understood he couldn't possibly convince all these people he was innocent. They'd all something against him, they'd put his own evil jigsaw together and he knew they'd got him. Aston considered saying he was not responsible for the crashing aircraft but again, they wouldn't believe him and besides that, the Al-Hassans would have covered their tracks. He realised they would leave all evidence for that crash pointing directly towards himself.

Slowly Aston could feel his case for living disintegrate, his plan for fame and fortune was no longer. Mohamid Van Jonger moved closer to him and as he did so ripped away Aston's jacket, shirt and tie, exposing his bare flesh. Appleton now understood how he was going to die but could do nothing to stop his execution.

With caftan flowing Mohamid reached for a full syringe and with a single stabbing motion emptied its contents into Appleton's bare, weedy arm. He pulled the needle out, stood back and beckoned the others to follow his lead.

One by one they all emptied a full syringe into Aston's body with Winston guiding his father's hand until there was no more life left. It was an eerie few moments as they stood around their prey still seated at the leather-topped desk and watched him die in disturbing agony.

As Aston Appleton finally drifted from this world an enormous clap of thunder shook the window and was almost instantly followed by rays of intense sunlight streaming into the room.

This was the second dawning of that day, the first in the rest of their lives.

EPILOGUE

Molly Soon

The death of Aston Appleton came as a great shock to Molly Soon when she eventually found out many months later. She saw all her well laid plans for a good, wealthy life blow away like dust in the wind. Her scheme to blackmail him could no longer be realised but instead she was to produce a son, which although giving her immense pleasure created a greater financial burden than she'd ever known. Molly returned to working the streets.

As the years ticked past and her young son grew, Molly's bitterness at being cheated flourished until she could stand it no longer. She poured her heart out to the youngster one night after having been on the booze and told him all about her past. Her feelings were of a twisted, broken and cheated woman.

At the tender age of thirteen he was very impressionable and an image of Aston Appleton had been created within his mind but although still not understanding all the events his mother had related, promised one day to even up the score and make her proud of him.

Molly Soon grew to be a ripe old bitch spending most of her time drinking with a broken heart and crooked mind. Her son watched her age and decay with a bewitched vindictive seed of passion growing deep inside him.

The chip of hatred had been passed on, he was determined his mother would die a happy woman no matter what the incurred cost.

Dan Sung

Dan Sung never saw Mohamid Van Jonger again, in fact he never saw any of those kangaroo court members again with just one exception. When the police finally arrived at Rosco International's office there was no trace of any dark, dirty deeds but they hadn't expected to find any since the phone call which alerted them came from an old lady in search of her adopted daughter.

Dan tried to find out what actually had been going on that morning but since he was not in charge of any investigation drew a blank in every respect. His only break occurred when three bodies were found in the Thames some considerable time later but their identification proved difficult since decomposition had taken its grip. Consulting dental records proved the only means open to them and as time passed the three bodies were named as Aston Appleton, Hans Zenna and an old lady known as Martha.

Brett Watson was grilled many times by Dan Sung but eventually the case was closed and the file placed in a dusty cabinet marked "Murders Unsolved".

Dan stayed with the New Scotland Yard police force for only a few more years after the Appleton case before returning to his native Hong Kong. His years of longing to return and marry were fulfilled but he never forgot the scene he witnessed in London.

Dan Sung lived to be a real old man, happy with his lot in life, his memories, a wife who was twenty years his junior and a son who was born within their first year of marriage.

Alexis Matos

The relief of Aston's death was like a worldly weight being lifted from her silken shoulders. She'd turned to Winston Al-Hassan for support after that grim death scene had been concluded and as they embraced with tender loving intentions only known by newlyweds, Mohamid finally told them both they were related by a strong, healthy bloodline. At first they both stood in total silence while the remaining members of Appleton's death squad looked on. Neither Winston nor Alexis could at first believe Mohamid's words but Berber Al-Hassan confirmed Winston and the mother of Alexis were in fact brother and sister.

It took many months for Alexis to overcome the shock of being related to the only man she'd ever really wanted but in time she came to terms with the reality of the situation and returning to Tangiers, lived with Mohamid Van Jonger as before. Alexis had aged in every sense but she was now a woman of the world, but could the world ever be ready for Alexis?

As Mohamid grew older she took control of the Rembrant with his blessing and it continued to thrive with increasing glitter; she proved to be an excellent asset but continued to write and keep in touch with Winston Al-Hassan. After all, he was family!

The Berber Of Marrakesh

With their revenge against Aston Appleton complete, the Berber realised he must make his peace with Mohamid Van Jonger since it was many years since their two families had fought. More than that, however, the old man was delighted to see how his granddaughter had developed; she was a credit to Mohamid in every way but he felt relieved she could no longer distract Winston.

After a long period of negotiation with the Moroccan authorities, Mohamid Van Jonger secured a pardon for the Berber in respect of his expulsion all those years ago. The old man was delighted to return to his native beloved country and spend his last days at Mohamid's villa overlooking the Mediterranean.

He died a happy man, contented and satisfied, only six months after the Appleton event.

Winston Al-Hassan

Having learnt about his blood relationship with Alexis, Winston Al-Hassan felt like a man who'd lost everything with nothing to gain. He became very distant from all those around him, especially his old father, and from the moment Mohamid had pronounced the family tie Winston had an urge to live and work on his own.

Like Alexis, he considered his past family history had finally caught up with the current generation and although resenting his forefathers' lustful desires knew Alexis was now out of his reach.

After the Berber died back in his beloved Morocco, Winston sold *Brave Goose* and elected to remain in London. He relocated his old friends from many years before, purchased a smart Mews property in the heart of the city and became totally involved in the world's financial markets.

Winston Al-Hassan loved the letters and meetings he continued to encourage from Alexis, they remained the highlight of his life for many years to come. He drifted into his middle years a wealthy man in material terms but in love represented an empty desert. Winston never loved again, remained the world's most eligible bachelor and a true virgin. Intercourse was a pleasure he would never encounter.

Mohamid Van Jonger

As Aston Appleton died the relief which filled Mohamid's heart was awesome and so pleasurable it almost made him weep. However, the exposure of his past life to both Alexis and Winston really hurt. It was then he understood the past must die and with it a huge chunk of his own very personal life.

Mohamid Van Jonger spent many hours in the company of Berber Al-Hassan talking of past events and of how Alexis came into this cruel, evil world. Both men had much to say and in some ways much to apologise for, yet they grew to be very close friends. It was Mohamid pulling his influence within the corridors of Moroccan society which had gained a pardon for the old Berber and as a gesture of his hopeful goodwill he offered the old man a permanent place in his own home.

On returning to Tangiers Mohamid viewed his hotel in a different light. He felt tired and rejected but having rebuilt the damaged foyer decided it was time for Alexis to take over his empire. From making that decision, Mohamid never looked back but began to enjoy himself as he considered a gentleman of his calibre should do during the twilight years of life.

Mohamid retained a back seat and while Alexis developed the hotel he began to see less and less of her. His only real regret was she could never marry the one man in her life who she'd found true love for and that, Mohamid considered was entirely his own fault.

After Appleton's death scene Van Jonger remained in close contact with the Watsons for many years. He felt them to be a part of his own family and treated them as if they were his favourite children. They visited each other on frequent occasions but never again did he venture into the United Kingdom.

Mohamid Van Jonger had developed and carried out a premeditated murder, it was a part of his memory he couldn't erase no matter how hard he tried, but lived on in the hope Allah would one day forgive him.

The Watsons

Being back together again meant all the world to these two people. They both realised they had to make admissions to each other but initially felt their immediate future must be put into a correct perspective.

After Aston's death Brett had been questioned by Dan Sung many times but he didn't disclose the events of that morning. Brett had never seen a man die before and in witnessing the death he'd taken part in performing, understood life to be truly precious. Rebecca, on the other hand, had been mentally disturbed to a far greater degree by the events of those four days; she wanted to forget it all and start a new life totally devoted to Brett himself. Rebecca no longer cared for anyone else, she'd learnt a valuable lesson.

As soon as the death squad had succeeded in their mission, Mohamid made arrangements for the bodies to be removed. Winston had been pleased to help and instructed Yiannis, who'd remained in that circular reception lobby of the office throughout the killing, to visit the Watsons' house, collect the two bodies and dump them alongside that of Appleton himself in some quiet backwater of the Thames.

Even when the house on Lenton Parva had been cleaned up both Brett and Rebecca couldn't settle, the memories wouldn't leave them. In an attempt to overcome their feelings they sold that delightful place they'd both enjoyed from their early marriage and chose to live in a rented flat around the Mayfair area of London until their aching hearts eased. However, this still did not clear their minds and Brett suggested a far more radical change in their lifestyle which had crossed his mind during the latter part of their ordeal.

Initially Rebecca didn't know what to do for the best but with a little help from Brett, understood him to be right. Her small perfumery shop was almost given to Alice McDonnald, the price was a gift but despite being heartbroken Alice knew the reasons and continued to develop the business. Rebecca's departure saddened her greatly but she was to be with Brett and that was all that really mattered.

Brett Watson entered into serious negotiations with a large American company and sold Rosco International lock, stock and barrel with the sale making him into a multi-millionaire many times over. He walked away from that office building with a sole briefcase containing only a single cheque, never looked back, never flinched as he passed what used to be his own Aston Martin and never considered that company anymore. In his mind it was dead.

For the first time since leaving university Brett Watson took a bus home and laughed out loud as he closed the door on his past career.

*

Brett and Rebecca purchased from Winston Al-Hassan *Brave Goose* inclusive of the crew and all its fittings. They left London to join their new floating home which although still moored in Larnaca offered them fresh hope in life.

Brett changed very little about that magnificent vessel and Rebecca loved it. The crew grew to admire the new owners and were pleased the ship was again to be used on the high seas rather than as a static hotel. Everything was beginning to flourish in the Watsons' life but still they both had a nagging desire to tell their unspoken secrets. Each of them knew it must be done sooner or later.

Eight Months Later

As *Brave Goose* made its way around the small Greek islands after leaving Larnaca, the urge to talk came to both their minds. They had no other distractions, they had only themselves and a concrete relationship which they both wanted to maintain.

It was a particularly hot, sweltering afternoon in early summer and they'd spent much of that day lying in the sun, relaxing and enjoying their newfound lifestyle. The warm, clear blue sea played against the side of the ship with monotonous effervescent music as Brett cleared his throat and began relating to Rebecca his heated night of passion in Athens. She listened but could show no emotion and when he'd concluded his tale she told him of her own encounter with Hans Zenna. Both confessions were over and a silence drifted around them broken only by the gentle throbbing of the ship's engines. For many moments they just looked at each other, uncertain of a reaction. It had taken much courage to divulge these events when they could both have so easily said nothing despite their knowing undertones.

Brett made the first move; he stood up and without saying a single word gently took Rebecca's hand. He led her though the ship to their grand cabin and with hungry eyes removed her scant swimsuit, laid her slender body down on the bed and admired his woman. He removed his white shorts and showing signs of a growing gigantic erection lay down beside her. They made love like no pair of matching human beings had ever conceived was possible. They enjoyed each other, they loved each other and they respected each other as the seed for the next generation was sown.

Brave Goose sailed on into a glowing red sunset, proud and content. Life was good.

THE END

ABOUT THE AUTHOR

Attention to detail in all aspects of life describes the Author in both this novel and in the professional world of business. The irresistible craving for perfection coupled with the desire to succeed perfectly describes how this Author flourishes in today's fast flowing world.

Born and raised in Chesterfield, Derbyshire the Author has a passion for the better things in life with an eye for meticulous manicured yet relentless jaw-dropping excellence.

Printed in Poland
by Amazon Fulfillment
Poland Sp. z o.o., Wrocław